NATALIE CLARKE

Lost In You

First edition

This book was professionally typeset on Reedsy.
Find out more at reedsy.com

Contents

LOST in You

Author Note

Lost In You is book 2 in the Hudson Hearts series. It is a single dad, friends-to-lovers romance. It is **not** a standalone. This series must be read in order as the subplot continues throughout. This book ends on a cliffhanger. It is intended for readers 18+ due to explicit sexual content, self-harm, mental illness and themes that some readers may find triggering.

This book in no way glamorises or glorifies self-harm, but simply seeks to raise awareness of an issue that affects so many people across the world in so many different ways.

Please excuse some British spellings of certain words, please remember I am a British author writing American characters set in the USA.

Prologue

Rafe

Three Months Ago

"Wow, you look shittier than usual." A familiar female voice draws my attention from the sticky mahogany bar top under my hand and up to a pair of emerald green eyes that have the power to see right through me.

Reese fucking Reynolds.

A red-headed devil of a woman who could lure any man into the depths of hell with just one look, one swish of her copper hair and one sway of those deliciously curvy hips. A woman who could bring even the strongest of men crashing to their knees.

My sister-in-law's best friend.

Rather than answer, I down the amber liquid in the glass in front of me in one, biting back the burn as it scorches my throat before sliding the empty glass towards her.

She raises an eyebrow, pursing her lips as she takes the glass and refills it, passing it back to me a second later. "That's not gonna get you out of answering. Come on, tell me what's up."

"It's not your problem."

I can't help but steal a look at her breasts that spill over her low-cut shirt as she leans forward on the bar across from me. "Drowning yourself in booze is one slippery slope you don't wanna go down, my friend. Besides, I'm a barmaid, it comes with the job. I could qualify as a shrink with all the shit I have to listen to night after night."

"Maybe I should pay you for your services."

"Nah. You're practically family, it'd be wrong to extort you of your hard-earned money."

I laugh, shaking my head as I take a sip of my drink.

"I'm still waiting for an answer," she says.

I blow out a long breath. I've never been one to talk about my problems and how I'm feeling, and I'm not sure if it's the drink or the beautiful woman in front of me that's compelling me to do it. "My dad's dying."

Her face softens. "Yeah, Della mentioned that. How is he?"

"Not good. I had to get out of the house, I... I just couldn't do it. For months we've been watching him getting worse and I can't stand it."

"Losing someone you love is never easy. I guess that's why they call it losing. You don't just lose *them*, but you lose a part of yourself too when they leave." She speaks like she knows the feeling.

I never thought of it like that before.

As bad and cruel as it sounds, sometimes I wish he'd just die. Not because I don't love my dad, because I *do*, more than anything. But these past few months have been grueling and painful for everyone. He's suffering and so are we and I just want it all to end. I hate seeing him in pain, a weakened shell of the man I looked up to, a man who can barely find the strength to leave his bedroom some days, which is why I had to get out, it hurts too much to see him like that.

My phone buzzes in my pocket, my brother's name lighting up my screen with an incoming call.

"Fuck," I mumble.

"What?"

"Gage is calling me."

"You gonna answer? It could be important."

I shake my head, turning my phone off completely. "He'll be calling to tell me what a selfish prick I am, I don't need him to tell me what I already know."

Reese places her hand over mine, it's soft and gentle against my skin. "You're not selfish, Rafe. You're just trying to cope the best way you know how."

Another customer catches her eye and with a tentative smile, she excuses herself to go and serve them.

I tip the glass up to my lips, letting my eyes remain on Reese as she laughs at something the older guy at the other end of the bar has said. It's a dirty, cackle of a laugh that's infectious as fuck and a sound I'm desperate to hear again.

The first time I met her was at my brother's wedding a few months back, dressed in a beautiful green gown that was made for her, hugging every gorgeous curve of her body. I didn't think I'd see her again, that was up until I walked into this bar a couple of weeks ago only to find out she works here. Since then, it's not just been the liquor and the friendly atmosphere in here that keeps me coming back. It's the hope of seeing her, seeking the warm feeling that fills me when she smiles and how she has an uncanny knack of making me laugh when it feels like the last thing in the world I want to do.

For a few short hours, I can escape in this tiny watering hole and forget about the shit storm that is my life, and it's all down to her.

Reese returns, leaning casually against the bar. "Blondie over there hasn't taken her eyes off you since you walked in," she says, inclining her head to the table nearest the window.

I glance to my left at the leggy blonde nursing a Margarita. Her black sequinned dress is so small that her tits are practically spilling over the top, and so short I bet I could see what she ate for breakfast this morning. I have to admit, she's hot, and on any other day, I'd gladly follow her out of this bar, drive to her house and fuck her all night long. But not tonight.

"She's always in here, dressed in that belt she calls a dress looking for a guy to take her home for the night. Surprised she hasn't come over to talk to you yet. Sad, lonely guys are exactly her type."

"And what's your type?" I ask.

"I don't have one, but if I did, you definitely wouldn't be it, I can assure you," she replies playfully.

I grin. "Oh yeah? And why's that?"

Her smile drops. "Because I've known enough guys like you to last me a lifetime. The guys who promise me the world only to be gone the next morning. I've heard all about your playboy antics from your sister-in-law."

"I'm not the kind of guy to make promises I can't keep. One night of wild, no-strings sex is the only offer on the table. *Ever.*"

She leans forward. "It's a good thing relationships are the last thing on my mind right now," she replies with a mischievous glint in her eye that has my sex-starved mind working in overdrive.

I guarantee every story Della has told her are true. I like women and I *love* sex. I've never wanted to settle down or enter into a relationship. I'm not cut out for the married with children, two dogs, and a little white picket fence bullshit. One-night stands are easy, they don't involve strings or complications or commitments. Feelings aren't required, but goddamn this woman makes me feel things I don't want to, things I can't *allow* myself to.

But I'm almost certain a woman like Reese Reynolds would make even a man like me want to stay.

∞∞∞

My eyes open to a darkened room, my head thick and cloggy from lack of sleep and however many drinks I chugged back at the bar. My limbs feel like they each weight a ton and a marching band has taken up residence inside my skull. I move to roll over onto my side but something stops me, something heavy lying across my arm that's stretched out beside me on the mattress.

I blink a few times until my eyes adjust to the dark, just enough to make out the silhouette of her face from the light that bleeds through the blinds.

Reese.

The bed sheet is draped over her body but I know she's as naked as I am underneath it.

Fuck. What have I done?

I manage to slide my arm out from under her and pull myself out of bed without waking her, and gathering my clothes from the floor, I head into the bathroom.

I flip on the light and get dressed before splashing some

cold water on my face to try to sober myself up.

How did I get here?

I search through my mind, trying to fill in the huge gaps in my memory and soon enough, images flash through my mind, tiny snippets of events coming into focus.

We left the bar after her shift... Drank some more at her apartment... I kissed her... She kissed me back... And we had the most amazing sex of my life...

I reach for my phone from my trouser pocket and turn it on and I'm hit with a string of texts and missed calls that light up my screen. I click on one of the many voicemails, only to be met with my brother's voice bellowing down the phone.

"Where are you? Answer your fucking phone for once."

"How could you just walk away from him?"

"Rafe, get your fucking ass home, now. It's time."

"Rafe, it's Della. I uh... I'm sorry. I'm so sorry. He's gone."

My heart slams to a halt as I hear that last message, and my phone slips from my hand, crashing to the floor with a clatter.

No...

No.

I sink down to the cool tiled bathroom floor, clutching my stomach as pain slices through me like a knife. It's like someone has cut me wide open and is pulling out my insides one by one.

He's gone...

My eyes burn with tears but I force them back, digging my fingernails into the palm of my hands enough to draw blood, willing myself not to cry.

Don't cry.

Don't be a pussy.

I can't remember the last time I cried. I never cry. It never did anyone any good or made anybody feel better, so what's the fucking point? But fuck, I could cry a Niagara Falls worth of tears right about now.

He's dead and I wasn't there.

Instead, I was getting wasted at a bar and fucking the night away with a woman I should never have touched, a woman who deserves better than a fuck-up like me.

I guess I am selfish, just like my brother said I am.

A waste of space.

Worthless.

And now my selfishness has cost me saying goodbye to my father, one of the few people in this world who matter to me. And I don't think I could feel any worse than I do right now.

The darkness is closing in on me, swallowing up that tiny bit of happiness I had left.

I'm just… *empty.*

I pull myself up and stare at my reflection in the mirror above the sink.

Selfish... Useless... Worthless… The voice inside my head taunts me.

The words play on a repeating cycle in my mind and I can feel the pain, the anger, the frustration building up inside me like a kettle ready to boil.

I spot the razor lying on the glass shelf in front of me and my stomach twists. My fists tighten on the edge of the porcelain basin so tight my knuckles are turning white as the urge to do something I haven't done in years grips me. The need to find a release to rid this awful feeling inside of me is so strong.

I want it.

I *need* it.

I go to reach for it, but it's the thought of the woman on the other side of the door that stops me.

No. Not now.

Not here.

So far, Reese is the one person in my life I haven't let down, and I'd like to keep it that way for a little while longer.

I leave the bathroom, stopping at the side of the bed where Reese lies deep in sleep, her copper hair fanned across the ivory pillow, the tops of her breasts peeking out from underneath the sheet like a tease.

A memory pops in my mind of her beneath me. Her smile wide, her lips parted on a gasp as I dip down to kiss her mouth while I move inside her, and a strange feeling settles in my gut. A feeling that screams at me to climb back into bed with her, to do the thing that I never do…

Stay.

I want to crawl in beside her, hold her, drown in her warmth and let it ease the agony that cripples me from head to toe.

She can do better than your worthless ass. Let her go while you still can...

She deserves better than you...

The voice is louder than ever, but every word is true. She *does* deserve better than me. If I stay, I'll only end up letting her down like everyone else in my life, but will leaving in the middle of the night hurt her more?

Probably, but ripping the band aid off now is better than hurting her later on down the line like I know I will.

It's inevitable.

So I do the one thing I always do. The one thing I know best.

I leave.

1

Reese

Present

Is this shift over yet?

I'm six hours into a nine-hour shift and it's dragging on longer than *Titanic*. Not that I didn't like that movie, it's actually pretty good, it's just so unnecessarily long.

I keep watching the clock on the wall that seems to have stopped ticking, but I guess that's what they say right? A watched clock never ticks? Or is it a watched kettle never boils? I don't know. Whatever. You get the picture.

I just want to go home, crawl into bed and sleep for the next week because there's nothing worse than standing around doing nothing.

I've worked at *The Watering Hole* for almost two and a half years. I started off picking up random shifts on evenings and weekends in between college until I graduated when my boss, Wayne, took me on full time. The shifts are long but considering its location on the outskirts of Halston, the pay is surprisingly decent. Not to mention the tips our customers give, I guess it helps to look pretty.

"Jesus. I don't think I've ever been so bored in my life," Sadie complains. She's been working here a little longer than me and she took me under her wing to show me the ropes. She's in her early thirties but doesn't look a day older than me. "Actually, the last time I was this bored was the last time me and my ex-husband had sex. I think if I was fucked by a mannequin I would've come harder."

A full-on belly laugh escapes me and it feels good. I haven't had much to laugh about recently.

She flips her strawberry blonde hair over her shoulder, leaning over the bar top that separates us. "Speaking of lousy exes. What happened to Jack? Or Jerry? What the fuck was his name again?"

"Jay? Ugh. Don't even. A waste of time and effort just like all the rest."

"Well you know what they say about a guy who's name begins with a J... Hell, my ex-husband's name was Justin, can't get more of an asshole with *that* name."

Jay was the latest in a long line of mistakes that stretches the length of the Nile. Mistakes that I keep making time and time again.

Will I ever learn? Probably not. Attracting assholes and falling for their bullshit is starting to become a full time job, and every time it ends the same way.

I'm not looking for marriage for crying out loud, but a guy who makes me happy, a guy who's proud to call me his girl. But they all seem to want the benefits of a relationship without actually committing to one and I always wind up alone and disappointed.

Is it the fear of commitment that has them running for the hills, or do they find it fun to toy with a girl's emotions, dangling a carrot in front of her while holding her at arms length?

Modern dating is a minefield, and don't get me started on dating apps, they are the literal bane of my existence.

I'm tired of getting hurt, getting my hopes up for them to be thrown on the ground and trampled over the second I start catching feelings.

I just want to be happy. Is that so much to ask?

One night when I was at my lowest; sat on my bathroom floor fully naked after *'boyfriend who didn't want to be labelled boyfriend'* number one hundred had given me the brush off, I made an executive decision to put myself and my heart first. I've officially sworn off relationships for the foreseeable future and chosen to stick solely to no commitment hook-ups. That way I can still have fun but protect my heart in the process.

No commitments. No expectations. No room for heart-break.

Just take a page out of the *Assholes' Playbook*.

"Yo, baby. Get me a beer over here?" a man calls from behind me.

"Is he talking to me?" I ask Sadie.

She glances in his direction for a split-second then looks back at me. "Yup."

"Sugar? A little service over here," he calls louder, tapping his empty bottle on the bar.

My fists clench as I continue to ignore him. *Baby? Sugar?* Who the fuck does he think he's talking to?

"What a dick," Sadie comments.

The asshole actually clicks his fingers. "Hello? Sweetheart, can you fucking hear me?"

I whirl around. "When you ask politely and stop hollering like a child, I'll serve you. And the next time you click your fingers at me, you're out of here. I'm not a dog."

His mouth clamps shut, his eyes wide with surprise. He obviously didn't expect me to stand up for myself, but I don't take shit like that from anyone, especially not misogynistic assholes like him, God knows I've known enough of them.

He clears his throat. "I apologise. May I have a beer?"

I make my way over to him, digging into the fridge for a bottle of *Bud* and sliding it over to him. "Better," I say with a wink before heading back to Sadie, standing a little taller.

"Nice work, babe."

"Thanks."

The front door swings open and my boss, Wayne bursts through, a deep frown etched onto his face as he takes in the half a dozen customers sat in here tonight.

Wayne is in his late forties and he's a pretty decent guy. He takes care of his employees which is more than I can say for some of my bosses I've had before him.

He forces a smile. "Evening Ladies. Slow night tonight?"

"Like you wouldn't believe," I comment.

"Shit. Well, I'll be in the back if you need me." He heads behind the bar and into his office in the back.

"Ooh, I forgot to ask you, my mom's watching Connor on Friday so I've got a child free night. Want to get food or something? Maybe hit up a club?" Sadie asks.

"That sounds great, but um... I'm gonna have to pass. Things are pretty tight right now, you know?" *Tight* would be a colossal understatement. "Rain check?"

"Babe, no worries. I get it. Maybe next time."

"Absolutely." I force a smile, because everything inside is screaming at me to go. I'd love nothing more than a night out on the town but my bank account already hates me, and my overdraft even more.

Just lately it's a struggle to keep above the red and sometimes I can't help but cry myself to sleep. I have no idea what to do.

The FINAL NOTICE that was stuck my front door this morning was more like my FINAL FINAL FINAL *FINAL* NOTICE seeing as I've ignored every single one.

I could ask Della for help, she said it herself she'd do whatever she could. But I can't. I've never accepted charity and I'm not about to start now, especially not from a friend. I can't take advantage like that.

It'll be fine, I tell myself.

It has to be.

∞∞∞

An hour later, a few more customers have come in, but it's not anywhere close to how busy it should be for this time of night on a weekend.

"Have a good night! Thank you!" I call as one of our regulars heads for the exit, probably deciding to stop off at a different bar on the way home, one with a better atmosphere, unlike the staleness of the one in here.

I've had more fun actually watching paint dry. If it carries on like this for much longer, we're all gonna be out on our asses and looking for a new job.

"How is it out here?" Wayne asks, appearing from the back

room, but I'm pretty sure the picture of Sadie and I scrolling through TikTok videos is the only answer he needs. "I uh… I need to talk to you girls a sec."

Sadie and I shoot each other a look.

Judging by the regret on his face, whatever it is, isn't good. He presses his lips together in a tight line, stuffing his hands into the pockets of his jeans. "It's been like this for quite a while now, and I had hoped that business would pick up around here, but to be honest we're barely scraping by. I've been going over the numbers and the bar is losing more money than it's making. I've tried everything to turn this place around to draw in new business, but if it stays like this for much longer… there's not gonna be any shifts for anyone, let alone a functioning bar." He sighs heavily. "I really hate to say this, I hoped I'd never have to but… I'm cutting hours."

"*What?*" Sadie and I shriek in unison.

"Wayne, are you serious?" I ask.

He nods regretfully. "I'm sorry, I know it's not ideal, but at the end of the day, I've got a business to run. You know I wouldn't do this unless I had to."

Shit. He's serious.

Cutting hours? I can't even afford to lose *one*. At this point, I need every cent I can get my hands on.

"No, I get it. It's fine, Wayne," I lie. It's definitely *not* fine. None of this is fine.

What the hell am I gonna do?

2

Rafe

I raise my empty glass in the air and shake it, the ice cubes clinking against the sides of the glass. "Another, thanks."

I toss it back down onto the bar and let my head hang forward. I don't know how many drinks I've had since I got here over an hour ago, but I know it's not nearly enough.

I'm sat at the bar in the *Hudson Casino,* letting another shitty day fade into a distant memory, and since my family own every square inch of this place, I can drink to my heart's content with no worries of getting thrown out.

"You good, Mr. Hudson?" Jonathan, our head bartender asks as he slides a drink across the bar towards me.

"Never better." Sarcasm drips from my voice as I bring the glass up to my lips, my taste buds now immune to the bitter taste of the alcohol as I take a sip.

I always pitied people that would spend night after night in a bar like this. I always wondered what a person could be going through, what troubles could have led them to the point that alcohol was the only answer. People with nothing better to do, no family to go home to, no motivation or drive to do anything other than drown their sorrows in the bottom of a glass, letting the alcohol wash away their problems.

People like *me*.

An unknown number flashes up on my screen, and rather than answer it like any sane person, I Google it. They must have the wrong number because it's some social services group based in Austin. *Who the fuck do I know in Austin?*

I take a swig of my drink, letting the cool liquid slide down my throat. These past few months, alcohol has quickly become a crutch, something that I can rely on when reality just gets too much to handle. I know it's a bad habit, but drinking is the only thing that numbs the pain, the guilt.

The *regret*.

It calms me, like a balm washing over me and it stops me from overthinking so damn much. It's an escape, albeit a temporary one, I'll take whatever I can get.

I take a look around at all the happy, smiling faces that surround me, people with not a care in the world as the sound of their laughter fills the space. How the fuck can everyone be so happy when I feel the complete opposite? My life is a total train wreck and not one person seems to notice.

"I thought I might find you here." My brother's voice steals me from my thoughts as he slides into the seat to my left, motioning to the bartender and ordering himself a drink. He says nothing as he unbuttons his jacket, straightening it out and resting his elbows on the bar top.

The bartender returns a few moments later with his drink, and I order another for myself.

Still, Gage says nothing.

"What's this? Not gonna chastise me on my choice of extra-curricular activities outside of work?" I ask, lifting my glass before taking a swig.

"Why beat 'em when you can join them?" he replies with a shrug, taking a sip of his own drink.

Gage has made it no secret of his disapproval of my drinking, but I'm sure to some degree he understands the reason. Losing Dad was hard on us all, but I've never been one to handle grief well. While Gage has always been much more in touch with his feelings than I am, I tend to bury them down, not wanting to confront them, but it's getting harder and harder with every passing day.

"It would have been their anniversary today," I say.

"Si and I visited their graves earlier, put down some flowers from the garden. You should have come with us."

I shake my head. "I don't belong there."

He turns his face to me. "What are you talking about? Of course you do."

I slam my drink down on the bar a little too hard and some of the liquid spills out. "You don't get it," I grit out. "You were all there at the end. I wasn't." Guilt churns in my gut at the mention of it.

"Then you more than any of us need that closure, Rafe. Dad wouldn't resent you for not being there at the end, he loved you and knows you loved him."

"It doesn't make me feel any better."

"It's been three months and you've mourned enough, you've beaten yourself up long enough and drowned in enough booze to last you a lifetime."

"*I'll* decide when I've had enough."

"Spoken like a true alcoholic," he shoots back.

"I'm not an alcoholic."

"*Again*, spoken like an alcoholic."

I rise to my feet, my chair screeching across the floor. "Fuck this. I'm out of here."

I push my way through the bar and the casino floor before bursting out the door into the cool evening air. I cross the parking lot towards my car, not that I should be driving given the amount of alcohol I've consumed, but when has that ever stopped me? I feel perfectly fine.

"Rafe! Come on, wait." Gage calls behind me.

I speed up, my shoes eating up the dirt, but he's faster. His hand clamps on my shoulder, and I shrug off his grip, spinning out of his hold until my back collides with the side of my Corvette.

"Why the fuck are you even here, Gage? I moved out and got my own place to get away from your smothering, I don't need you following me all over the city, too." I sigh heavily. "I just need space for Christ's sake."

"Am I not allowed to be worried about you? Forgive me for not wanting to find my little brother choking on his own vomit from alcohol poisoning in some dirty alleyway."

"Don't be so dramatic."

Gage has made it his mission to fill my dad's very large shoes since he's the head of our family now. He has a habit of making everyone's problems his own, wanting to make everything right, but what he doesn't understand is that there's some things he can't fix. There are some things he can't control and he hates it.

"Della's always asking after you, worried about you being alone all the time and Sierra… She misses her brother, as do

I."

I swallow hard. I miss them too. I've barely seen them since our dad died, if anything I've been avoiding them. At work, I stay barricaded in my office or I just stay at home altogether and work from there.

"You can't carry on like this, brother. It's not healthy. This guilt you're carrying is going to kill you, and you have *nothing* to be guilty about."

I wish I could believe him, but he'll never know the feeling of letting someone down and not being able to make amends.

"Listen, it's Si's twenty-first birthday this coming Friday. We're having a party at *De La Rosa.* She'd love it if you came." His eyes are hopeful as he searches mine.

"I'll be there," I promise. I won't let my sister down, I won't allow myself to.

He smiles, and much to my dismay, he brings me in for a hug, and while his arms go around me, mine stay glued to my sides, discomfort crawling in my skin. I hate PDA and all the cushy, huggy shit. It's just not me. Nothing makes me more uncomfortable, and my brother knows this, he just chooses to ignore it.

The hug only lasts a few seconds before Gage pulls back. "I hope you don't think you're driving home by yourself."

"I'm fi—"

"If you say you're fine, I'm going to punch you in the face. Come on, I'm driving."

Rather than enter into an argument I will undoubtedly lose, I follow him to his car and when we pull up outside my apartment building, a huge skyscraper in the middle of Halston, I nod goodbye to Gage and climb out.

As I head towards the entrance, I look back over my

shoulder at my brother, his car idling on the curb like he doesn't want to leave, but after a long minute, he pulls away and disappears down the street.

When I enter my apartment, it's the empty quietness that hits me first. Don't get me wrong, I love living alone, having my own space without being under the watchful eye of my brother, but I can't help but feel... *lonely*.

Stripping off my clothes I head into the bathroom and turn on the shower. It was a hot and humid day today and sweat clings to every inch of my body, and as I step under the warm spray of the shower, I feel this shitty day washing away, swirling down the plug hole.

After my shower, I move into my bedroom, and dropping the towel that was wrapped around my waist on the floor, I go to pull out a pair of sweatpants from the dresser. My stomach drops when my eyes land on a photo sat on top. It was Della and Gage's wedding, a photo of all of us together, including my dad. Gage is positively beaming, my sister smiling sweetly at the front, Della is rigid at Gage's side, forcing a smile while praying the whole thing would be over soon since marriage was *not* her idea. Me, I'm ruining the photo by not looking at the camera and instead eyeing up a woman from across the room. And then there's my dad, looking twice as old as he was, his body slowly letting him down, the pain crippling him and yet he wears the biggest smile of all of us.

His courage in the face of death was the thing I admired most towards the end, though I couldn't be around him. Seeing him weak and in pain was something I couldn't stomach, and while I should have been by his side until the very end, I wasn't.

I missed out on the chance to say goodbye.

Selfish...

Pathetic...

I disappointed him, I know I did, but that's what I am, I'm a disappointment, constantly letting people down even though I try my hardest not to. Maybe it was best I wasn't there at the end, by his bedside like the rest of my family.

The worst part of all of this? I can't even remember the last time I spoke to him or what I said. I can't remember ever telling him that I love him.

How bad is that?

He deserved better than a son like me, which is exactly the reason I'm not cut out to have kids of my own. I wouldn't know the first thing about how to care for them and not be a disappointment to them too.

In the background of the photo, my eyes catch on something I had never noticed before. A woman in a green dress, stood with her back to the camera, a waterfall of soft copper hair cascading down to the middle of her back.

Reese. There's no doubt that it's her, I touched every inch of her perfect body and committed it all to memory enough to recognise her luscious curves and long, toned legs.

Guilt punches me in the gut as I think back to the last time I saw her, how I left her without so much as a goodbye. Just another person in my life I let down, another person who didn't deserve how I treated them.

Jesus, what a total fuck-up I am.

I head into the kitchen and drag out a half-empty bottle of vodka, and I spend the rest of the night making sure I drink every last drop.

3

Reese

Where the hell is my earring?

Sierra's birthday party is in less than an hour and after hunting high and low for the last ten minutes for my runaway earring, I'm about to tear my hair out. Hair I just spent the last hour on, curling my copper locks into thick waves that fall down my back.

I've searched everywhere I can think of. Where the hell could it be? I've only worn them a handful of times and it's not like it's tiny, it's a two-inch-wide gold hoop for crying out loud. It can't have gotten far.

I check the time. I have forty minutes to find my earring, finish off the final touches of makeup, make a final decision between the four possible outfits that hang from my wardrobe doors and get to the other side of Halston. Which reminds me, I don't even have money for a taxi. Why did I not think of this before?

3

I toss myself onto my bed, bouncing against the springy mattress and let out a frustrated sigh.

What the hell am I going to do? I can't exactly walk, it's way too far for that, even in flats let alone in heels. I can't flag down some random stranger to give me a ride without running the risk of him kidnapping and killing me then dumping my body in the lake.

I'm fucked, but you know what? I'm going to do what I always do. I'm going to finish getting ready, and then when the time comes to leave, I'll think on my feet.

It'll be fine, I convince myself.

On the upside it's a free bar, all expenses paid for by her brother which is like music to my ears.

I finish off my makeup and decide on the black dress with a built-in corset to accentuate the curve of my hips and tits, because who can resist a little black dress? It ends mid-thigh, showing enough skin to look sexy but not enough to go flashing anyone since I've had to forgo wearing panties. That happened once, it wasn't pretty.

Once I'm satisfied with my appearance, I give my apartment one last going over in an attempt to find my earring, which just happens to be wedged between the couch cushions.

How the hell did it get there? My stomach lurches. Oh yeah, I remember. Let's gloss over that memory for now.

As well as finding my earring, luck seems to be on my side because stuffed down the back of the couch is a collection of loose change, just enough, save for a few quarters, to be able to afford a taxi.

I put in my earring and grab my clutch, making sure I have everything when my phone rings.

Without looking at the caller ID, I answer and instantly

regret it. "Hello?"

"Ah! Miss Reynolds. It's Simon."

Shit.

Shit. Shit. *Shit!*

"Oh, uh… Hi." I try to keep my tone light and not let the dread that sinks like a lead weight into my stomach slip through my voice.

I've done my best for the past few weeks to avoid answering my landlord's calls, I guess this time I just wasn't careful enough.

Every rent payment for the last six months or so have been late and my landlord has been up my ass about it. I've done my best to pay them on time but life has a funny way of fucking me in the ass. It's not like I haven't been making the effort. I've done everything I can to keep on top of the payments and I'm exhausted.

The point here, is he gets paid, even if it is a little late. Let's face it, it's not like he's not good for it. Has he ever lived hand to mouth a day in his life? While he sits up in his four-bedroom house in the better part of the city, I'm stuck here wondering where my next meal is coming from and how I'm supposed to scrape enough money together to pay for my shitty apartment. Not to mention he's a creepy bastard who gives me the shivers every time I'm within five feet of him, and *not* the good kind of shivers either. The ones that make my skin crawl when he so much at looks at me. How the fuck is a perv like him even married?

"What can I do for you?" I ask.

"Reese, I think you know. I don't think I have to tell you that this really is your final warning. I've tried to be understanding but your late payments and blatant avoidance on the subject is becoming a habit."

There are a number of ways I can play this, but ultimately I opt for the one that might come back to bite me on the ass in the near future.

"Si— hell?— C— yo— hear m—" My disjointed words fall from my lips easier than I thought.

"Reese? Hello? You're breaking up," Simon says on the other end.

"Can't hea— y-you. I—" I hang up, my heart hammering in my chest.

It's not the first time I've pulled that shit, and from previous experience, it works quite well.

Crap, I only have ten minutes until the party starts. I guess I'm going to have to be fashionably late, that's if I make it at all.

I order an Uber and within five minutes, it pulls up outside my building.

"Where we headed?" the driver asks.

"De La Rosa."

I make it to Gage's club fifteen minutes later, and after the bouncer on the door checks my ID, he waves me inside. The deep bass of the music pumps through me, reverberating through my chest as strobe neon lights shine down from every direction.

The dancefloor is already full. Hot, sweaty bodies moving to the rhythm of the music as I weave my way through the crowd. How the hell does Sierra know so many people?

I'm not sure how many people she invited tonight, but it doesn't surprise me that she's so popular.

I head for the bar, figuring Sierra wouldn't be far considering it's the first time she can legally drink. But before I've even found Della or Sierra, my eyes catch on a familiar face that I'd completely forgotten would be here tonight. Of course, he'd be here, he's Sierra's brother after all.

That list of mistakes I mentioned a while ago? The ones I make a habit of repeating over and over again? Well, there's one man who sits at the top of that list, and from across the dancefloor he's staring right back at me.

Rafe Hudson.

His face falls in recognition as his eyes land on me, and even from where I'm standing I see him suck in a breath. He's surprised to see me. Did he think I wouldn't be here? Sierra is my friend, how could I not show on such an important night for her?

Well, screw him.

I tear my eyes from him and continue towards the bar, spotting Sierra downing a shot while my pregnant best friend, Della, nurses an orange juice. Sierra turns and her eyes go wide when she sees me.

"Happy Birthday!"

"Oh my God! You made it!" Her arms go around my neck as she pulls me in for a hug.

"As if I'd miss your party. What do you take me for?"

Sierra's wearing the dress we picked out on our girly shopping trip a couple of weeks ago. A white, sequined party dress with spaghetti straps, a stark contrast to her raven black hair that falls loosely in bouncy curls.

I turn to Della, tugging her into my arms, careful of her baby bump. "Hey, babe."

Della is almost five months pregnant, but her pregnancy has been anything but easy.

"Hey," she says with a weary smile. "You look beautiful."

"So do you." I grab Della and Sierra's hands in *mine. "Both* of you."

"Selfie time!" Sierra pulls out her phone and ushers us closer. "Smile!" She snaps the photo of the three of us smiling. "Aww! I love it. That's one for Instagram."

"Can you send that to me?" I ask.

"Sure!" Her eyes catch on someone over my shoulder. "Oh! I need to go say hi to somebody but I'll be back. Grab a drink, or two or three. It's a free bar tonight, courtesy of my eldest brother so help yourselves!"

There are many perks when your best friends are the wife and sister to a man who owns half of Halston, and a free bar at one of his clubs is definitely one of them.

I order a vodka and coke and take a seat at one of the tables as Della lowers herself into a chair across from me, letting her hand wander over her swollen belly.

"Do you remember the last time we were here?" I ask.

Della smiles fondly. "Yeah. That was the first time I saw Gage, right up there." She points to the wall of glass windows on the first floor. Gage's office.

Speaking of Gage, he parts the crowd as he heads towards our table. Jesus, this family and their devastatingly beautiful genetics. Gage is tall and commanding, in some ways almost intimidating, but that image diminishes whenever he's within a foot of his wife. I've never seen two people more in love with each other than Gage and Della.

He presses a kiss to the top of Della's head when he reaches us. "Hey, angel."

She cranes her neck up and beams at her husband, biting her bottom lip. "Hi."

He leans in and brushes his lips over hers.

"Still in that mushy honeymoon phase, I see. Do you ever make yourselves nauseous with your PDA?" I joke with a wink.

"We actually have some exciting news. I didn't want to say anything in front of Sierra what with it being her birthday, but um... We're having a boy."

"Oh my gosh!" I gasp. "Congratulations!"

"They told us at the scan earlier. We were going to wait and find out at the birth, but we thought, what the hell!"

I reach across and take her hand. "I'm so happy for you, both of you."

"Thanks," Gage says.

"After everything you've both been through, you deserve some happiness."

"So do you, Ree." Della smiles softly, squeezing my hand.

Yeah, I could do with a little happiness right about now.

I'm on my fourth drink of the night that I don't even manage to finish before Sierra is tugging me onto the dancefloor, and we weave our way through the crowd as the heavy thump from the sound system vibrates through my chest.

We sway to the beat of the music, letting the freedom I feel while I'm dancing wash over me.

I've always loved dancing, how it invigorates the mind and body and liberates the soul. It's so freeing. I could dance forever if I could.

Growing up I wanted to go to dance lessons, I didn't care about what type of dance it was, I just wanted to dance, but we could never afford it. Or rather, we *could* afford it, but my mom had other ideas on what to spend it on.

"Ugh! Alec is looking so hot tonight," Sierra says, and I

follow her eyes to find him stood against the wall talking with Rafe.

Alec is Gage's personal bodyguard, though I think if Sierra had any say in it, she'd make him her own. It's obvious to anyone who's not Stevie Wonder that she's got the hots for him and I don't blame her, he's fucking gorgeous. All tattoos and muscle wrapped up in a sexy six-foot-four package of pure masculinity. An ex-soldier so I've been told.

I lean in close to her ear. "So, go get him! You're both adults, go get your man and jump his bones already."

She takes a sip of her drink through her straw. "Gage would literally kill me, and then *him*."

"Gage has no right to interfere with your life, *or* your happiness," I point out.

Wouldn't Gage want his sister to be happy?

Since their dad died a few months ago, Sierra's been struggling. She thinks she's hiding it well, pretending she's okay, but behind the smile, I know deep down she's finding it hard to let go.

According to Della, Sierra didn't leave his bedside for hours, she just kept his hand in hers until they came to take his body away, and even then they had to prise her away of him.

I can't imagine what it feels like to lose someone you love, but I know how it feels to watch them getting worse and knowing you're powerless to stop it.

My skin tingles, the hairs on the back of my neck standing to attention, and I don't have to look up to know that Rafe's eyes are on me.

Jesus, why does he have to look so delicious?

He's wearing a plain white button-up shirt, paired with faded black jeans and a leather jacket. His hair is tousled perfectly and it's almost annoying how quickly my panties grow damp whenever we're in the same vicinity. After the last time I saw him, I should want to hack off his balls with a blunt dinner knife, but I don't.

Why is that?

Probably for the same reason it always is, because I'm a sucker for a pretty face and a huge dick and that red flags are more like an invitation than a warning.

"Rafe literally can't keep his eyes off you. Is there something going on between you two?"

My eyes shoot to hers. "What? No. Of course not."

She shrugs. "I just wondered."

"Let's skip boy talk and let's dance!" I say in an attempt to deflect.

"Hell yes!"

We dance through a couple of songs, twirling and singing along to the lyrics until two strong arms band around my waist from behind. "Wanna dance, gorgeous?"

I crane my neck to see a handsome guy with shaggy blonde hair peering down at me.

"Sure."

His face drops into the crook of my neck as we sway to the song, his hands at my hips, my ass tight against his crotch.

"You're so fucking sexy," he says against my ear, his breath hot on my neck.

My eyes catch Rafe standing in the same spot as before, and I can't help notice his hand clenched tight around the bottle of beer he's holding.

Is he... jealous?

He has no right *nor* the need to be. I'm not his. I never was. But I wouldn't be me if I didn't make him even more so, and now I have his undivided attention, I'll show him what he's missing.

4

Rafe

"You know you don't have to stand against the wall all night like you've got a stick shoved up your ass, right?" I tell Alec, handing him a beer.

One corner of his mouth curves up as he takes the bottle, his shoulders relaxing. "Sorry, force of habit, I guess."

Despite being under the employ of my brother, Alec is more of a friend to both Gage and I rather than just one of the guys who work for us. He's been by our side through a lot of shit lately, and not once has he failed us, not once has he given us reason to doubt him.

For the first time in a while, he's been given the night off to enjoy my sister's birthday party as a guest rather than the security, at the personal request of Sierra. But his protective instincts must be hard to shift because I still notice his eyes scanning the crowd for threats, his senses on overdrive.

I watch as his attention lands on my sister who is currently in the centre of the dancefloor, her head thrown back as she twirls on the spot. His eyes soften as he takes her in. I know he cares about her, maybe more than he should, but I don't think he's ever acted on his feelings, scared of the wrath my brother would rain down on him if he ever touched her. But I'm sure even Gage can admit that Alec would never hurt her or put her in danger.

Alec catches me eyeing him and he does his best to school his features, darting his eyes away as he takes a swig of his beer.

My eyes fall on the woman dancing beside Sierra and my fist tightens around the neck of the bottle in my hand. I've never been what you'd call a jealous guy. I've never had any reason to be, given that I've never been with a girl long enough to warrant the feeling. Never *cared* enough. But Reese Reynolds has the potential to be the first girl that ever made me want to kill because of it. The dyed-blonde prick she's dancing with has his dirty hands all over her and my fists clench at my sides, wanting to break every fucking finger on both his hands for touching what isn't is, and what also *isn't* mine.

I watch as she grinds her ass against the prick's crotch, leaning back into his touch while his hand dips south, skimming the hem of her short strappy barely-there dress. She laughs at something he said, for a second I'm almost certain I can hear it over the music that pulses through the speakers and I curse under my breath.

He's a sleaze, anyone can see that. I don't even know why he's here. I don't remember Sierra saying that he was a friend, if he was he'd be dead already, I don't want this scumbag anywhere near my sister *or* Reese for that matter. He's giving off a vibe, a vibe that has me on high alert.

Reese's eyes flick to mine and my skin heats under her gaze. A hint of a smirk touches her red lips. She knows exactly what she's doing. She's trying to make me jealous. And as much as I don't want to admit it, it's working.

"Please tell me you didn't," Alec says, side-eyeing me with a knowing look.

"What?"

"You know what. Della's friend, the redhead."

"Don't know what you're talking about, man," I lie.

"Yeah, yeah." He chuckles, shaking his head. I can tell by his face he's not believing a word of my bullshit, though I'm surprised, I tell myself enough bullshit that I sometimes have myself believing it. "I'm gonna hazard a guess, so go with me on this," he begins, "You fucked her, and judging by that look you're giving the guy she's dancing with, I'd say you care more than you like to let on."

"There's only four people on this planet I care about. My brother, my sister, Della and myself. I don't have enough room to care about anyone else."

"I don't believe that."

"The more people you care about, the more chance you have of getting hurt."

The blonde prick whispers something into Reese's ear, squeezes her ass and walks away. I watch him leave and before I know it, my feet are on the move. I push my way through the crowd and follow him down the corridor that leads to the exit.

I follow him outside, doing my best to stay out of sight as he turns the corner into the alley at the side of the building. It's not until I get closer I realise he's talking to someone on the phone.

"Fuck, man. She's exactly what I'm after. Built like a whore with the mouth made for sucking cock."

His vulgar language about Reese has me feeling for the gun that I have tucked into the waistband of my trousers. With everything that's happened lately, and despite it all being over with, I don't go anywhere unless I'm carrying.

He laughs loudly. "She looks like a feisty one, gonna have to make sure I take care of that," he continues.

I poke my head around the corner just enough that I make out the tiny bag of pills he's pulled out of his pocket to inspect before putting it back.

"Yeah. Once it's done and I'll send you the address. Might as well make the most of her while she's out cold. Pussy is pussy whether she's awake or not."

Fuck. The asshole's going to drug her.

"You too, dude. Don't sweat. It'll be easy." He stuffs his phone back into his pocket before pulling out a cigarette and lighting it.

There's no way in hell I'm letting him get within a hundred feet of her.

"Got a spare one of those?" I ask, shuffling around the corner to stand alongside him, my hands thrust in his pockets.

Something flashes in his eyes when he sees me. Recognition? Well, I sure as fuck don't know him.

"Uh, yeah. Sure." He pulls one out and gives me a light. I don't smoke, but he doesn't have to know that.

"Hopping party, right?" I give him a toothy smile. "There are some *real* beautiful girls in there. Don't think I'll be going home alone, know what I'm sayin'?"

He rubs his face, laughing, though it dies quickly. "Sure is. I uh… better get back inside. Gotta get back to my girl."

He flicks his cigarette to the ground, pushes off the wall and begins to walk past me but I stop him, my hand against his shoulder. "The fuck, man?"

"She's not really *your girl* though, is she?" I ask.

"What?"

"'*Pussy is pussy whether she's awake or not*'? That sounds a lot like rape, and with those little pills you've got in your pocket, I'd say that's exactly what it is."

"Fuck you, Hudson."

"You know me, then?" I slam the side of my hand into his throat hard, and he falls to his knees, clutching his neck, choking and gasping for breath.

I crouch in front of him and take him by the hair, yanking up his head, forcing him to look at me. I take a puff of my cigarette and blow the rancid smoke into his face, making him cough even more before putting it out on his face. He screams as the burning end of my cigarette sears into his skin.

"Never really liked smoking anyway." I toss it away.

"The fuck, bro?"

"Let's get one thing straight, I'm *not* your 'bro', I'm your worst fucking nightmare. You see, that girl you plan on drugging in there, she's important to me, and you're not gonna touch her or any other woman in my club again, you understand me?" I grip his hair in my fist tighter, and he winces. "Pieces of shit like you make me sick. Just how many girls have you drugged and passed around your friends, huh? I bet you can't even count them on both hands. You're scum and I should just kill you right now. It'd make the world a better place if you were wiped off the face of it." I pull out my gun, making sure he can see it.

He recoils from it, the fear in his eyes only spurring me on.

4

"Don't hurt me, man."

"Do you listen to the women you hurt when they beg you not to? Is that what turns you on, prick?" Men who hurt women don't deserve to breathe, and this guy is breathing on borrowed time.

He wouldn't be the first guy I've killed and I'm sure he won't be the last, and ever since then, I've had a thirst for it, as fucked up as it sounds. I crave the adrenaline, the excitement and the satisfaction of knowing the guy I was killing was a piece of shit that's better off dead. Killing isn't okay, by any means, but in most cases, it's justifiable. Fuck with my family and the people I care about and see what happens.

"Give me one reason I shouldn't put a bullet in your head right now."

"What's going on?" My head shoots around to find Alec standing over me, his brows furrowed as he takes in the sight in front of him.

"Help me take out the trash."

Ten minutes later, I'm back in the club. Sweat clings to my skin, my heart still pounding a heavy beat in my chest as I scan the space. My eyes fall on a wave of red hair and I move towards it.

Reese is sat at the bar, tapping her fingers on the marble bar top as she glances over her shoulder in the opposite direction, no doubt looking for that piece of shit I just disposed of.

I slide in beside her and in an instant her spine stiffens, her eyes meeting mine.

She rolls her eyes, signalling over to the bartender. "*Double* gin and tonic please."

"Of course."

"Good night?" I ask.

"It was better before I saw you," she shoots back and my pulse races. I forgot how much I enjoyed her sass and her smart mouth.

The bartender brings her drink over and she tips it back.

"Am I really that bad?" I'm a little offended.

"Do you want something? I'm waiting for someone."

"Ah, that blonde prick you were dancing with. You know, for a moment there, I thought you were trying to make me jealous."

"And why would I do that?"

I shrug. "You tell me. It was *his* dick you were rubbing against and *me* you were looking at so go figure."

She scoffs. "Don't flatter yourself, Rafe. I wouldn't waste my energy trying to make you jealous."

"If you say so." I lean in closer, the scent of her sweet perfume intoxicating my senses. "But we both know the truth, don't we? Where is that guy anyway? He's been gone an *awful* long time."

She studies my face and her shoulders drop. "What have you done?"

"Me? Nothing, besides take out the trash."

Her eyes narrow. "I know you did something, Rafe. Where is he?"

"Like I said, I took out the trash," I reply, my face giving nothing away, but I know she can tell something through my tone. "You don't know who you were dealing with. He's a piece of shit."

"Says who?"

"Says *me*. You should be fucking thanking me," I say.

She slams her glass down onto the bar. "Thanking you?

What for? For screwing up a perfectly good night for me?"

"You don't know what you're talking about," I sigh.

"So enlighten me."

"He was gonna fucking rape you!" It slips out before I can take it back. I wanted to ease into it slowly, give her the news gently, but of course my mouth jumped the gun before my brain kicked in.

She jerks back like I slapped across the face. "W-What?"

"Shit, I… I didn't mean it to come out like that." I pinch the bridge of my nose. "I followed him outside when he left you. Was gonna run him off, don't ask me why. I overheard him on the phone, bragging about how he was gonna drug you then use your body before sharing you with his friends."

Her eyes go wide. "Are you serious?"

"Why would I lie?" I swallow hard. "He had a packet of pills in his pocket. He was gonna spike your drink."

"Oh my God," she mutters, her gaze dropping to the bar. "I don't feel so good."

"Come on, let me take you home."

To my surprise, she doesn't argue as I lead her out of the club and after vomiting into a hedge, she lets me help her into my car.

As I drive, I'm hyper-aware that her dress has ridden further up her thighs, exposing miles of long creamy legs that has my dick twitching in my pants, but I force my gaze back onto the road. After what's already happened tonight, a car accident is definitely not on the table.

Neither one of us speaks on the way to her apartment, not even when I pull up outside and walk her to her door. It's not until she shoves the key in the lock and turns to me, her emerald eyes shimmering under the harsh lights in the corridor.

"Thank you," she says softly.

"You're welcome."

She goes to say something else, but must think better of it because without another word she disappears inside and shuts the door behind her.

I never expected to be invited inside when I offered her a ride home, my only motive to make sure she got home safe, and content with that knowledge, I head back to my car.

Before going back to the party, I meet Alec a few miles out of town at an old abandoned power plant. It's pitch-black, no other person besides us for miles, the only light is the headlights of the car.

The blonde prick is lying on the ground, his hands and ankles bound so he can't move, a gag in his mouth muffling his voice as he shouts.

"What do you wanna do with him? We let him walk, he'll talk," Alec says, folding his arms across his chest.

"He wouldn't risk it. If he did, he'd risk getting found out. I'm gonna send a message."

I drop down in front of him. I can just about make out a bruise that's darkening around his left eye, this lid swelling shut. "You're gonna wish you'd never laid eyes on her."

5

Rafe

A high-pitched screech pierces my eardrums, shocking me out of the deep, alcohol-induced coma I drank myself into last night at Sierra's party.

After I'd finished with the blonde piece of shit who dared try to hurt Reese, I returned to the party and proceeded to drink myself into oblivion.

I have no idea how much I had to drink, or how I even got home, but judging how my head thumps like someone is slamming it into a brick wall and how my eyes feel like they've been gouged out with a spoon, I'd say I had my fair share.

It's all a blur.

I guess you could call it self-pity or self-harm if you look at it from a certain angle. Unlike most people who use alcohol as a way to forget all the shit in their lives, I use it as a way to numb the pain. It's the only time I allow myself to feel all of the things I deny myself when I'm stone-cold sober, things I can't bring myself to face, because at least when I'm drink it doesn't hurt so fucking much. Weirdly, in my drunken haze, it makes it easier than if I wasn't.

Truth is, I don't know how to handle feelings, so I don't let myself feel. I don't let people in. Simple, right? Except the feelings that churn and grind in my guts make me nauseous, slowly eating away at my insides which is why I force them down like I do, or I try to at least.

Seeing Reese last night made me feel things again and I didn't like it.

The screech starts up again, punishing my eardrums and I realise it's my phone ringing. I look at the caller, it's the same number that's called me three times this week, and every single call I've ignored, but the person calling doesn't seem to know when to give up.

Fuck sake.

"Yeah?"

"Is this a Mr. Hudson?" a lady asks on the other end of the line.

I recline further back into my chair. "Depends on which Hudson you're after and who's asking."

"Oh, my apologies, Sir. I'm looking for Rafe Hudson."

"That's me."

"Oh, hello. I'm sorry to bother you but I'm glad I finally managed to get a hold of you. My name is Amanda Sampson, I work for Social Services. I was hoping I could speak with you in regards to your daughter."

I sit up straight in my chair, my heart skipping a beat. "Is this some sort of a joke?"

Have I drank way too much and I'm stuck in some sort of nightmare I can't wake up from?

5

"What? Oh, no. Mr. Hudson, I assure you, this isn't a joke. Like I said, I work for the Department of Child and Family Services here in Austin. I've been trying to contact you about your daughter."

What the fuck is going on?

"I don't understand what you're talking about. I… I don't have a daughter." *Do I?*

This has to be a wind up.

"According to the child's birth certificate, it says you are. You are named as her biological father. Her mother, Yvonne Harrison was involved in a fatal accident a few weeks ago and as far as we understand it, you're her next of kin."

Yvonne Harrison? That name seems vaguely familiar, but there's been so many women in and out of my life, they soon all blend into one.

Is it bad that I can't remember her? I can't even picture what she looks like.

"I… I don't even know what to say." I lean forward on my knees, rubbing the stubble that prickles on my face.

"I understand this must come as quite a shock to you, but I was hoping to meet with you soon regarding Ivy."

"Ivy…" Her name falls from my lips on an exhale, the image of a little girl scared and alone, not knowing where her mother is. "Um… Yeah. Uh… When would you like to meet? I can be there tomorrow?"

"Tomorrow would be wonderful. Two o'clock? I will send you details of the address and documents that you will need to bring with you."

"I'll be there."

"I'll schedule the appointment. Thank you for your time, Mr. Hudson. I'll see you tomorrow."

My mind is reeling.

I have a daughter?

A million questions pop into my head, firing at me all at the same time like a machine gun.

When did this happen? How old is she? What does she look like? What colour hair does she have? Does she have my eyes?

I can't believe it.

I have a daughter... I mull that thought over in my brain.

Despite my brother who is soon going to become a father in a few months time, having kids of my own was the furthest thought from my mind.

Well, if I wasn't sober before, I sure as fuck am now.

An hour and a half later, I burst through my brother's office door and it slams back against the wall, swinging on its hinges.

"You sure know how to make an entrance," he says with a smirk, not bothering to take his eyes off his computer screen. "Nice of you to finally join us today. Sleep off that hangover?" When I don't answer, he stops typing and looks up at me, his expression of amusement morphing into one of worry. "Rafe? What's happened?"

I make my way towards the chairs opposite his desk and lower myself into one. "I..."

"Rafe?" he presses.

"I... have a daughter." The words are barely a whisper.

He blinks a few times as my words sink in. "What?"

"I have a daughter."

His eyes widen as he rounds the desk and drops into the chair beside me.

"I got a call from a lady from the CPS or some shit in Austin. A woman, someone from my past died recently, leaving her kid and I'm named as the father," I explain.

"The mother? Who was she?"

"I can't remember. Yvonne Harrison, I think her name was. She was in some sort of accident."

He rubs his forehead. "Holy shit... I don't know what to say."

"I've gotta uh... fly down to Austin tomorrow for a meeting at two o'clock."

"Do you want me to come with you? I can clear my calendar, reschedule my meetings."

"You don't have to."

"I want to. This is big, Rafe. *Huge*. Let me come with you." I can see the sincerity in his eyes and he searches my face.

I nod. "Okay."

"Do you know her name? The kid?" he asks.

"Ivy. Her name's Ivy." I can't deny the warmth that spreads through me as I speak her name. My *daughter's* name.

A small smile spreads across his face. "Ivy Hudson, I like it." He stands, straightening his blazer. "I'll book us a flight and a rental. I'll also contact Kevin Worth, I think he still lives in Austin. He's a lawyer who specialises in family affairs. He'll help us."

"A lawyer?"

"They're not just gonna hand the kid over to you. There's legal procedures they have to go through."

"Shit. I hadn't thought of that." My mind is a total mess.

"They might even require a paternity test and background checks to make sure you're fit to acquire custody."

Custody.

My stomach lurches.

How could I have let that part slip from my mind? Where

did I expect her to go? If I'm her only living relative, that means she doesn't have a home. But how the hell am I supposed to take care of her? I can barely take care of myself as it is.

Gage must see the fear written across my face as my mind spirals into overdrive because he moves closer, squeezing my shoulder. "Hey, it'll be okay, brother. You're not alone in this."

That may be true, but why does it feel like I am?

∞∞∞

My foot taps nervously against the floor as Gage and I sit in the Social Services waiting room. We landed two hours ago and ever since we stepped off that plane, my stomach has been in knots. I didn't get much in the way of sleep last night, hovering between the state of awake and unconscious all night long, but when I did manage to fall asleep, I dreamed, the image of a little girl playing a starring role.

A frightened little girl calling out for her daddy.

I never really thought about having kids, never entertained the idea, but now I can't think of anything else. There's a little girl here who needs someone, needs *me*. She needs a home, a family. What kind of prick would I be if I turned my back on her now after losing her mother?

Before we came here, we consulted with the lawyer Gage contacted yesterday, running through everything we needed to know and the standard procedure for all of this. I'm expecting to have to give a DNA test to prove Ivy is mine. Though the lawyer, Kevin, seems to be pretty confident I'll gain custody considering my clean record, my family name holding the reputation it does, with the reassurance of providing her with a safe, stable home.

A door to the left opens and a lady steps out. She looks to be in her late forties, blonde hair cropped into a bob, and glasses perched high on her nose. "Mr. Hudson?"

"Yeah." Gage and I both stand and make our way into her office. "This is my brother, Gage, I hope it's okay he be with me."

"Of course. This can be a very challenging time given the circumstances, so whatever support you need is absolutely fine. Please have a seat." She ushers us over to the chairs in front of her desk before taking a seat behind it.

I clear my throat. "I apologise for not returning your calls sooner, had I known the importance, I would have."

"No apologies necessary. As I said on the phone, my name is Amanda Sampson and I'll be handling your daughter's case. I want to thank you for meeting me so quickly, cases such as these are best resolved as soon as possible. I'd like to start by asking how you knew the mother of the child."

I shift in my chair. "I'm gonna be honest, I can't really remember her and we parted ways soon after our... *encounter*. Had I known she was pregnant, I'd never have let her face it on her own." I may be an asshole, but I'm not that much of an asshole that I'd leave a pregnant woman to raise my kid by herself.

She nods understandingly. "Miss Harrison was involved in a fatal accident, it seems she'd taken a nasty fall down the stairs at her home. Unfortunately, Ivy was the one who found her. Despite how young she is and how scared she must have been, she was able to call an ambulance."

Ivy found her mom...

Oh my God.

"She fell?" Gage asks beside me.

"It seems so, and unfortunately when the ambulance arrived, it was too late to save her. It seems that Miss Harrison was unmarried, and no family has come forward to claim her estate or petition for custody."

"Petition for custody? She's *my* daughter, why would she be placed with anyone else other than her family?" *What the fuck?*

"Please understand that biological parent or not, we have to establish that the environment the child will be entered into is safe, loving and that she will be looked after with the utmost care."

"And me? Where do I stand in all of this?" I ask.

"Given that your name is on the birth certificate, and the mother's wishes were that you gain custody of the child, that's a huge step forward and will make this whole process simpler. However, it would be recommended to complete a paternity test to rule out any doubts. After that, it is up to you whether you would like to press for custody."

In other words, do I want my daughter? What kind of fucked up question is that? Of course, I want her.

"She's my daughter, why would I want her to be anywhere else other than with me?"

Gage clears his throat. "Ms. Sampson. Ivy should be with us, her *family*. She will never receive as much love as she will with my brother. My wife and I, along with our sister will make sure of that."

Amanda smiles. "I have no doubt about that. But please understand we have procedures and guidelines to follow but provided paternity is established and you're found to be fit to take care of her, I see no reason why Ivy can't be placed in your care."

My chest lightens. "Can you um... Can you tell me about her?"

"I can do one better." She flips open a manila folder and slides something across her desk. "This is Ivy."

My heart stops. It literally stops beating as I stare down at the little girl smiling back at me in the photo.

My little girl.

"She's five years old. She's very quiet and reserved but that is to be expected given the circumstances," Amanda explains. "She's very polite and in the last few days she's started coming out of her shell."

There is no doubt in my mind that she's mine. She has my eyes for crying out, topaz blue as bright as the ocean and a wave of raven hair just like my sister, and my mother.

She's beautiful.

I have no other way to describe the feeling inside me other than it feels like I just took a sledgehammer to the gut as my heart thunders wildly in my chest.

"Can you excuse me for a moment?" I'm out the door before she can answer, and once I'm out in the corridor, I rest my head against the wall.

This is all too much.

My mind is spinning.

Tears burn in the backs of my eyes and I have to bite down on my fist to stop from breaking down completely.

Keep it together... I tell myself. Keep it together not just for me, but for that little girl.

This is real. Now that I have a face to go with the name, this shit just got a hell of a lot more real.

Her face flashes behind my eyelids and my knees threaten

to buckle. I can see so much of myself in her. I can see so much of my mother.

Even without that DNA test, Ivy is mine, that I have no doubt.

The door opens next to me and Gage steps out. "Are you okay?"

"Yeah. Just needed a minute."

"It's a lot to take in, that's for damn sure. She's a beautiful kid."

"That she is. She's got Mom's hair."

"And your eyes," he adds with a smile. "Like I said yesterday, you're not alone in this. We're all going to help you, brother."

"Thanks."

"Come on." He takes my shoulder and guides me back towards Amanda's office.

"Everything alright?" she asks.

"Yes. Just a little… *overwhelmed* with all of this. How long will it all take before she can come home with me?"

"Well, I assume you would like to provide a DNA sample voluntarily?"

"Of course."

"That speeds things up significantly. Provided paternity is established and the case remains uncontested meaning no extended family come forward or there are no objections to you gaining custody, it can take as little as a couple of months, if not sooner. Hopefully, we can get a court hearing soon."

"And if it *is* contested?" Gage asks.

"Contested cases can take upwards of six to eighteen months," Amanda tells us.

"No way," I start. "She can't spend that long in foster care. She needs to be at home with me. I know I have no experience with children, but I'm certain I'm her best option."

"I'll make a call to the local clinic to have you come down and provide a sample. Results should be back within a few days and we can go from there. Off the record, Mr. Hudson, your daughter will be coming home with you once all the legal stuff is out of the way. Your family's reputation travels far further afield than in Halston. Personally, I can't think of a better fit for her."

"Can I meet her?" I ask.

Amanda smiles. "I'm sure that can be arranged."

"Thank you, Amanda," I say.

"I'll be in touch."

Gage and I both shake her hand as she walks us out of her office and once we're outside, I heave a deep sigh.

Gage slaps a hand in my shoulder. "I don't think I've ever been prouder of you, brother. Dad would be too."

6

Reese

I both cherish and dread days like these. They're both heart warming and heart breaking, usually leaning towards the latter. But isn't that what happens when you love someone? It almost always ends in heartbreak, and yet we love them regardless, because a life without love isn't worth living.

"Hi, Nanna," I say, poking my head around the door. She's sat in her armchair set beside the window as she gazes out. She doesn't hear me come in, even with the hearing aids we sorted her out with last year.

"How is she today, Gloria?" I ask my grandmother's carer who follows me inside.

"She's had a good morning so far, she's in very high spirits." Gloria has been caring for her since she arrived at *Cedar Tree* almost two years ago.

I was forced to have my grandmother admitted into a nursing home after she was diagnosed with dementia. At the beginning it was manageable. She'd forget the neighbour's name or lose her train of thought once or twice, but even *I* do those things occasionally. She soon spiralled, and I came home one day after college to find an ambulance and a fire truck parked up outside and our front door wide open. Turns out, my grandma had turned the stove on in the kitchen to cook her lunch and had forgotten about it and left it on. It was then that I realised things couldn't carry on the way they were, and the day I brought her here is one I'll never forget. She begged me not to leave her and my heart broke in ways I never thought possible. I cried all the way home and well into the night, the guilt eating away at me from the inside out.

I was forced to sell her house and use the money from the sale to pay for her care, but that money is rapidly running dry. Another couple of months and there'll be nothing left to cover the ten-thousand-dollar monthly cost for her care, and I have no idea what I'm going to do after that. I've considered stripping at the local gentleman's club, auctioning off a kidney or finding myself a sugar daddy. I don't think what I make at the bar will suffice considering I can barely cover my own rent. Whatever happens, I won't allow my grandmother to suffer.

I move further into the room, taking slow steps so as not to spook her.

"Mavis, Reese has come to visit, isn't that lovely?" Gloria says, placing a gentle hand on Nanna's shoulder.

"Nanna? How are you?" I ask, taking a seat on the bay window across from her.

Her face brightens when she sees me, the wrinkles around her eyes deepening when she smiles. "Reesie? That you?"

"It's me. How are you?"

She leans forward in her armchair and pats my hand. "Just fine, dear. Just fine."

"I'll leave you to it. Would you like something to drink?" Gloria asks me.

"No, thank you."

She leaves the room, leaving Nanna and I alone. My grandmother is the only family I have left. I never knew my sperm-donor of a father, he packed up and left before his sperm even reached the egg, and my mom... the less said about her, the better. I might as well have grown up without her for all the good she did me. My grandmother was the only stable person in my life, the only one I could count on to always be there for me.

"How do you like my hair? The lady came yesterday to give me a perm."

"I love it! It looks great," I tell her, noticing her short silvery locks curled into tight rings close to her head.

I take in the vase of fresh lilies on my grandma's window sill, the sunlight hitting the vibrant orange petals. They're almost the colour of my hair. "These are beautiful flowers, Nanna. Do you have a secret admirer I'm not aware of?"

She smiles softly, letting her gaze drift towards the window. She doesn't talk much these days and when she does, her sentences are usually disjointed or broken, and sometimes they don't even make sense at all.

"Do you need me to bring you anything the next time I visit? A book maybe? A crossword puzzle? What about some moisturiser, your skin is looking a little dry?"

"Don't worry about me, Reesie. I'm just fine. Oh, I forgot to tell you, I got my hair done yesterday."

My smile falters slightly. "You already told me, Nanna. It

looks lovely."

Her smile fades and her gaze returns to the window. She gets tired very quickly, and I can always tell when she's too tired to talk, because she'll stare out of that window overlooking the gardens for hours if you let her.

I go about tidying up, folding some of her clothes and making her bed. I pour a fresh glass of water from the jug on her bedside table and plump her pillows.

"There you go, Nanna. Nice and tidy." I place my hand on her arm and she jumps, startling me.

Her brown eyes meet mine but something has changed, she shows no sign of recognition or recollection of who I am at all. "Who are you? You leave me alone!"

"Nanna, please. It's me, your granddaughter, Reese."

"Get out of here!" she yells. "Help!"

A sob rips through me, a waterfall of tears cascading down my face as Gloria rushes into the room, hurrying to my grandma in an attempt to calm her down.

"Get her out of here! I don't know her! She's come to steal from me, I'm telling you!" she rants, waving her arms in the air growing more and more distressed by the second.

Gloria tosses a sorrowful glance over her shoulder at me, while another carer comes into the room to help with the commotion.

"Nanna…" My heart cracks, and the more distressed my grandmother gets, the harder I cry and I'm taking off into a run before I realise it.

I don't stop running until I'm down the stairs and out into the fresh air, clutching my hand to my chest, my knees giving way beneath me as I sink to the ground.

Tears blur my eyes as my cries turn hysterical, my breaths

coming in short, sharp bursts of air.

I hate this, but it's not the first time it's happened. It's happened a few times and every week I visit, I pray that it won't, and every time it does, it never gets any easier. It still hurts the same. This woman who loved me, raised me better than my own mother ever did doesn't know who I am.

To her, I'm a stranger, just a nameless face among many who come in and out of her life everyday, but to me, she's everything.

I need for this day to fade into a distant memory. I need something to fill the gaping hole in my chest that has been with me the second my grandmother looked at me with no recognition of who I am in her eyes.

I need to forget.

The walls in my apartment were suffocating and I had to escape. Which is why it only took a guy I met not even half an hour ago buying me one drink at the bar to find myself bent over the sinks in the ladies room, my dress bunched up around my waist while he pounds into me from behind.

I don't usually do the whole, fuck a stranger before you even get to know their name thing, but tonight it was just what the doctor ordered, or so I thought. His fingernails bite into my bare hips as I hang onto the edge of the counter for dear life, but not out of pleasure or unbridled ecstasy like I imagined, but because his hurried movements and his tight grip has me struggling to remain upright.

He's one of those, 'talk a big game' kinda guys when in actual fact he's got a three-inch dick the width of a pencil that is barely touching the inside of my vagina. I'm not even sure he can feel anything himself because I sure can't. The only thing that tells me what's going on is the hands on my hips, the sound of slapping flesh that bounces off the walls along with his exaggerated grunts at my ear.

A few minutes later, he comes with a roar and I do my best to sound convincing as I fake my own orgasm. It's not my first rodeo, I've had to do it many times before, forced into finishing myself off later.

He tucks himself back into his pants while I straighten out my dress and smoothing down my hair.

"I uh… I've gotta go." Without even looking at him and without waiting for a reply, I unlock the door and rush out of the bathroom.

I don't stop until my feet are covered in blisters from my high heels I'm wearing as I limp the twenty-minute walk back home to my apartment. Not a smart move since it's past ten-thirty but what other choice did I have?

After taking a long hot shower, scrubbing off any remnants of that guy from my body, I crash face first into bed, not even bothering to dry my damp hair.

My chin wobbles as I force back a wave of tears.

I feel worthless. *Used.* It's my own fault, I *did* ask for it. My plan to forget my shitty day backfired because I feel even worse now than I did earlier.

∞∞∞

The next day, I'm woken by loud rapping on my front door. I lie in bed hoping that whoever it is will assume I'm not home and go away, and when it stops, I sink back against my pillow, drifting off to sleep when the shrill sound of my ringtone has me flying out of bed.

"Ree, I can hear your phone ringing from the other side of this door. I may be pregnant but I'm still able to kick it down," Della shouts from the hallway.

Pulling my robe around me, I head for the front door, greeted by my best friend with a hand on her hip. "Were you still in bed? It's almost noon," she says, slipping inside my apartment. I swear her bump gets bigger every time I see her.

"Sorry, *Mom*," I draw out, closing the door behind her.

"You forgot, didn't you?"

"Forgot what?" It's then that I remember I was supposed to meet her for coffee this morning for our weekly catch up. "Oh shit! I'm so sorry. It completely slipped my mind."

"It's no big deal. We can have coffee here," she offers, heading for the kitchen and opening one of the many cupboards that are empty save for a half-empty bag of pasta.

"Good luck finding some, I haven't had time to go shopping in a while so I don't have much in."

"We'll order something in." She pulls out her phone and begins tapping away.

"I can't pay you back, babe."

Her eyes lift to meet mine. "You don't have to, Ree. It's my treat."

"It's *always* your treat," I point out.

"When you're married to one of the wealthiest men in the city, it's allowed to be my treat. Besides, what are friends for?"

I love my best friend more than words can express, but it's times like these I feel like the shittiest friend in the world.

A loud drawn-out meow fills the space as Merlin trots towards Della, brushing himself up against her ankles, purring softly as he rubs his head on her leg.

Merlin is my grandmother's beloved cat until she couldn't

take care of him anymore, and despite not being a lover of cats myself, I couldn't bear to give him up when she went into a care home, so I took him in.

While we eat, she tells me how her and Gage have a list of baby names as long as her arm ready for when their little boy comes along. Although they're both undecided, the one thing they have agreed on is that his middle name will be Joseph, after Gage's dad.

"We've narrowed down a few names we both like. There's Alexander... Caleb... Theo..."

"Theo, like your old bodyguard?" I ask. Theo was killed last year when some shit went down resulting in Della being kidnapped and sadly, he was caught in the crossfire.

"Yeah. He was like a friend to me, and I don't know, Theodore Joseph sounds kinda nice. We also like the name Edward."

"As in Edward Cullen? Is your *Twilight* obsession from when we were thirteen about to make a comeback?" I joke and she swats my arm playfully.

"It's a nice name!" she insists, and even I have to admit that Edward Joseph has a ring to it.

"What about Isaac?" I suggest.

Her lips twist. "Huh... I quite like that name."

"Better yet, why not call him Rhys after your amazing and incredible best friend."

"It's already on our list. Rafe suggested it "

What? "He did?"

"Uh-huh." She nods. "Oh! I forgot to tell you, we found out that Rafe has a daughter," she tells me.

What? "Are you serious?" Rafe has a daughter? I never in a million years saw *that* curve ball coming.

"He got a call from Social Services saying that a woman was involved in an accident, leaving her five year-old daughter without a mom and turns out his name is on the birth certificate. He had no clue. Can you believe it?"

"What's he gonna do?"

"He wants her. I'm going down to Austin with him next week to meet her. He has a court hearing coming up soon when they decide if he can have custody of her. He's in with a good shot."

I never saw Rafe being the family man, and I thought for sure having kids would be the furthest thing from his mind, but it might do him good to have someone depend on him, someone to care for. He's still grieving the loss of his dad, so maybe this will help to ground him somehow, give him something to focus on and give him a reason to keep moving forward.

It might even show him what he's missing.

7

Rafe

"Ivy's a little apprehensive about meeting you, which is understandable. My advice is to take things slowly and let her get used to you. We also discourage telling her you're her father until she's grown accustomed to being around you. It's an incredibly confusing time for her and we want her to be as comfortable as possible."

"Of course."

A few days after the meeting with Amanda, the DNA tests that were carried out at the clinic came back positive.

Just as I already knew, Ivy is my daughter.

Since losing her mom, she's been staying with a foster family not far from the centre of Austin, but the sooner I'm allowed to take her home the better.

A court date has been set for two weeks from today, which is a lot sooner than any of us expected, it also helped that Gage managed to call in a few favours and have it moved forward.

The lawyer Gage found believes I'll have no problems gaining custody and in his experience, uncontested cases such as ours are pretty much cut and dry. A home visit has been scheduled for next week so they can inspect my apartment and ensure it's a suitable home for her.

It's all so surreal, sat in a stranger's living room waiting to meet the daughter I never knew I had up until a week and a half ago. My little girl is on the other side of the door and I have no idea what to do or say to her.

My leg begins to bounce and I pull at the collar of my shirt. It's getting way too hot in here. I opted for a casual t-shirt and jeans, I thought it might seem a little intimidating if I rocked up in my usual three-piece suit.

As if sensing my nerves, Della sets a gentle hand on my arm. "You've got this, Rafe."

Della flew out with me to meet Ivy, while Gage stayed back in Halston to handle the business. Della was so excited that I thought for sure she was going to give birth prematurely, but I figured if she were here, Ivy might respond better if there was a woman around.

"Are you ready?" Amanda asks, and taking in a lung-full of air, I nod.

Amanda moves off the sofa and leaves the room, returning a moment later with a little girl's hand clasped tightly in hers.

If I wasn't sitting down, I'm positive my knees would have buckled at the sight of Ivy, clutching a worn-out teddy bear close to her chest as she's led into the room. Her raven hair is styled in thick braids either side of her head, her bright pink floral dress matching her shoes exactly.

Ivy shuffles awkwardly from one foot to the other before her crystal blue eyes find mine and my heart skips a beat.

7

Amanda drops into a crouch beside Ivy. "Ivy, this here is Rafe and Della. Do you want to say hi?"

"Hello," she mumbles.

"It's really nice to meet you, Ivy. I'm Della." She gives my daughter a wide smile. "This is my husband's brother, Rafe."

"Rafe? That's a silly name," she says shyly.

"Well, he's a super silly person," Della replies, making Ivy giggle.

Well, if that isn't the best sound in the world...

Della's eyes find mine, encouraging me to say something. *Like what?* I don't know the first thing about talking to kids.

Everybody looks at each other awkwardly, waiting for someone to speak first.

After a long stretch of silence, I clear my throat. "It's so good to meet you, Ivy. Um... Who've you got there?" I point to her bear that she holds tighter to her body.

"His name is Bobby," she answers quietly, her eyes not wanting to hold mine for too long.

"Bobby Bear? I like that. My sister had a bear that looked like Bobby when she was your age."

She smiles, then looks towards Della. "Are you having a baby?" Ivy asks Della, pointing a tiny finger towards her swollen belly.

Della laughs. "I sure am. It's a boy. Do you want to feel?"

Ivy glances up at Amanda who nods, urging her gently towards us. Ivy takes a few hesitant steps closer as Della reaches for her hand before placing it on her belly.

Ivy stares at the bump inquisitively, leaning in closer to inspect it. "Ellooo, baby," she whispers, moments before she gasps, jumping back a step with a giggle. "He moved!"

"He felt your hand, Ivy. He's saying hello back. He must

really like you because he hasn't kicked all day."

Ivy finds Della's eyes and she breaks out into a wide grin. I knew it was a good idea to have Della come along.

"I brought you something," I tell her, reaching around the side of the chair for the gift box.

Her eyes widen. "You got me a present?"

"I did. I heard that you're not a fan of the dark so I thought you might like it." I hand her the gift box and she sinks down to the floor at our feet, tearing open the wrapping.

"What is it?" she asks, lifting the lid.

I join her on the carpet and take her gift out of the box. "It's a nightlight, and when it lights up, it plays a melody to help you sleep." It's clear acrylic cut out in the shape of a unicorn with a number of tiny bulbs in the circular base the illuminates the unicorn in a neon shade of pink. "Shall we see if it works?"

"Sure!"

I plug it in at the socket on the wall and flick the switch, the unicorn lighting up pink while playing a soothing tune.

"It's pink!" Ivy stares in awe, a smile tugging at the corners of her mouth.

"Is that your favourite colour?" I ask.

She nods. "Pink is the colour of princesses."

"It sure is." And this little girl is the prettiest princess of all.

"You're my real daddy, aren't you?" Ivy asks, her mouth twisting as she chews on the inside of her lip, her blue eyes wide as they flick back and forth between mine.

I falter, her question taking me by surprise. I glance up to Amanda whose expression is one of panic.

"I heard Sally and Toby talking about you. Said you was my daddy and that you want to take me home with you."

There's no point in denying it, no matter what Amanda or

anyone says. Lying would only confuse her more. "Would that be okay?"

She shrugs. "I guess so. Would I get my own room?" she quizzes.

"Yes."

"Will it be pink?"

I laugh. "If you want."

"What ab-"

"Ivy, let's not get too excited, okay? There are still a few things to sort out before that can happen," Amanda interrupts, causing Ivy to frown.

"Okay," she replies sadly, her little shoulders sinking.

"I think that's enough for today. Ivy, do you want to say goodbye?" Amanda's clipped tone irks me. She's a curious child, you can't fault her for that.

Ivy's eyes meet mine. "Thank you for my present, Mister."

"You're welcome, sweet girl."

I watch as Amanda leads Ivy out of the living room to rejoin her foster family, but not before she tosses a glance back over her shoulder and waves goodbye.

That goodbye stabs me in the heart like a knife, the pain I feel completely unexpected. I don't want to be waving goodbye, I want her to be with me.

Tears prickle in the backs of my eyes and I feel a soft hand take mine and I glance beside me at Della whose eyes, like mine, are swimming with unshed tears.

"She's absolutely incredible, Rafe," Della says, a single tear trickling down her cheek.

Incredible... Adorable... Beautiful... There are a hundred other words to describe that little girl, and you would still be scratching the surface because she's *everything*.

Everything I never anticipated and everything I never realised I wanted. I never expected to feel like this. I never anticipated how much this little girl would come to mean to me in such a short amount of time.

Is this what love feels like?

They say that the love you feel for your children is unlike anything else you'll experience in your life, and I never believed it until now. How the instinct to love and protect them from harm consumes every fibre of your being. How I'd do anything for her.

It's safe to say that my heart's been stolen by a little girl with black hair and an infectious smile, because there's no doubt that I'm irrevocably in love with my daughter.

8

Rafe

A whirlwind…

A literal whirlwind is what my life has turned into in a matter of weeks. I thought I had my life all figured out, that was until a five year-old angel with raven black hair and eyes the colour of the ocean came along and turned my world upside down.

It's been almost a month since I found out I had a daughter that I never knew existed. Two and a half weeks since I met her for the first time. Four days since the court hearing where I was found fit to care for her permanently and awarded sole custody.

And finally, today, my daughter came home.

She and Amanda arrived just under half an hour ago and she's yet to say something other than 'yes', 'okay' or just nodding her head silently, but I don't blame her. All this is new to her, and I can't imagine how scared she must be in a strange house surrounded by strangers telling her they're her family.

Since the hearing, Gage has been more suffocating than a plastic bag wrapped around my head as we readied for her arrival, going over everything down to the tiniest detail. Sierra has been like an excitable puppy on steroids, foaming at the mouth to meet her new niece. So much so, she's spent the past few days buying out every toy store in Halston and bossing around the decorators, making sure Ivy's room is perfect.

I have to say, Sierra did an excellent job on Ivy's room. It's been fully decorated and furnished in pink, because what other colour was it going to be? The walls are a soft blush pink while the curtains, bedspread and rug are all a deeper shade.

There's a sheer canopy that hangs around her bed with pink fairy lights woven through it. The room itself is filled with different toys and games so she'll never get bored. A doll house sits in the corner of the room by the window, a small bookcase stands opposite filled with books, and glow in the dark stars scatter across the ceiling, so she'll never have to be afraid of the dark again.

It's a palace fit for a princess.

You could say she's spoilt, but why shouldn't I spoil her after everything she's been through?

"Ivy, why don't you get your Auntie Della to show your new room while I talk to your dad?" Amanda offers.

"Okay," she replies shyly, shuffling off the couch as she lets Della lead her down to the room at the very end of the hallway.

"How are you feeling, Rafe?" Amanda asks.

"Fine. Yeah... Good." It's not a total lie. One half of me has me thinking I've got this, that it can't be that hard, but the other half is freaking the fuck out. Even with the handful of self-help books Della bought me for new parents and how to care for a child as a single parent, I still have no clue what I'm doing.

A single parent...

How the fuck did that happen?

"Well, everything here seems to be in order. It may take some time for Ivy to adjust so be patient with her. It's a very stressful time for both of you and you need time to get to know each other. I'll call each week to check in, and I'll arrange a time in the next couple of months when I can drop by and see how she's settling in and how you're getting along. If you need anything, I'm only a phone call away, and remember, there's no shame in asking for help. Being a parent for the first time is daunting for everybody, so use your friends and family you have around you should you need them."

I do my best to ignore the patronising tone in her voice and remind myself she means well, so I choose to simply smile. "Thank you. I really appreciate all your help."

"You're welcome." She smiles. "I'm going to go and say goodbye to Ivy and I'll be on my way." She rises off the sofa and disappears down the hallway, returning a few minutes later and I move to show her out.

"I think she'll do just fine here with you," she tells me. "I'll be in touch."

I close the door behind her and head to Ivy's room where I find her exploring her new toys while Della unpacks her things.

"Hey, how do you like your new room?" I ask Ivy, joining her on the floor beside her doll house.

"Is this all for me?" she asks, fiddling with one of the dolls.

I nod. "It's all yours. This is your home now, I want you to be happy here."

I turn back to find Della watching us with a tear in her eye. "I think we all ought to leave you guys to it, get out of your hair."

"Do you have to go?" Ivy asks, her chin wobbling.

"I'm afraid so, sweetheart. I don't live here, but I'll come back."

"Pinky swear?" Ivy holds out her little finger in the air as Della makes her way over.

"Pinky swear," Della replies, linking her finger with Ivy's. "Try keeping me away."

Leaving Ivy to play with her new toys, I follow Della from her room to join my siblings.

"*Parenting for Dummies... The Secrets of Parenting... How to be a Single Dad?* Where did you get these?" Sierra asks, inspecting my almost empty bookshelf.

"I bought them for him, thought they might help," Della replies.

"That's assuming he's ever read a book in his life that didn't contain illustrations and pop-up pictures," Sierra jibes with a cheeky wink. The little shit has always known how to push my buttons.

"Says the girl who thinks *Fifty Shades of Grey* is a literary masterpiece."

She flips me the finger and I can't help laughing.

"I uh..." I run a hand through my hair. "I wanna thank you for everything, guys. I appreciate it."

Gage steps forward. "You don't have to thank us for anything, brother. That's what families do." He insists on pulling me into one of his hugs and I stand there frozen until he pulls away. "Call if you need us, alright? Like I said, you're not alone."

"I will."

"She's amazing, Rafe," Sierra says with a wide smile before pulling me in for a hug herself. "I know I tease a lot, but I love you, and you're going to do great."

Della presses a kiss to my cheek before the three of them filter out of my apartment and the second the front door closes my chest tightens. Things just got a lot more real. I'm a single dad with a daughter I barely know and no clue what to do next.

∞∞∞

Della: How are things? Xx

It's only been three hours since they left and I can't help but love how much she cares.

Me: She hasn't left her room since you left.

Every time I check on her I find her sat in the same place in front of her doll house. I put it down to just exhaustion, nerves and being overwhelmed from moving half way across the country and to a strange house. It'll take time to digest, so I leave her alone, not wanting to smother her.

Della: Give her time. She'll come out of her room when she's hungry.

Crap!

What the fuck do I cook for dinner? *How* the fuck do I cook dinner? My mom did all the cooking growing up, then when she died, Viola, my mom's best friend and our live-in housekeeper took over. The only thing I've ever cooked in my life came out of a can, a plastic tray or in a takeout box.

I search through the kitchen cupboards for ingredients I can use to make something out of, but given I haven't actually grocery shopped since I moved in, opting to eat out every night, unsurprisingly, I have nothing in.

Shit.

I can't expect my daughter to live on all that crap every day. But I guess it'll have to do for just one night.

I poke my head around her door to find her in the same spot she's been in since she got here.

"Are you hungry?" I ask. "I was thinking burgers?"

She shakes her head, not shifting a muscle to face me. "No."

"Would you like a drink maybe?"

"Not thirsty."

"You've gotta eat, sweetheart. Need you to be big and strong, don't we?"

I get nothing. Jesus, it's not even been half a day and I'm already struggling.

"Okay… Um… Well, I'll order some food anyway and it's there if you decide you want some. Okay?"

She shrugs, and I figure that's all I'm going to get so I leave her to it.

Luckily, when the food arrives an hour later, she's hungry enough to find me in the dining room. We eat in silence and once she's finished eating, she retreats back into her bedroom without even speaking a word.

This is going to be a long fucking night.

I manage to get her bathed and dressed into her pyjamas before tucking her into bed.

"Do you want me to read you a story?" I offer.

"My mommy always read to me before I fell asleep. I miss

her."

"I know, sweetheart."

"Did you love my mommy?" Her question catches me off guard.

"No, I didn't," I admit. "I didn't know her well enough to love her."

"Do you love me?"

This little girl... My heart swells in my chest as she peers up at me with wide, hopeful eyes. "Yes. Yes, I do."

"Are you going to leave me too?"

A lump forms in my throat. "No. No, I am never going to leave you. I'm here for as long as you need me to be."

"Okay."

"You get some sleep, alright? I'm only down the hall if you need me." The want to kiss her forehead surges through me, but maybe it's too soon for that, so instead I flick off her light, and turn on the unicorn nightlight I bought her, bathing the room in a dim pink glow.

Just as I reach the door, Ivy stops me.

"What's that?" she asks, pointing to the ceiling and I look up at the glow in the dark star stickers I forgot I had put there.

I smile, making my way back over to her, dropping to my knees at the side of her bed. "I read somewhere that stars can't shine without the darkness and it made me think of you."

When Sierra and I saw them in the store, I knew right then I had to buy them. She's scared of the dark, so what better way to take her mind off it than luminous stars that shine bright when the lights are off?

"They're pretty."

"They sure are. Goodnight, sweetheart," I say before pulling the door closed behind me.

I stand outside her room for a moment and just as I'm about to walk away, I hear a whimper on the other side of the door. A faint sound that pierces straight through my heart.

A cry.

I swallow hard, resting my forehead against the door. My daughter's suffering and there's nothing I can do to stop it.

9

Rafe

My brother's barbecue is in full swing by the time Ivy and I arrive at my family's home, the wide back yard bathed in the warm summer sunshine as the smell of burgers sizzling on the grill drifts into my nose.

I drop to a crouch in front of Ivy, whose clutching her teddy bear like a security blanket so hard if it was alive, it would've died by strangulation by now.

"Hey, why don't you go sit on that chair over there and I'll get you something to drink?"

"Okay," she says quietly before shuffling towards the circle of chairs around the garden table, shaded from the sun by the parasol.

She wasn't overly thrilled about having to come here with me, and in all honesty, I wasn't excited at the prospect of having to pretend to know what I'm doing in front of my family, but I couldn't let them down. I just have to suck up the next couple of hours before we can go home, but I figure seeing Della and Sierra again will do Ivy some good. In the short time she's known them, they appeared to have made an impression on her.

"How's she doing?" Gage asks as I near him, and I follow his gaze that rests on my daughter while he flips the burgers on the grill.

This past week has been rough to say the least. Trying to get her to talk is like trying to pull blood from a stone, and trying to coax her out of her room is proving just as difficult. It's like she's shut down. I expected that shy but curious little girl I met that first day would slowly but steadily come out of her shell, but she's closed herself off from me entirely and I'm at a loss at what to do.

I've barely slept, having had to listen to her faint whimpers from down the hall as she cries herself to sleep almost every night. We should be going forward, not backwards.

I can't help but wonder whether I made the right choice by her. Maybe she would have been better off being with someone who knows what they're doing, someone with more experience with children. Children who have suffered loss and trauma. Maybe she wouldn't be so withdrawn and distant. The doubts have been on a repeating cycle in my mind for the past few days and I can't help but feel like a failure.

I'm her dad, I should be everything she needs, right? So why do I feel like I'm the exact opposite?

"She's good. Quiet, but I'm hoping she'll open up soon."

"And you? How are *you* doing?"

"Fine. I'm fine," I lie, giving him my most convincing smile.

He narrows his eyes. "Pull the other one, brother. You're not fooling me. What's wrong?" Gage has always been able to read me like a book.

I sigh, pinching the bridge of my nose. "I'm at a loss, bro. She won't talk to me, she cries herself to sleep most nights, she eats as fast as she can and then disappears into her room straight after… I don't know what to do."

"It's only been a week, give her time. Her whole life has been turned upside down and been uprooted halfway across the country, it's going to take time to settle in. It's a lot to process for anybody, let alone a five year-old who just lost her mom."

"I can't help thinking that she's better off without me."

"What are you talking about? You're her dad, and the fact you didn't even hesitate taking her in after finding out you had a daughter you never knew about, shows that you are *exactly* who she needs. Someone who is dedicated and cares about her. Someone who loves her."

He's right, there was no hesitation. Ivy belongs with me and nobody else.

"Where's Della?" I ask, not having seen her since we got here.

"Resting. The morning sickness is really taking it out of her. Sierra and Reese have gone to check in on her."

I don't miss the flip of my stomach at the sound of Reese's name.

"I thought morning sickness was only at the beginning of a pregnancy?" I ask.

"We've been assured by the doctor that there's nothing to worry about. It can happen with some women, I'm just hoping it'll pass soon. I hate seeing her so sick knowing there's nothing I can do to help her."

"I'm sure having her overprotective husband by her side is doing her wonders," I joke and he shoves his elbow into my side and I laugh.

I hear the sound of a giggle and I glance over my shoulder to see Ivy's face lit up in a huge smile, a smile created by Reese, who sits opposite her, matching my daughter's expression.

I head to the drinks table and pour Ivy some orange juice and make my way over to her.

"...you got hair just like *The Little Mermaid*," Ivy says to Reese, reaching across to twirl a lock of her copper hair around her little fingers.

"I guess my mom should've called me Ariel, huh?"

"Me and my mommy used to watch it all the time, sometimes even two times a day!"

"Wow! That's a whole lot of *The Little Mermaid*!"

"Do you have a tail too?"

"Sadly, I don't. But you know, if I spend too long in the bath, I go all wrinkly and scaly like a fish!"

"Ew!" Ivy giggles, scrunching up her nose and a laugh falls from my lips.

I clear my throat as I approach their table, placing Ivy's drink down onto it.

"Reese," I greet with a small smile as her eyes find mine.

Her smile falters slightly as her eyes lift to mine and the moment they connect, something flutters deep in my belly. "Hey."

"Uh, Rafe?" Ivy fidgets with her hands in her lap. It hurts a little that she uses my name to address me, but I guess we're gonna have to work up to *Daddy* slowly.

"Yeah, sweetheart?"

"May I please have one of those?" She points over my shoulder where Gage is cooking up a storm on the barbecue.

"A burger?" She nods. "Of course you can. Why don't you go

and ask Uncle Gage, and he can fix you up with some food?"

She gives me a small nod. "Okay." She shifts off the chair and starts towards Gage.

"It was really nice to meet you, Ivy," Reese calls after her before her eyes return to mine. "She's adorable, Rafe."

"She's certainly something, isn't she?" I take a seat opposite Reese, letting my eyes follow Ivy as she tugs on Gage's pants and points to the burgers on the grill. I turn back to Reese. "You know, that's the first time I've seen her smile since she came to live with me. You've known her all of five minutes and you've already got her smiling." I can't ignore the pang of jealousy that stabs me in the gut.

"What can I say? I'm a natural," she boasts, sitting up straighter.

Got any pointers? I want to ask.

"I heard what happened to her mom, I'm so sorry," she says, and I know she's not just saying it out of politeness like everybody does, she says it because she genuinely cares.

"Don't be. As bad as it sounds, I can barely remember her. It was a long time ago and I hate that it took her death to bring Ivy and I together."

I'd like to have known her as a baby, to watch her grow up, take her first steps and speak her first words. Hell, I'm bummed I even missed out on the vomit and dirty diaper years. I've missed out on all of it, all of the things a parent should experience. I don't even have any photos of her back then. As much as I hate to admit it, and as much as a bastard it makes me sound to say it now she's gone, a part of me resents Yvonne for that. For robbing me of the first few years of my daughter's life, memories I should be able to cherish.

Why did she never try to contact me? Did she think I

wouldn't care?

"I um..." Reese's voice pulls me from my thoughts. "I wanted to thank you again, for what you did at Sierra's party."

"There's no need. He was an asshole, no way was I letting him touch you."

"I hate to think what would've happened had you not been a jealous ass and followed him outside to warn him off."

"I wasn't jealous," I deny.

"Oh, you weren't?" Her mouth twists into a smirk.

"No, absolutely not," I scoff.

"*Hmmm...* you kinda were." She laughs, a faint blush tinging her cheeks. "Either way, thank you."

"You're welcome."

My eyes fall back to my daughter who stands besides my brother, stuffing her face with a burger as Gage laughs.

"Hey, uh... You know if you need any help with Ivy, there's support groups and online forums and stuff that can help with that."

"What makes you think I need help?" I shoot back a little too harshly.

She's rendered speechless for a split second, taken aback by my harsh tone. "N-Nothing I... It's just that, I guess it can be a little overwhelming, becoming a new parent so quickly. It might help to know you're not alone."

I blow out a breath. "Yeah. I'll keep that in mind. Thanks." I know she's only trying to help, but is it that obvious I'm failing before I've even begun?

∞∞∞

"Come on, Ivy. You need to eat something," I encourage as she stares at the sandwich in front of her, her arms folded as a frown contorts her face.

Since we got back from the barbecue, the light in her eyes from being surrounded by my family, in particular my sister and Della, together with Reese has faded. She's shrunk back into herself, settled back into the same habit she's been in since the day she arrived.

The not talking. The barely eating. The constant sadness she carries with her all day and then cries for hours at night.

She's adamant she's not hungry, and as much as I don't like it, I don't want to force her.

"Do you want to watch a movie with me tonight? *The Little Mermaid,* maybe?"

She shakes her head. "No, that was mine and mommy's movie."

My shoulders deflate. It's always *'Mommy did this'* and *'me and Mommy always used to do that'*...

How the fuck am I supposed to compete with a dead woman? A woman who raised her, who was her whole life to just be ripped away from her?

I know I'm sounding like an asshole, I just don't know what to do.

"Okay... What about another movie? You can pick any one you want. Just name it."

"Um... *Beauty and the Beast?*"

I smile. "*Beauty and the Beast* it is."

She snuggles up on the sofa while I head into the kitchen in search of snacks, carrying an armful back and depositing them on the coffee table before downloading the movie onto the TV.

I've never been much of a movie buff, but I have to admit

it's not a bad film if you're a kid. Ivy's eyes stay glued to the screen, her face lighting up in a smile whenever the candlestick comes on screen. But whenever the beast enters the screen, I can't help but notice Ivy edging ever so slowly towards me across the sofa, right up until the point she's almost completely tucked into my side.

My heart swells, the heat of her tiny body warming something deep within me, something I never knew was there.

I don't think I could love my little girl any more than I already do. I can't believe how quickly she's become the centre of my world in such a short space of time.

It's not long after the movie's over that she falls asleep beside me, and as gently and quietly as I can, I lift her into my arms and carry her into her room, placing her on her bed before bringing the covers up to her chin.

"Goodnight, sweetheart," I whisper, pressing my lips to her forehead, this time without hesitation.

She stirs, rubbing her eyes with the back of her hands. "My mommy's dead isn't she? Gone up to heaven?"

"Do you know what that means?" I ask, perching on the edge of her bed.

"It means she's gone to go live in the sky."

I nod slowly. "It means that she's left this world because it wasn't right for her anymore. She's gone to a place that's calm and peaceful now."

She frowns. "Is that why she was on the floor and she didn't wake up? I kept calling her, pushing her, but she didn't move." Her eyes swim with tears.

"I'm so sorry you had to see that, sweetheart."

"I want my Mommy!" Ivy wails, her piercing cry stabbing me through the chest as tears cascade down her face.

A lump forms in my throat. "I know, sweetie. I know how much you miss her and I'm so sorry." I lean in to hug her but she shrinks away and my heart sinks.

She rolls over onto her side away from me, clutching her teddy bear as it's furry body muffles her whimpers.

"Get some sleep, sweetheart. You know where I am if you need me."

Leaving her room, I pull the door closed and breathe out a long heavy sigh. A small glimmer of hope, a tiny light at the end of the tunnel, just ever so out of reach, and it's ripped away quicker than I can blink.

I thought we'd made progress tonight. Not a lot, but some. I thought I was getting somewhere when she curled herself into my body when we watched the movie, only to be dragged back to square one not an hour later.

After crawling into bed, I listen to her cry through the wall and it takes almost an hour for them to die down as she finally goes to sleep and every minute was agony.

The helplessness crushing against my chest, the stab of rejection from her slicing through me like a knife.

Am I really cut out to be a father?

10

Reese

"Well, someone's looking radiant," I greet, as Della stands in the hallway wearing a wide smile, her skin glowing and her eyes brighter than I've seen in months.

I pull her into a hug and she squeezes me tighter than she has in a while.

"It's the first morning in months I haven't thrown up everything bar my liver," she replies.

"I'm glad you're feelings better. Drink?"

She nods. "Orange juice is fine, thanks."

I head into my open plan kitchen as Della takes a seat on the couch with her feet propped up on my coffee table.

"Thought anymore on those baby names?"

She nods before rattling off a reel of awful names only to end on Adonis, Gage's suggestion. *Are you kidding me?*

I join her on the couch, passing her a glass of orange juice as I take a swig from my coffee. "Do not call him that unless you want him to be bullied. Kids are brutal."

"I told him I'd file for divorce before I ever called my son Adonis." She chuckles. "Speaking of kids, I have a really big favour to ask you."

"Sure, name it."

"Rafe's been struggling with Ivy. It's been almost two weeks and she barely leaves her room. He's tried engaging with her but apparently he's getting nowhere. I was wondering since you used to babysit when we were younger and how well I hear Ivy took to you at the barbecue, that you might be able to help?"

Shit, I should have seen this one coming.

"I'm not a child whisperer, Del. I'm not really sure what you expect me to do." I looked after a few kids during high-school when their parents wanted some alone time and did the same to give me some extra cash to get me through college, but I'm far from what you could call experienced, I'm a novice at best.

"Ivy seems to respond better around women, I thought you might be able to bring her out of her shell a little, make her feel more comfortable."

"Why can't you do it? Or Sierra?"

"Aside from the chronic morning sickness and lack of energy most of the time, and the fact we live elsewhere, there's not a lot we can do."

"And you automatically thought of me? I don't know, Del," I sigh.

"Just think about it, okay? Ivy's a special kid and what with losing her mom and being sent halfway across the country..." she trails off, and I know what she's doing. She's trying to appeal to my better nature, knowing that I'll cave because I lost my mom too, in a way. I know how it feels to have an absent parent.

It sucks.

But the thought of spending more time with Rafe, being in his space, that's exactly what I need to avoid. Seeing him at Sierra's party proves that he gets under my skin, he always has and I can't allow him to have that much control over me.

"Why do I sense there's more to this story?" Della asks, eyeing me curiously, as if reading my mind. "Has something happened between you two?"

"What? *No!* Of course not. What makes you think that?" I lie, but Della has a knack of seeing through the cloud of bullshit that surrounds me, and now is no different.

Her eyes narrow, her scrutinising gaze never wavering from mine.

"Ugh, fine. We slept together a few months ago," I admit.

Her jaw drops. "Holy shit. Wh… *How?*"

How? "Do you want a play-by-play? He kissed me like no one has *ever* kissed me before. He ate my pussy like he was on death row and gave me the hardest orgasm I've ever had. Satisfied?" I'm almost ashamed to admit that even though he was drunk that night, it was still the best sex I'd ever had. Out of all the guys that have come and gone in my life, no one holds a candle to the night I spent with Rafe, despite how it ended.

"When did it happen?"

"He came to the bar one night, he was as surprised to see me as I was him. We talked and then he kept coming back most nights after that. That night… I guess things just got out of control, and the next morning he was gone. He didn't even say goodbye."

"He just left?"

"Yup. It felt like shit. The first time I spoke to him since it happened was Sierra's party and it was like it never happened. I tried to help him at the barbecue but he threw it back in my face, why would this time be any different?"

"Please. Don't do it for Rafe, do it for her."

I mull the thought over for a long moment before I give in. I can never say no to her and she knows it. "Fine, I'll try. Send me his address."

"Thank you, Ree. Truly. I owe you one."

"I'm holding you to that."

∞∞∞

What the fuck am I doing here?

My hand hovers next to the door for a good minute as I try to figure out if this is a good idea or not.

The answer is no, but most of my ideas aren't, so why would this be any different?

Ivy. I'm here for Ivy, I remind myself as my pulse pounds out a beat in my eardrums. I knock on the door before I have the chance to talk myself out of it. A moment later, the door opens, and judging by Rafe's confused expression, he wasn't expecting me.

"Reese?"

"Did Della not tell you I was coming over?"

"No, she didn't. Uh... come in." He widens the door and allows me inside.

"Sorry to just drop by, I assumed she called to say I was coming."

"What's up?"

"Della mentioned you were struggling with your daughter

and asked if I could do anything to help."

"'Course she did..." he scoffs, with a shake of his head. "She shouldn't have told you."

"She was just trying to help," I argue.

"Well, she needn't have bothered, I don't need anyone's help."

"You don't *need* my help, or you don't want to *admit* you need my help? I'm sensing it's the latter."

A wave of anger rises up in me. Della only meant well because she cares. Could he sound any more ungrateful? I think he needs help but is too stubborn to admit it.

"I'm not here to judge you for your parenting skills, Rafe."

"So why did you come here? Are you really here to help or are you hoping I'll jump back into bed with you?"

"I can't believe you just said that." His words hit me like a slap to the face and I take a step back. "You know what, I'm out of here. Sorry to burst your bubble, but I'm here because Della thought I might be able to help your little girl, I'll just tell her she wasted her time. I figured after what happened at Sierra's party that I owed you a favour, *that's* why I'm here, not to inflate your ego even more. You are so *not* who I thought you were."

"Fuck," I hear him mumble under his breath as I head for the door. "Reese, wait."

My hand hovers on the door handle before I turn to look back over my shoulder. "Feel free to give me a call when your ego returns to its original size." And with that, I pull open the door and slam it shut behind me, marching down the corridor towards the elevator without looking back.

11

Reese

Work dragged like a camel's ass in the desert and all I can think about as I lock up the bar is getting home and crawling into bed. It's just passed one in the morning when I begin the long walk back to my apartment, and as much as I hate walking alone at night, it's my only option seeing how my car is without gas. But I make sure to keep my hand tight around the can of pepper spray in my pocket. A girl can't be too careful nowadays.

I have to admit, this walking crap has some perks. My thighs have never been so toned and my ass looks amazing. I'm lazy, I drive literally anywhere and walk only if I have to, but I might take walking up on the regular.

My phone buzzes in my pocket and I reach in to answer it without even look at who's calling.

"Hello?"

"Reese, it's uh… Rafe."

My pace slows. Of all people to call me, he was the last person I expected. "Yeah?"

"Sorry, I know it's late—"

In the background I can hear screaming, the high-pitched sound goes straight through me. "What's that noise?"

"It's Ivy. I think she had a nightmare and she won't stop crying, every time I go near her she starts screaming. I… I don't know what to do."

"Is this you finally admitting you need my help?" I can't help but be a little smug seeing how I'm still pissed off at how he spoke to me earlier. I was there to help, and no matter how many times he said he didn't need it, deep down he knew he did.

"*Yes.* Okay? I need your help. *Please.*"

I consider telling him no to make him squirm, have him get down on his knees and beg for my help, though that's a little dramatic even for me. But it's that little *'please'* at the end that has something inside of me melting.

Ivy screams again, a heart-breaking cry that claws at my heart. "Okay, I'm on my way."

Fifteen minutes later I'm outside his door and even before it opens I can hear Ivy wailing.

"Hey," I say, forcing a smile as he widens the door to let me through. He's dressed in a plain black t-shirt and grey sweatpants, his hair messy in the best way, the way that has me wanting to glide my fingers through it.

I shrug off my coat and drape it over the back of the couch along with my bag.

"She's just through there. Last door at the end of the hall," Rafe directs, following a few paces behind me.

Ivy's cries grow louder as I get nearer and when I enter

her bedroom I find her curled up in the middle of her bed clutching a teddy bear to her chest with her face buried in its fur.

I glance back at Rafe who looks... lost. His eyes are bloodshot as he hovers by the door, watching over his daughter, his jaw clenching. His face is pained, like a man at a total loss of what to do.

"Ivy?" I get closer, crouching beside her bed. "Ivy? Do you remember me? It's Reese, Daddy's friend."

She peers up at me over her bear, her eyes swimming in tears. "Don't let the bad man get me," she says with a sniff.

"What bad man?"

"Don't let him get me," she cries and I draw her into my arms as she sobs against my chest, her tears soaking through my shirt.

I shift onto the bed, pulling her with me, her legs are draped over mine as I sit propped up against her headboard, rocking her gently back and forth. I press a kiss to the top of her head. "You're safe, sweetie. Your daddy's not gonna let anybody hurt you. It was just a bad dream. You're okay."

I look over at Rafe and usher him closer, and after a moment's hesitation, he nears the bed, dropping to his knees. "Ivy?"

She nestles closer to my chest and Rafe looks broken at the rejection. I can't help feeling sorry for him. He's all new to this and it's clear by the look of hurt on his face that he adores his daughter and it's killing him not being able to help her. With a small shake of his head, he rises to his feet and leaves the room without another word.

I run my hand soothingly up and down her back. "Who's the bad man, sweetie? Is it..." I hate to ask, but I have to, I have to know what's going on. "Is it Daddy? Is Daddy the bad man?"

"No," she replies, her little voice muffled in my shirt and I release a relieved sigh.

"You know he'd never hurt you though, right?" After a moment she nods. "Good."

Ivy's cries have stopped now, reduced to a sniffle and she yawns, rubbing her eyes.

"Are you tired?" She nods. "I'll let you get some sleep."

"No, don't go!" She grips my shirt in her little fists in panic.

"I'll only be next door. Just shout if you need me or your daddy, okay?"

She sniffs, and after a long moment, she nods. "Okay."

I shift off her bed and tuck her into bed. "Sweet dreams, Ivy," I say before leaving her room and closing the door behind me.

I find Rafe sat at the kitchen island nursing a glass of vodka, beside him a half-full bottle.

"Nice, Rafe," I comment.

"Don't fucking judge me." He necks the contents in one and slams the glass back down onto the grey marble top with a clang.

"So what? When things get a little tough you turn to the bottle? I didn't come here to help your daughter so you could get wasted. I'm outta here."

I turn away, swiping my coat and my bag and storm towards the door.

"Reese, wait," he calls behind me, but I keep walking, ignoring him calling my name.

How can he be so selfish?

Heavy footsteps grow closer as a hand grips my arm, spinning me around as my back collides with the door.

11

"Just fucking wait, okay?" He sighs heavily as he leans against the door, his hands either side of my head as he brackets me in. "I'm sorry. I just... I don't know what to fucking do."

I hate the fact that my body doesn't seem to mind how close he is to me. How he's close enough that I can feel his body heat, I can smell the faint scent of his cologne and my mind travels back to that night, how that night started out almost exactly like this.

I shake the thought away.

"Do you think any new parent does? It was never intended to be easy, it's a learning curve for everyone. Most parents have nine months to prepare for it, you had less than a month. I get it's hard, but you don't have just yourself to think about anymore, you have *her*."

He eases away, heading back into the kitchen. "Yeah, a daughter who hates me."

"She doesn't hate you, Rafe. Not yet, but she will if you carry on down this road, I know it firsthand," I say, following behind him.

"Oh yeah?"

"My mom was a drunk," I begin, and his eyes snap to mine. "I don't have a single memory of her where there wasn't a bottle of booze in her hand or she wasn't passed out on the couch completely. She might as well have not even been there. I've had to fend for myself for longer than I should've and it was shit not having a parent to rely on." I take the bottle on the counter and fill the glass in front of Rafe. "Now, if you want that beautiful little girl in there to have the same childhood I did, then by all means, keep drinking. But if you love her even a fraction of what I think you do... *stop*."

I see something flicker in his eyes as they hold mine. Sadness? Pity? "I had no idea, Reese."

"Of course you didn't, it's not something I like to open with when I meet someone. It's not really a great icebreaker."

He snorts a laugh.

"Look, I know you're still struggling with losing your dad, and this whole thing with Ivy came as a shock, but drinking yourself into an early grave isn't the answer. Fight. Keep fighting and you'll get through this, I promise." I don't know why I do it, maybe to show him he's not on his own or simply because I wanted to, but I lay my hand on top of his.

He looks down at where we're touching and nudges my fingers with his thumb. "I'm sorry I spoke to you the way I did earlier."

His apology takes me by surprise. "So you should be. You were an asshole."

"I know, and I am grateful you're here, truly," he says. "I guess I don't like to admit I'm wrong."

"That's one thing we have in common at least," I say with a smile. "Why did you call me? Why not Si or Della?"

"I guess I just wanted to see you." His blue eyes flick up to mine and the way he's looking at me has me wishing for so many things to be different. They're the kind of eyes that are as deep as the ocean, eyes a girl could get lost in, and under different circumstances, I'd be one of those girls, but I can't ever be. Not again.

I look away, pulling my hand off his and sliding off the chair. "I better be going."

"What? Reese, it's the middle of the night. Sleep here. You can stay in my room."

I cross my arms over my chest. "You're not getting me into

bed *that* easily, Hudson."

He laughs with a shake of his head. "I'll take the couch."

"It's fine, really. I—"

"I insist, stay here until morning." I can see he's not going to take no for an answer, I suppose that's one more thing we have in common.

"Okay, fine," I relent.

"It's the first door on the left, it's an en-suite," he tells me.

We say goodnight, but before I twist the handle of his bedroom door, I turn to look back over my shoulder. Rafe carries the bottle of vodka and the glass over to the sink, tipping the contents of both down the drain.

I smile, silently punching the air as I turn and head inside the bedroom.

12

Rafe

The thought of Reese lying in my bed, her body nestled between my dark satin sheets just a few short meters away from me is enough to keep me wide awake for most of the night. *That* and the fact the couch is uncomfortable as fuck and I ended up sleeping on the floor.

I was wide awake at six a.m., and not seeing any reason to lie on my back staring up at the ceiling, I got in a couple of hours work in my office while the girls slept. The past few weeks, I haven't been in the right head space and the company has largely been left to Gage to deal with, but it's time I get back into it. I've never been a slacker, and I'm not about to start now.

It's almost nine o'clock before I head into Ivy's room to wake her up and announce I'm making breakfast. Still dressed in her pink striped pyjamas, I lift her onto the stool at the kitchen island. "How are you this morning? Sleep okay?"

"Uh-huh." She nods, stretching lazily.

I set about making breakfast, with my phone set beside me on the counter as I follow the recipe step by step, and it's not long before a door opens and closes down the hall behind me.

I toss a glance over my shoulder to find Reese padding barefoot into the kitchen. My eyes wander over her, taking in my white t-shirt that's three sizes too big for her, long enough to pass for a dress. I also can't help noticing the outlines of her tight nipples poking through the thin fabric and my dick jerks in my pants.

"Is something burning?" Reese asks with a yawn she doesn't even try to hide. She smiles when her eyes land on Ivy who's sat at the kitchen island watching me. "Good morning!"

"Hi, Reese!" Ivy responds. She seems happier this morning, and the smile on her face when Reese walked in tells me it's all because of her.

"You're wearing my shirt," I say.

She glances down. "So I am. Well spotted."

"Why?"

"I couldn't exactly sleep in my corset top and denim shorts, could I? That would've been *way* too uncomfortable."

"You could've slept naked," I suggest, the words out of my mouth before I can stop them. Seems my dick has taken control of my brain at the sight of those nipples and my mouth waters from the memory of how they tasted that night.

The corners of her mouth curve up into a smile. "I could've, but that would have been a bit weird, don't you think?"

I run a hand through my hair. "Yeah, maybe."

"You've got yourself one hell of a bachelor pad here. That bed alone could persuade me to move in permanently," she says.

"No one but me has slept in that bed," I say.

Her eyes widen. "Seriously?"

I nod. "You're the first woman who's ever been here. This place is mine, I don't just bring *anyone* here."

She seems surprised by my admission, but it's true. This isn't a place with a revolving door of women passing through, that's what the hotel was for. I haven't been with anyone since my dad died months ago. To me, sex was always a way to deflect from the pain that rocks me inside, but not even pussy could mask the pain of losing my dad, so I turned to a guy named Jack Daniels for help instead. I think this is the longest I've ever gone without sex which is an achievement in itself, and I've been surprisingly okay with it, but with Reese dressed like a wet dream, my abstinence is waning.

Her eyes hold mine for a long moment before she breaks the contact. "What are you doing?"

"I'm cooking breakfast." Or at least *attempting* to.

"Whatever it is, it smells like you're cremating it rather than *actually* cooking it." She rounds the counter and peers over my shoulder. "Yep. *Definitely* cremating it."

"Well then, I guess the instructions are wrong. I followed the damn thing to the letter."

She shoots me a look. "You need instructions to make pancakes?"

"Hey, don't judge the rookie, cut me some slack, yeah? I'm new to all this."

"Come here, give me the spoon," she says, holding out her palm.

"I can do it," I insist.

"Yeah, it sure looks like it, now move." She bumps my hip with hers, nudging me out of the way. "This is just... I can't with this." She scoops at the slop in the pan and ultimately gives in, tossing the spoon down. "Well, eight points for trying, zero points for the execution." She tosses the contents of the pan in the trash and sets about making breakfast the right way with me hovering beside her watching everything she does.

I want to learn, I *need* to learn this shit because Reese isn't going to be here forever.

"You okay this morning, sweetie?" Reese asks, taking a seat next to Ivy on the couch after we've eaten, running a hand through my daughter's hair.

"Uh-huh."

"Can I ask who the man in your dream was?"

She fiddles with the sleeve of her pyjama top. "Mommy's boyfriend."

What? I move closer, taking a seat on the edge of the coffee table in front of them.

Reese shoots me a worried look. "Did he hurt her?"

She nods. "He shouted a lot. Mommy would tell me to go to my room and not come out until she came and got me."

"Did he…" I swallow hard. "Did he ever hurt you?"

She shakes her head. "No, but he was scary. Not a nice man. He called Mommy bad names and made her cry a whole lot. I didn't like seeing my mommy cry." Her chin wobbles as her eyes fill with tears.

I touch her knee and give it a comforting squeeze. "You have nothing and no one to be frightened of now, Ivy. You're safe here, you know that right? I will never let anyone hurt you."

She nods again.

"Do you remember his name?"

"I think it was Stephen," she replies.

I dig out my phone and bring up Gage's number.

Me: Can you get Derek to look into Yvonne's boyfriend? See if we can track him down? Name's Stephen but I don't know any more than that. Ivy's having nightmares about him. He abused Yvonne. I want the animal put down.

A few minutes later, he replies.

Gage: Consider it done.

Reese rises from the couch. "I uh, should probably get going. I'm gonna go get changed."

"Don't go!" Ivy jumps up and clings to Reese's legs, banding her arms around her to hold her in place.

"I'm sorry, sweetie. I don't live here."

"But why? Why can't you live here?" Ivy's eyes seek mine, slowly filling with tears again. "Can she stay? *Please*."

"She has her own house to go back to, sweetheart, but she can come around to see you anytime, how does that sound?"

Her arms return to her sides as her shoulders drop. "Okay."

"Where are you parked?" I ask Reese and her face falters slightly.

"Oh no, I... I walked."

"You walked? Why?"

"I haven't had chance to fill my car up with gas, I keep forgetting," I lie. "I don't mind walking. It's not far."

"Screw that, I'm driving you. Ives, get dressed, we're going for a ride."

Ivy dashes down the hall towards her room. The new nickname came out of nowhere, but I like it.

"Rafe, it's fine. I can walk."

"Take a look out the window," I tell her, where a torrent of rain lashes at the windows. "You'll get soaked the second you step outside. So quit being stubborn and say yes for once."

I can see the want to protest in her eyes but after a minute she gives in. "Okay. Thanks."

It's still pouring with rain outside when Reese and Ivy are dressed and ready to go, and once Ivy is strapped into her booster seat, I peel out of the underground parking lot.

As I drive, I can't help but catch a glimpse of her thick creamy thighs in those cut off denim shorts of hers as she sits in the passenger seat. You can't blame a guy for looking, they're just too good to *not* look at.

God, this woman...

"Eyes on the road, sport. You want us to crash?" My eyes flick up to her face where I find her smirking. She caught me checking her out. *Fuck.* There is however a faint blush on her cheeks that tells me she liked me checking her out.

The rain has slowed to a drizzle as I pull up outside her apartment building, killing the engine.

"We'll walk you in," I say, unclipping my seat belt.

"You don't have to."

"I want to."

Once I've got Ivy out of the car, the three of us dash towards the building out of the rain that's starting to get heavy again.

"Do you really have to go, Reese?" Ivy asks with a pout, peering up at Reese with wide eyes.

"Yeah, sweetie. But I'll visit all the time, I promise," Reese replies while digging through her bag for her keys as we reach her floor, and when she turns back toward her door, her steps falter. "What the hell?"

A bright yellow sticker reading **EVICTION NOTICE** in thick black font is stuck to her door.

"You're being evicted?" I ask.

"It's nothing." She rips off the sticker and shoves the door open.

"It's not nothing, Reese. It's serious," I say, following her inside, Ivy's hand clasped in mine.

She tosses the sticker in the trash and slumps onto the couch. "I didn't think it would come to this."

"I didn't know you were in trouble. What can I do?"

"Nothing. I'm not your problem or your responsibility, Rafe. This is my mess, I'll deal with it."

"They can't just evict you without notice or reason."

"But there is. I've been late on my rent for a while now. My assho— *idiot* landlord has been looking for an excuse to get rid of me for months."

"Is this why you've got no gas in your car? Why you walk everywhere?"

She nods slowly. "I guess I had it coming. I've got a stack of letters from him that I've never even opened. I think I knew what they were threatening, I just chose to ignore them and according to this," she holds up the yellow sticker, "I have two weeks to get out."

"What's evicted?" Ivy asks innocently.

"It means I'm being kicked out of my house, sweetie," Reese answers.

"But you can come live with us at our house, right?" The question is aimed more at me than it is Reese.

That's not a bad idea...

Reese goes to protest but I cut her off. "You're coming to stay with us."

"Yay!" Ivy cheers.

"I can't do that, Rafe," she protests.

"Why not? Give me one good reason." She needs somewhere to stay, I have the space and means to help her...

"I... I just can't."

"You wanna be sleeping in a cardboard box in a shop doorway?"

She clamps her mouth shut.

"Thought not," I say. "How deep in shit are you?"

"Deep?" she scoffs. "The gravedigger is filling in the hole with me buried six feet under."

"Why didn't you say anything? I could've helped."

"Because I don't take charity, I don't even take money from Della. I don't care if it makes me stubborn or stupid or whatever, but I refuse to take money from anyone. I won't be a burden."

"I think it's your pride telling you not to."

Her jaw drops open. "Excuse me?"

"What? You're allowed to call me out on my bullshit, but I can't do the same for you? I think you want to prove to yourself and everyone else that you're not a failure, that you're not your mother and accepting help from anyone admits that you are."

"And you'd know all about that, wouldn't you? Being too proud to accept help from anyone?" she shoots back.

"Maybe so, but either way, you know I'm right."

She jumps up from the couch and forces her way past me, shoving my shoulder and I follow her into the kitchen. With her back to me, she's quiet for a long minute and her silence tells me she knows I'm right, even if she doesn't want to admit it out loud.

She turns to me. "The bar is cutting hours and I can't keep up with the rent, among other things. I'm drowning. I'm trying to stay above the surface but it keeps dragging me down."

"I didn't know things were so bad."

"Why would you? It's not like you're my boyfriend or anything, we're barely even friends." Her words sting more than I thought they would.

"Come and work for me," I suggest, the idea popping into my head a split second before the words leave my mouth.

She blinks up at me. "What?"

"Think about it, you can help me take care of Ivy while living with us, rent free. All I ask is you help me get Ivy settled and more at ease."

"Like a nanny?"

"Technically. When I'm at work, you can keep her company, help take her to school and after school clubs and all that parent-y stuff I have no clue about. Come on, it's a win-win for both of us. I'll pay you, of course."

Her hands find her hips as she mulls the thought over in her mind. "How much?"

"Name your price."

"You want me to just say a number, no matter how ridiculous it is?"

"Yep. Give me a ballpark figure." I cross my arms over my chest.

She blows out a long breath. "Fifteen grand."

"Done."

Her eyes bug-out. "*What!?* I was kidding."

"I'm not. The money's not an issue, Reese."

"You can't be serious about paying me fifteen grand to take care of your daughter?"

"Fifteen grand a *month*," I correct and her eyes bulge. "Reese, I'm deadly serious about you coming to live with us, it's in all of our best interests."

She studies me for a moment. "You're really not joking are you?"

I shake my head.

"Why me?" she asks.

I take a step closer. "Because my daughter likes you, I trust you have her best interests at heart, same as I do. And because there's no way I'd let you become homeless. You're important to Della which makes you important to me." I brush a strand of hair from her face with my thumb, and I don't miss the gasp when our skin touches. "I might be a dick sometimes, but it doesn't mean I don't c—"

Her eyes are widen as they hold mine. "Were you about to say you care?"

"No." I frown, jerking my hand back.

A smirk crosses her face seeing right through my lie and she laughs softly. "I think you were. But it's okay, your secret's safe with me."

I extend my hand. "Do we have a deal?"

After a moment, her hand takes mine. "Deal, *Boss*."

She closes the space and presses a kiss to my cheek, her sweet feminine scent wafting into my nose as she brushes past me, heading back into the living room.

Danger.

This woman is a danger to my very existence. She should come with a warning sign because she holds the power to bring my life as I know it crashing down around my feet.

But you know what? It's a risk I think I'm willing to take.

13

Reese

It's taken me the better part of a week to get all of my stuff out of my apartment.

Rafe wanted to help me pack up my stuff, but being the stubborn independent woman I am, I insisted I was fine and to take care of Ivy instead, so I settled on letting him help me move my things over when I was ready.

I'm loading up my car that now has a tank full of gas in it when Rafe pulls up in his Corvette behind me.

"Hey," I greet, my full arms balancing two boxes that weigh about as much as I do as I lug them to the car.

"Here, let me get that." He lifts the boxes out of my arms like they weigh nothing and slides them onto the backseat.

"There's a cat in your car," he says.

"You know, I've been wondering what that fluffy thing sat on my passenger seat was. Thanks for clearing up that mystery for me," I reply sarcastically, not managing to cover up my grin.

The horrified look on his face is almost comical. "But *why* is there a cat in your car?"

"He's my grandmother's, I'm taking care of him."

"Right, and why can't she do it?"

My throat locks up. "She uh… she's not able to at the moment." She can't even take care of herself let alone a cat.

"Since when did you have a cat? I don't remember seeing it the night that…" he trails off, his face falling as though he said more than he intended, like he didn't want to remember.

"That night I brought you home with me where we fucked for hours, then you left while I was still asleep? I think you were a little drunk and too busy making me come to notice."

His eyes flare, telling me my little trip down memory lane had the effect I was aiming for.

I huff. "Sometimes my elderly neighbour takes care of him when I'm pulling a long shift at work, I think he makes him feel less lonely," I explain.

"Right, well, just so you know, I hate cats."

"Well, I hate your stupid face, do you see me complaining?"

He tries to hide a smile, but I don't miss the tiny shake of his shoulders as a laugh slips through.

"Merlin and I are a package deal, take it or leave it," I say, placing my hands on my hips.

"Merlin? *That's* its name?"

"He's a Maine Coone cat, it fits him perfectly." He's huge, a mass of long grey, white and black fur with a full thick tail, pointed ears and a deep, soulful face. He's like a miniature lion the way his fur is set and how he sits up straight and proud, like he commands the room.

"If you say so."

"You know, animals have been shown to help reduce stress and anxiety. There's some sort of chemical that's released in the body when petting an animal that's calming and therapeutic. I think having him around will help Ivy too." I was skeptical at the beginning, wondering what all the fuss of owning a pet was all about, but I soon learned that having Merlin around, I wasn't so lonely and all my anxieties faded away whenever he brushed up against me or lay across my lap.

Rafe glances through the window of my car where Merlin gazes up at him. "*Fuck me...*" he groans on an exhale. "Fine, bring the fucking cat, but if it shits on my carpet or scratches my sofa, I'm tossing it off the balcony."

"Stop being such a grouch," I say as we start back towards my building to gather the last of my stuff with Rafe in step beside me. "You'll learn to love him, you'll see."

"I can bet you I won't."

I toss him a glance. "You'll love having both of us around so much you'll never wanna let us go."

"I can assure you, I *won't*."

I don't know why my stomach drops and my heart sinks at his words. I know I'm doing this for Ivy. I know that whatever this is between us is strictly platonic, but there's still that flicker inside me that hopes a tiny part of him wants me there for *him*.

What happens when this arrangement is all over? Hell, one night with him was enough to have my heart splintering, but spending every day with him, in his home, in his space, sleeping in his bed... Will I be strong enough to walk away with my heart in tact?

I guess only time will tell, but I'm starting to wonder

whether accepting his offer was a good idea after all.

∞∞∞

My hunch about Merlin being good for Ivy was spot on. I knew the two of them would be inseparable the second I introduced them. Maine Coone cats are people oriented, so within seconds of letting him loose in the apartment, he gravitated towards Ivy like he's known her all his life, and *she* looked as excited as a kid on Christmas morning the moment she laid eyes on him.

Ivy claps excitedly. "He's so pretty! Is he yours, Reesie?"

My heart jumps. The only other person who ever calls me by that nickname is Nanna, and something in my heart warms. "He belongs to my grandma, but he lives with me now."

"I love him so so much! We're gonna be bestest friends!"

Merlin brushes his face against Ivy's arm as she sits cross-legged on the floor before he climbs into her lap and snuggles against her.

Since I met her, I've never seen Ivy so excited, and by the expression on Rafe's face as he watches the two of them together, he hasn't either.

I shoot him a look that says *I told you so,* and he answers me with a roll of his eyes, one corner of his mouth quirking up. He knows I'm right, and whether he likes Merlin or not, he can't deny that he's good for her.

"Thanks for coming over, Si," Rafe says to his sister. It wasn't practical moving my stuff out of my apartment while having to watch over Ivy, and Sierra jumped at the chance to get to know her new niece better.

She smiles. "No problem. Ivy and I had a great time! Didn't

we, munchkin?"

"We sure did!" Ivy beams up at her from the floor where she continues to pet Merlin.

"Do you need any help unpacking?" Si offers me.

"Uh, sure. Thanks."

She helps me carry my bags and my suitcase full to the brim with clothes and shoes, and drops them at the foot of the bed.

"Isn't this Rafe's room?"

Her eyes take in the black satin sheets on the king-sized mattress, the black feature wall and she screws up her nose. "What is it about guys with black bed sheets? Like, what's wrong with white?"

"No clue, but whatever gets you off, I guess."

"Okay, *ew.* I do not want to think of my brother doing anything like *that.*" She shudders at the mental image. "So, how's this gonna work? Like, are you and him…"

"What? No! Did you think we'd be sleeping in here…. *together*?" I ask. She nods. "Absolutely not. I'm staying in here and Rafe's taking the couch. Why on earth would you think that?"

She chews on her lower lip. "Della may have mentioned that you two…" she trails off, but I know exactly what she's hinting at.

I groan. "Of course, she did. God forbid my sex life remains private. Rafe and I… It's nothing. It was one time that won't be repeated. He's offering me a job and a place to stay. We're just friends."

"I'm not judging. I'm just saying be careful."

"Careful of what?"

"The jury is still out on how many women's hearts are still in one piece after a night with my brother."

I'm not dumb, I know Rafe has a history, and I'm not here to judge because so have I. I have more history than I care to admit, and a lot of that history, I severely regret, but I can't ignore the stab of jealousy that cuts through me at the mention of his.

I straighten my spine. "Yeah well, like I said. We're friends."

"Then why did your face drop at the mention of the other girls he's been with?"

"Sierra, seriously. *Lay off.* I'm here for Ivy. Our history is exactly that, *history,* and it's going to stay that way." I only hope my words convince Sierra more than they do me, because I'm not at all sure I believe them myself.

As much as I'm here for Ivy, there's a part of me that agreed to this arrangement for Rafe too. I don't know what I'm expecting, probably nothing, but I like the back and forth banter between us. I like the way we bounce off each other and how he makes me laugh, it's one of the things that drew me to him in the first place. It's almost impossible for any girl not to fall for his sarcastic, bad boy charm, that killer smile and his skills when the lights are off. But since his dad died and as much as he hates to let his emotions show, a part of him died too. His heart broke, and I want to do whatever I can to help piece it back together.

But will trying to piece his heart back together be the breaking of mine?

14

Rafe

I head through the entrance to some fancy-ass restaurant downtown my brother insisted we meet at. He's taken a recent liking to it, probably because it's a place that's special to him and Della—the sentimental bastard. Soft classical music plays quietly in the background as chatter fills the space. The room is dimly lit, giving it a sultry atmosphere, and as nice as it looks, my nose scrunches as the faint tinge of fish permeates the air.

I fucking hate fish.

I spot Gage sat at the bar on the other side of the room, tossing back a swig of his drink.

"Moving up in the world, brother. Dining with the elite now, I see." I smirk as I drop into the seat beside him as he slides a glass of whiskey in my direction. I wave it away. "You drink it, man. Just a soda for me, thanks," I say to the bartender.

His brows lift, the corners of his mouth curving upward.

"You are Rafe Hudson, right?"

I laugh. "One and only, I've parted ways with alcohol for the time being. Trying to stay on the straight and narrow, a hungover dad isn't the impression I want to give my daughter."

"Good for you, bro. You want to eat?" he asks, passing me a menu.

My eyes scan over the page and I'm almost sure my breakfast is going to make a surprise reappearance. I should have checked the menu out before I came here or I would've suggested meeting elsewhere. Sushi, wild salmon, mussels, prawns... Why the fuck did Gage pick here? He knows I hate fish. Give me a big juicy burger and fries any day of the week over this shit.

"Hard Pass, unless you wanna make the acquaintance of my breakfast from a few hours ago?"

He chuckles. "Not particularly. Drinks it is then."

The bartender sets my drink down on the bar.

"So, what's this I'm hearing about Reese coming to stay with you?" he asks.

I lean back in my seat, taking a swig of my soda. "I offered her a job to help take care of Ivy, sort of like a nanny. It's just temporary while Ivy gets settled."

He smirks into his glass. "Excuses, excuses. Do I detect my little brother is about to fall in love for the first time in his life?"

"No, I'm fucking *not*. Like I said, she's just coming to help with Ivy, as a *friend*."

He nods slowly like he doesn't believe a word and lifts his drink to his lips and shoots me a look.

"What?" I ask.

He shakes his head. "I still don't get it. We grew up in the same house, with parents who worshipped at each other's feet for Christ's sake. You must see the beauty in it."

"Beauty in what? Love? *That's* what you call it? Why would you give someone that much power over you? Are you forgetting the years Dad pined for Mom after she died? He was crushed. Why would you willingly put yourself through all that pain and heartache?"

Gage smiles softly. "Because it's better to feel a love so potent and all-consuming for even a brief moment than to never experience it at all. A life without love is full of emptiness. It's lonely. That's how I felt before I found Della, and now I wouldn't change a thing."

I'm not a pessimist, well, maybe I am, but above all, I'm a realist. All good things will inevitably come to an end, there's no denying that sad but true fact of life, so why set yourself up for that?

"You got anything on the boyfriend yet?" I ask, deflecting the conversation.

"Just a name. Stephen Thomas. But there could be thousands out there, Derek needs to narrow down the search to find the right one. We'll find him. I'm sorry it's not exactly what you wanted to hear."

I scrub a hand over my forehead. "It's okay. I just… I don't believe for one second Yvonne just fell. The whole thing just doesn't sit right with me."

"Me neither. Has Ivy said whether he hurt her too?"

"She says not, but she saw stuff, heard things. He terrified her."

"*Fuck…*" Gage breathes out. "How is she doing?"

"Better with Reese around. Her nightmares aren't as regular and she seems happier in herself, she's even started talking to me a little more."

He smiles, clapping a hand on my back. "Good, I'm glad. You know I never doubted for a second that Ivy would be the making of you. She's good for you, and I think Reese might be too."

"It's not like that between us. We're ju—"

"*Just friends,* yeah, I got that. Just don't close off your heart completely, brother, you might just be surprised."

∞∞∞

I pass Reese's piece of shit car parked up on the street beside the apartment complex. The thing belongs in a scrapyard, though I'm not sure you could sell any of it off for parts. I don't even know how it's legal to drive or how Reese hasn't been killed in an accident before now. It's a death-trap, but Reese is as stubborn as I am with a pride to match, and no amount of arguing is going to get her to buy a new one.

When I step through the front door, I'm greeted by the smell of baked cookies and the sound of laughter filtering in from the direction of the kitchen.

As I reach them, I see Ivy sat on the counter with a mixing bowl on her lap and a spatula in her hand while Reese is bent over, placing a baking tray inside the oven.

My eyes trail down to the full round globes of her ass wrapped up in her tight denim jeans and my dick jerks in my pants. I clear my throat, shaking the mental image of what I'd love to do with that ass from my mind. "Something smells good."

"Reese and I are baking cookies!" Ivy says excitedly, her hands, arms and clothes coated in a layer of flour. It's even in her hair.

"Well, *one* of us is." Reese plants a hand on her hip, her mouth curved into a smile. "The other is making the biggest mess with the flour. You're covered, Ivy!"

Ivy giggles. "Oops."

"Well everything is in the oven now. Why don't you go get cleaned up? And when the cookies have cooled, we can decorate them."

"Yay!" she cheers, leaping off the counter and tearing through the living room towards the bathroom.

My eyes follow my daughter as she disappears into the other room. "She seems happy today."

"Yeah, she does. It's a nice sight isn't it?"

"Definitely," I agree. "So, I passed that hunk of scrap metal you call a car on the way in. You know you don't have to park it on the street, right? There's a perfectly good parking spot next to mine in the garage."

"Yeah, my shitty sun-faded *Honda* with a missing door handle and dented bumper will look great parked next to your Corvette."

I laugh. "Fair point."

I help her load the dishwasher before pulling out the first batch of cookies from the oven and placing them on the counter.

"Have you always enjoyed cooking?"

"It was never really a hobby, I didn't have a choice. With my mom passed out on the couch night after night, I either learned how to cook or starve. I was making a turkey dinner for Thanksgiving by the time I was eight."

"How?"

"My uh... My grandmother taught me most of it. We used

to bake together all the time," she says fondly.

"If your mom was such a shitty parent, why did you never go and live with your grandma?"

"My mom was good at covering it up, she'd have anyone believing it was a glass or two of wine with a meal when in reality it was a bottle and a half of vodka or rum or whiskey, whatever she could get her hands on for breakfast, lunch *and* dinner. My grandmother had no idea how bad it was, *that* or she knew and didn't want to believe it."

I get it now, why she scolded me for drinking that night Ivy had her nightmare. She didn't want me to become a parent like her mother was. She didn't want Ivy to have to endure the same childhood she did.

"Even though I hated her, she was still my mom and no matter what she did, I still loved her. I was terrified that if I left for even a day, I'd come back to find her dead, poisoned by all the booze in her system. I couldn't leave."

"But you did eventually?"

She nods. "I used to babysit for some of our neighbours through high-school, I worked at Target on the weekends as well as odd jobs here and there, and one day all the money I saved up to one day move out, was all gone. My mom stole everything I had just so she could fund her fucking addiction. That was the day I left. I packed my shit and never looked back. I'd just turned eighteen when I went to live with my grandma."

"Have you seen your mother since?" I ask.

"No, and I never want to. She never cared about me, never appreciated me. She's dead to me."

I lay my hand on top of hers. "Well, *I* appreciate you, and I'm glad you're here with Ivy and me. And once you teach me how to cook, and I'm trusted in the kitchen by myself without burning the place to the ground, maybe you'll let me cook for you for once."

Her eyes lift from our hands to my eyes as a small smile touches her lips.

My heart thuds in my chest as she gazes at me, those beautiful emerald eyes holding me hostage. I can't seem to look away. There's so much to this woman, so many layers I never knew she had and I want to explore each of them.

The urge to lean in and take her mouth tugs at me, my lips tingling with the need to feel hers on mine but I stop myself.

I can't.

"I think we're a long way from letting you loose in this kitchen on your own. Let's learn to walk before we can run, yeah?"

15

Reese

"...he crept up to the door and called, *'Little pig, little pig, let me come in...'*" Ivy rests her head against my chest as I sit propped up on her bed against the headboard, reading from the book she picked out for me to read to her earlier.

My last shift at the bar starts in an hour, and Ivy insisted I read her a story before I go.

I gasp dramatically. "*'Oh no, not by the hair on my chinny chin chin!'* said the second little pig, as the first little pig hid *trembling* under the stairs..."

"The wolf is gonna eat him!" Ivy says, biting her fingernail in anticipation.

"*'Then I'll huff and I'll puff and I'll blow your house in!'*" I tickle her like mad and she squeals, giggling as she squirms in my hold, her laughter uncontrollable. She loves it when I do the different voices.

Cinderella... Red Riding Hood... Jack and the Beanstalk... I've read her a bedtime story every night this week and it's quickly turned into the one thing I can't seem to wait for. I'm wishing the days away for just twenty short minutes at the end of it where I can sit right here and read this little girl who has become such an important part of my life a bedtime story. I've become so attached to her that when this arrangement between Rafe and I comes to an end, I'm wondering how I'm ever going to walk away.

In the corner of my eye, I see Rafe hovering by the door, leaning up against the door frame with his arms folded. I can see the fondness in his eyes as he watches his daughter, but there's a sadness in his gaze too as he backs away down the hall.

I know that the fact he's been struggling to get close to her weighs on him. He's worried Ivy's not going to warm to him. He's scared that he'll lose her before he's even had the chance to get to know her. I see the longing in his eyes when he looks at her, and how desperately he hopes she'd let him in. He doesn't wear his heart on his sleeve, but I know him better than he thinks I do, I can see right through this mask he hides behind.

I finish up Ivy's story before shuffling out of her bed, placing a kiss to her forehead before leaving her room.

"How do you do it?" Rafe asks when I enter the living room. He's sat on the couch, his hands clasped together as his elbows rest on his knees.

"Do what?"

"Make it look so easy. An outsider would think *you're* her family, not me. I just can't seem to break through."

I join him on the couch. "Why, because I read her a bedtime story? It's hardly ground-breaking."

"But she asks for *you*." He shakes his head slowly, dropping his gaze to the floor. "She doesn't like me, does she?"

"Rafe, don't take it personally. She's never had a father figure in her life, it's all new to her. I was the same growing up. I was always surrounded by women, I felt more at ease with them. Just don't rush it. You're her dad, that's never gonna change and you have all the time in the world to get to know her."

"But how? How do I do that? You read her stories, she helps you cook, you play dolls together..."

"You just need to find something you can both enjoy together. Why not play dress up?"

"Dress up?" he scoffs. "Like put on a dress and pretend to be a princess?"

I force back the smile *that* image creates in my mind. "Cross dressing not your thing?"

He chokes out a laugh, shaking his head.

"I'm serious. Take interest in the things she likes. Dress up as Prince Charming and be the hero of her stories. Take her out, do something you can share together. I'll make myself scarce so you two can be alone." I place my hand on his arm. "You don't have to worry, you know. She's still learning, she's still all new to this. Her world just crashed down around her when her mom died. It's a lot to take in."

His eyes meet mine. "Thanks, Ree."

"No problem." I smile.

He places his hand on top of mine still on his arm and squeezes.

That mask I mentioned? I can see it slipping, and I'm not gonna stop until it slides to the ground completely.

∞∞∞

"I still can't believe you're leaving me!" Sadie whines, pulling me in for a tight hug, her arms cutting off my air supply as they wrap around my neck.

My last shift sailed by in the blink of an eye, the fastest shift I've worked in a long time and I have just a few short minutes before I walk through those doors I've passed through a thousand times for the final time. Sure, working in a bar has never been anyone's life dream, and I certainly never dreamed of schlepping drinks to strangers when I was lying in bed as a kid dreaming of my future, but I came to love this job, I loved the people and the banter, and I'm going to miss it.

"I'm gonna miss you so much. You're my work bestie, you're what gets me through the shift."

"I'll miss you, too. But I'll stay in touch, I might even come for a drink and see what it feels like to be on the other side of this bar."

Sadie laughs. "I don't think you'll give little old us a second thought when your panties are around your ankles with Rafe *fucking* Hudson between your legs. Get it girl!"

"It's not like that. I'm there to help his daughter. We're just fr—"

"*Just* friends," she finishes. "Uh-huh, sure. If you say so." A smirk grows on her face. She doesn't believe me. "I remember when he used to come in here every night not too long ago. He'd sit at the same bar stool and would only ever interact with you. He'd never take his eyes off you, wherever you were or whatever you were doing, he was always watching."

He was?

"I know he has a reputation, but why not have a little fun?"

"Already been there, Dee, and he did what all of them do. He left without saying goodbye."

"But he's here now. He opened his home to you, he trusts you with his little girl. That must mean something."

It *does* mean something. But I can't go there again, no matter how much my body hums whenever he's close to me, no matter how much I want him.

It can never be.

"No, Rafe Hudson is officially in the past," I say firmly, as if trying to convince both her *and* me.

"Well, if that's true then you won't mind doing me a favour."

"Okay?"

"So, I met this guy in the bar the other night and he also has a friend who's single too. I happened to mention my very beautiful and *very* single redheaded friend and he suggested we double date. Isn't that fun?"

I don't let it show on my face, but internally, I'm panicking, desperately trying to find a way out of this. I don't want to double date, I don't want to date, period.

"I really like this guy, Ree," Sadie continues. "Can you spare an hour or two to humour his friend and come with me? Then you can leave and you never have to see him again. *Please*. Hell, you might even come to like this guy."

Sadie is a hopeless romantic, and being a single parent, she has no social life outside of work, I've never even heard her mention any other friends besides me. I can sacrifice an evening for a friend, can't I? What's the harm? After all, I owe her a night out after turning her down last time.

"Can I at least think about it?"

"Of course, don't wait too long, though!"

I glance at the clock. Twelve-thirty-two. My last shift is officially over. A lump lodges itself in my throat as a wave of emotion grips me.

The end of an era. But you know what they say, as one door closes, another one opens.

∞∞∞

"Hey," I greet as I head into the living room, toeing off my shoes and shrugging off my coat.

I assumed Rafe would be fast asleep by now, but he's still up. He cranes his neck and smiles from where he's sat on the couch, illuminated by a single lamp beside him while the room is cast in dark shadows. He's reading a book.

"What are you reading?" I ask, dropping onto the couch beside him. I lift up the cover with my finger so I can read the title, *Adoption 101.*

"Thought I'd give this reading thing a try," he replies.

"Is it interesting?"

"Fuck no. I started falling asleep on the first page," he replies and I laugh.

"What are you still doing up? It's after one."

He closes the book and tosses it onto the coffee table. "I waited up for you."

"Wow, didn't realise we'd turned into such a boring married couple so quickly." It's crazy how Rafe and I have fallen into a routine so fast. An outsider would assume we've been married for years.

Rafe has just about mastered making scrambled eggs for breakfast without burning them while I help get Ivy dressed and ready for the day. Rafe spends the better part of the day in his office working from home while I busy myself tidying the house, doing the laundry and cooking dinner. And at night, I read Ivy a bedtime story.

He laughs. "Our marriage would never be boring, I guarantee it."

"That your way of proposing to me?"

"Reese, the only way I'd marry you is if you tied me to a chair and dragged me down the aisle gagged and bound."

"BDSM *and* exhibitionism. We never did get to explore this kinky side of yours, did we?"

He throws his head back in laughter. "You're unbelievable."

"You got a red room of pain like Christian Grey? Do chains and whips excite you?"

"What would you say if I told you they did?" he teases.

"I'd be pleasantly surprised. I have to admit a sex swing has always intrigued me, it could be kinda fun, though a riding crop to the ass, not so much. Suspended from the ceiling... I suppose I'll give it a try, and being tied to the headboard? Hell, I'm game. When do we start?"

He chuckles as he turns to me, his gaze hard and heated. "You'd like that, wouldn't you?"

He adjusts his position on the sofa and I don't miss the bulge at the front of his pants that seems considerably tighter than they did before.

Shit... He's turned on.

My blood spikes, my heart pounding in my chest.

"You're not so innocent as you lead people to believe, are you?" he asks.

I slap my palm to my chest dramatically. "*Me?* I'm a good girl!"

"Not from what I recall."

The mood shifts the second the words are out of his mouth and I dart my gaze away. The reminder of the morning I woke up to find him gone is like a bucket of ice water being tipped over me and just like that, the light, playful atmosphere is long gone.

"I um… I'm gonna head to bed. Goodnight, Rafe." No doubt he can sense my unease through my short, clipped tone as I rise from the sofa and high-tail it out of the room as fast as I can, seeking the sanctuary and solitude of the bedroom.

I stare at the blank white ceiling as I lie on the mattress, my heartbeat slowly returning to normal.

I don't know where exactly I expected the conversation to lead, entering into sex talk with an ex is never a good idea, but I'm glad it ended where it did. At least now to some degree he knows he hurt me, and by the look on his face he feels somewhat guilty of that fact.

Good. So he should be.

My attention catches at the sound of movement just outside the door. I know it's Rafe, but he makes no attempt to knock or enter, he just hovers for a long moment before his footsteps fade away into nothing.

I dig out my phone and pull up Sadie's number.

Me: The double date... Count me in. Set it up and I'll be there. Xxx

A few minutes later, my phone pings with a reply.

Dee: Yay! This is going to be so much fun! Love you forever. Xoxo

This is going to be so much fun... The very same words have landed me in trouble too many times before, and I'm certain this time will be no different.

16

Reese

"Wow, Reese, you look..." Rafe's wide eyes roam over me from head to toe and back up again as he takes in my appearance.

I'm wearing a pair of black leather pants that fit me like a second skin, a tight white top that shows off my tits, paired with black heeled boots and a black vintage leather jacket I found in a charity shop years ago. My eyes are rimmed in black, my lips painted ruby red, and my copper hair falling in loose waves down my back.

I look hot, but it's overkill. I thought by getting dolled-up it would make me more excited about tonight, but the only feeling in my stomach is dread that sinks like a lead weight.

I've typed out a message to Sadie three times now, making up excuses of why I can't go, but I've erased every single one. I can't let her down, but coming face to face with Rafe has made me even more apprehensive to go.

"What's the occasion?" he asks.

"I uh… I got roped into some double date with a girl I worked with at the bar."

"A date?" I don't miss the flicker of something akin to jealousy in his expression.

"Yeah. Sadie met some guy at the bar and she needs a plus one to double with one of his friends," I explain.

He leans forward where he's sitting. "Who's the guy?"

"I have no idea, I've never met him. What's with the twenty questions, anyway? It's just a date."

"I thought you didn't want to date anymore." He does his best to remain unaffected, but I can tell by the set of his jaw, how it clenches, that he's irritated.

"I'm helping out a friend, what's the big deal? It's just dinner, not that I have to justify myself to you." *Why is he acting like this?*

"It's never just dinner though, is it? There's expectations on what happens after. I mean-"

"Are you actually serious right now?" I cut him off. "Who the hell made you my keeper? Do I have to consult you on everything I do now? You keeping tabs on my every move?"

"Stop being ridiculous."

"*I'm* ridiculous?" I scoff. "I'm not the one grilling the other on something that doesn't concern them. We're friends, Rafe. You have your life and I have mine, just because I'm living under your roof does not give you the right to question and dictate my dating life. You know what? I'm out of here. Maybe snap out of acting like an asshole in case your daughter needs you."

I pull open the door and let it slam behind me without another word. I storm down the hall, the click of my boots echoing down the corridor with every heavy stomp.

Irritation itches at my skin as I replay the whole thing over in my head on the way to the restaurant, the whole thing leaving a bad taste in my mouth.

How dare he say all that shit to me like he has any say in what I do and where I go?

Who the hell does he think he is?

∞∞∞

The date goes smoothly, and the conversation between the four of us flows easily throughout dinner, and despite not wanting to be here, it's not actually as bad as I thought it would be. Declan, the guy I've been set up with is probably one of the nicest guys I've met. He's handsome in an Old Hollywood sort of way, he's kind and respectful, and on a different night and under different circumstances, I'd happily go on a second date with him, but there's no spark. There's no fire that burns in the pit of my stomach when we lock eyes from across the table. No butterflies that flip in my belly when he smiles at me. No ache between my legs at the thought of being with him. As much as I hate to admit, I've spent most of the night comparing him to the one man who makes me feel all of the above, the one man I *shouldn't* want.

While the guys order more drinks, Sadie and I excuse ourselves to use the ladies room.

She loops her arm through mine as we enter the restroom. "Oh my God! Oscar is *way* hotter than I remembered from the other night. God, his eyes make me want to melt into a puddle and his tattoos! I never found them attractive before, but on *him*, I'm ready to jump his bones right now!"

"Yeah, he seems great," I respond with zero feelings behind

my words.

"Ree, are you okay?" Sadie asks.

"I'm fine," I lie, forcing a smile as I glance at her reflection through the mirror above the row of basins.

"You don't seem fine, in fact since we got here it's like you've been planning out your escape route," she points out. "You're not really into him, are you?"

I turn to face her, leaning against the marble effect counter. "Declan's fine, in fact he's really sweet. He's just..."

"Safe? *Boring?*" she answers for me.

"I wouldn't say boring, just not..."

"Not *Rafe*. I get it."

"I'm so sorry, Dee. I'm not trying to be rude or ignorant. To tell you the truth I... I was so close to backing out of this whole thing. I had a fight with Rafe before I left and I knew me coming here would piss him off and..."

"You don't have to explain, babe. If you wanna ditch, I can make up some excuse of why you left."

"I can't let you do that. Besides, it's almost over anyway. Let's just go back out there, I'm not leaving until I'm certain you're onto a sure thing tonight with Oscar. You more than anyone need some dick inside you."

She slaps my arm with a laugh before disappearing into one of the stalls to pee.

An hour later, Sadie and Oscar speed off into the night on his motorcycle leaving Declan and I stood in the darkened parking lot beside my car.

Declan smiles down at me. "It was really nice to meet you, Reese. I'd really like to see you again."

My stomach twists with guilt. "It was nice to meet you too, but I'm... I'm going through some stuff right now and it's complicated and I—I don't want to hurt your feelings or lead you on or..."

"Hey," he stops me. "It's okay. Whoever he is, is a lucky guy, or an absolute idiot if he's messing you around. Don't settle for anything less than you deserve, Reese, you're the kind of girl a guy holds onto," he says.

The fact that he's being so nice makes me feel like an even bigger asshole.

I smile. "In a different life that guy would be you, Declan. You're the kind of guy a girl like me *should* hold onto."

"Tell that to my ex." He laughs softly, stuffing his hands into the pockets of his jeans. "But the heart wants what the heart wants, right? Hell, maybe the two of us are living it up together in some parallel universe somewhere. Lucky bastards."

A laugh slips free and he leans in and places a delicate kiss to my cheek and pulls open my car door.

"Goodnight, Reese," he says with a smile.

"'Night." I climb into my car and he closes the door behind me, and with a wave goodbye, he turns and heads towards his car parked across the lot.

I lean against the headrest and breathe a heavy sigh.

What the hell is wrong with me?

I must be an addict to heartbreak or unrequited love, a magnet to the type of guys who are all wrong for me, but like Declan said, the heart wants what the heart wants, and in my case, I guess old habits die a slow and painful death. I just turned down a man who would no doubt go to the ends of the earth to make me happy, a guy who would treat me the best anyone probably ever has, for a guy I shouldn't want, a guy who probably doesn't even want me back.

∞∞∞

It's just past eleven when I get in, and a part of me isn't surprised to find the lights are still on, but I had hoped Rafe hadn't waited up to avoid the awkwardness that will ensue between us.

He's sat on the sofa tapping away on his laptop with his feet propped up on the coffee table.

"How was your date?" He doesn't look up as he speaks, and I can almost hear the sarcasm drip from his voice.

"Don't start, Rafe. I don't wanna fight," I say on a sigh, kicking off my boots and shrugging off my jacket.

"It was just a question."

"I said I don't want to fight." I head through to the kitchen to get a drink. My mouth has suddenly turned dry, so I fill a glass of water at the sink and down the entire contents in one.

My spine stiffens when I feel Rafe stood behind me, the hairs on the back of my neck standing to attention under his gaze. "I didn't expect you back so early. Was he an asshole?"

"No, actually he was really nice."

"You gonna see him again?"

"I dunno, maybe." I shrug.

I catch a glimpse of him over my shoulder, enough to see my answer irritates him, but he tries his best not to show it.

"You wanna know what's funny?" I turn to him, leaning against the counter. "He's easily the nicest guy I've ever met, and I turned him down because he's not the man I want."

My confession surprises him. He knows exactly who I'm referring to.

"Why did you do it, Rafe? Leave like that, that morning?

Was I not even worth a goodbye?"

"I'm sorry I hurt you," he says, swallowing hard.

"You didn't even call or text. You ghosted me. Do you have any idea how that feels? I told you how much it hurts to wake up alone the morning after, how many times I've wondered if I'd done something wrong, and you did exactly that. More fool me for thinking you'd be different."

Silence falls between us as we stare at each other and it feels like hours as I wait for him to answer, but nothing comes.

I brush past him. "Forget it, I'm going to bed."

"My dad died that night." His words have me jerking to a halt.

I whirl around, searching his face as he casts his eyes down. "W-What?"

"I woke up and you were still asleep. My phone blew up with a dozen texts and voicemails... He died while I was at the bar getting drunk. How fucking selfish is that?" He collapses back against the counter, his hands fisting his hair, tugging harshly.

My heart cracks as I reach for his hand. "Oh my god, Rafe. I... I had no idea."

I knew his dad had passed away, but I didn't realise it was the same night we spent together.

"I didn't get to say goodbye to him."

"You couldn't have know what would happen."

He nods slowly. "Yeah, I did. He was sick when I left that afternoon and Gage begged me to stay, but I bolted. Deep down I knew he didn't have long left, I just... I couldn't handle it. I should've been there."

"Hey, look at me." I tip his chin up, forcing his eyes to connect with mine, the tip of his nose grazing ever so slightly against my own. "Don't beat yourself up. He knew you loved him at the end, take comfort in that. Maybe it was for the best that you weren't there. You can remember him how he was when you think about him, not lying motionless on some bed."

His eyes lift to mine. "I never wanted to hurt you, Reese."

"It's alright." Without thinking, I wrap my arms around him, my hands locking behind his neck and he melts into my touch, burying his face into my neck.

I get it now.

I get now why he left that morning. It wasn't like I first thought and regret churns in my stomach. I blamed him all this time, and a part of me hated him for leaving, but now I understand. He was in shock, grieving the loss of his dad while guilt ate him up inside.

"I know it's difficult for you to open up, but know that I'm here if you ever want to," I offer.

He pulls out of my hold gently, just enough to tip his head forward to rest against mine. "Reese…" he breathes out, tucking a stray piece of hair behind my ear.

"What?" I whisper, his warm breath fanning across my face, his lips so close my own tingle with the need to feel them on mine.

My heart thumps so hard in my chest I'm sure Rafe can feel it.

Kiss me… I will him silently. *Kiss me…*

I don't have to wait long for him to grant my wish when his mouth slams down on mine, stealing the breath from my lungs as he claim my lips.

I don't hesitate to kiss him back and I fall into it so easily, revelling in the feeling of his strong, soft lips gliding over mine, soaking it all up in case this is the last time it'll ever happen.

One of my hands rakes through his hair while the other fists his shirt, tugging him closer as he walks me backwards. My back hits the fridge as his mouth continues to devour mine in a chaotic, frenzied kiss. I'm so lost in him, in his lips, in his touch that I can't think straight, not a single coherent through passes through my mind because all I can feel is him.

"Did you let that guy kiss you tonight?" he pants against my mouth, his hands squeezing my ass. "Hmm? Did you let him kiss you like this?" I shake my head. "Good."

He bends to lift me, my legs banding around his waist as he places me on the kitchen counter, the glass I was using earlier toppling over with a clatter beside me.

We're a mass of lips and hands that can't seem to get enough, hungry to touch, to *feel* as his tongue slips into my mouth to tangle with mine.

My heart is beating out of my chest as I reach between us to grip the bottom of his shirt, but before I get the chance to pull it off him there's a piercing scream from Ivy's room and we break apart. Rafe jerks back like he can't get away from me quick enough, his back colliding with the edge of the counter.

A long pregnant silence falls between us, the both of us panting like we just ran a mile uphill, our lips swollen and bruised while staring at each other dumbstruck.

Ivy screams again and I clear my throat. "I um... I should go check on her." I'm out of the kitchen before he can respond.

I stop just outside Ivy's room and press my forehead against the door, my heart still hammering away in my chest.

Did that really just happen?

17

Rafe

In what universe did I think having Reese living under my roof was a good idea? In what universe did I think I think I'd be able to live alongside her and *not* want to touch her every five seconds.

I highly overestimated my self-control when it comes to her. I thought I could do it. I thought I could keep our relationship professional, given she's technically my employee now, but most of all, I thought I could keep it friendly. But I'd be lying to myself because the more I'm around her, the more I want to take us out of the friend zone, throw her on my bed and do wicked, wicked things to her body.

She doesn't notice that in the middle of the night, when she pads through to the kitchen to get a drink wearing just a thin tank top and a pair of panties, that my eyes follow her every move. How her top lifts, when she reaches up for an empty glass in one of the cupboards, showing off her beautiful ass, her full hips and the flat planes of her stomach.

She doesn't notice when her back is to me while she cooks away on the stove, swaying to a song she likes on the radio that all I can think about is bending her over the counter with her hair wrapped in my fist, pounding into her from behind, imagining all the sounds she'd make as I made her come over and over again on my cock.

My fingers itch to touch her, my dick hardening at every instance where I find myself way too close. Take the other day, she was teaching me how to cook some dish I can't fucking remember the name of because my mind was *very* much elsewhere. She'd brush against me with her body as she shuffled past and my dick would come alive behind my zipper. I've never been so responsive to a woman's touch before, such an innocent touch like a hand on my arm has my body charged with electricity.

She's been sent from hell to test me, I'm sure of it. And unsurprisingly, I'm failing.

She's a temptation too dangerous to indulge in, a distraction I can't afford to have in my life, but above all else, the one thing that scares me the most... She's the first and only woman who has the power to steal my heart—something I've never allowed before.

The tension has been brewing between us for some time now and the rope pulls tighter every time we're in the same room.

Take last night, I couldn't help myself from stealing a kiss, a kiss that still lingers on my lips a full eight hours after it happened and plays on my mind whenever I think about her.

A kiss I want to happen again.

But it can't.

I can't allow myself to go there, because I know one touch would never been enough to quell this ache, this burning need inside me that's been there since the night we spent together months ago. What would start out as lust would no doubt turn into something more—something I'm not ready for, but I'm not sure how long I'm going to be able to resist.

"Well, I did not expect to see you this morning." My brother blinks at me from across his desk as I sink down into the chair opposite him. He's been buried in work this past month or so since I took a break to deal with Ivy and all the custody shit and I feel bad. Della is pregnant for crying out loud, he shouldn't be spending in excess of twelve hours hauled up in his office at *De La Rosa*.

All because of me...

"I'm coming back to work," I announce.

"Seriously?"

"I mean, yeah. We're partners aren't we?"

"Of course we are, I just thought your head would be elsewhere is all."

"I've gotta come back sometime right? Might as well be now. I can still be at home some of the time and I can work from there if I have to."

"In that case, it's good to have you back, brother. How's Ivy getting on?"

"She's good, starting to come out of her shell a little, especially now she has Merlin around."

"Merlin?"

"Reese's fucking cat, it's actually her grandma's but she's taking care of it for her. You know, I woke up with the fucking thing rubbing itself against my face this morning?" Yeah, not the best wake up call I could have imagined.

Gage chokes a laugh.

"And it had a go at my leg like I was a goddamn scratching post. Look!" I swing my leg up and ledge my foot on the desk, pulling up my trouser leg where a series of red scratches are turning into welts on my calf. This only makes Gage laugh harder.

"How are things with that fiery redhead we know and love?"

"Sarcastic and feisty as ever. Ivy's really taken to having her around."

"And you?" he asks.

When I don't answer, he reclines back in his chair, eyeing me suspiciously. "What's your game with her, Rafe?"

"Nothing. She was being evicted, I needed help with Ivy so I offered her a job. It's a win-win for both of us."

"Since when were you and Reese friends?"

I don't think we were ever really friends.

"Does it even matter?" I shift my eyes to avoid his.

"Wait a minute... You've fucked her haven't you?"

"I'm not dignifying that question with an answer," I reply.

"I'll take that as a yes. When?"

He doesn't take his eyes off mine as he waits for an answer.

I huff. "Months ago. What does it fucking matter? She's there for Ivy and nothing more, and once she's settled and Reese has sorted out a place of her own... she'll be gone."

"And it'll be that easy to let her go?" he asks.

"Why wouldn't it be? Women have come and gone in less time, Reese is no different." I square my chin, trying to convince my brother of a lie I don't fully believe myself, because Reese *is* different.

He leans forward in his seat. "Then why aren't I convinced? She gets under your skin, doesn't she?"

"Yes, okay? *Fuck*. She gets under my skin and I wish she didn't but…"

"But you like having her around."

Too fucking much.

"Look, whatever you do, please just don't hurt her, alright? She's important to Della, she's practically family."

"The last thing I want is for her to get hurt, and it won't get to that. Nothing's gonna happen between us."

Nothing. Not again.

Rather than go straight back home, I decide to go for a walk first, leaving my car at work, and it's not long that I come across an old watering hole I used to drink in. My brain is telling me to keep on walking, but I've never been great at listening to reason.

The bar is dark and dingy, the floor sticky beneath my shoes and the smell of stale beer lingers heavily in the air mixed with the pungent stench of body odour.

"What'll it be?" the bartender asks as I slide onto the bar stool.

It's unsurprisingly quiet in here for a midweek afternoon and I'm glad. I'm not in the mood for conversation. I just want a couple of drinks, take an hour to myself before I return back to reality.

At that moment, my phone pings with an incoming text in my pocket.

Reese: Where are you?

My stomach twists. I can't avoid her forever, I'm gonna have to go home at some point, I just need to take the edge off first.

I pocket my phone and turn to the bartender. "Whiskey, neat."

17

∞∞∞

Reese is in the kitchen when I get back home, stirring something in the pan on the stove before placing a bowl of pasta in another, replacing the lid on top.

I clear my throat, moving closer. "Hi."

Her spine straightens and after a moment she turns to face me. "Where've you been? I've been worried. Did you not get my texts?"

"Work, then I went for a walk."

She folds her arms. "And evidently made a beeline to the nearest bar." I don't miss the disdain in her voice and the disapproving look in her eyes.

"You're really taking this whole housewife act a little too seriously considering you're not *actually* my wife, don't you think?" I regret the words as soon as they are out of my mouth.

She jerks back like I backhanded her across the face. "You're a real prick when you've had a drink, you know that?"

She spins around to shield herself from me, but even with her back to me I know I've hurt her. I promised my brother I wouldn't hurt her and within two minutes of getting home, that's exactly what I've done.

Asshole.

I reach out for her, placing my hand on her waist. "Ree."

"Don't." She sniffs, spinning from my hold and pushing past me to reach into the fridge. "Like I've said before, I'm not here to look after your daughter when you decide to go off and get shitfaced, if that's what you think then I'll pack my shit right now and leave."

"I don't want you to go, Reese. I'm sorry. The drink... It's a crutch whenever I need a pick-me-up."

"Was kissing me really that bad? Gee, thanks. Let's face it, that's what this is all about, right?"

I go to speak but my eyes fall on the pan behind her. "The uh... the pasta's boiling over."

She whips around to find the saucepan lid rattling as bubbles spill over the sides. She grabs for the handle but screams, dropping it with a loud clatter onto the counter. "Shit!"

I rush to her, immediately feeling myself stone cold sober. "Are you okay?"

She holds onto her wrist. "It feels like my hand's on fire."

"Let me see." I take her hand in mine, the skin of her palm bright red. I lead her over to the sink and let the cold water cool her burning skin.

"Jesus, it stings like a bitch."

"Reesie? Are you okay?" Ivy's standing across the room, her brows knitted with worry.

"I'm fine, sweetie. You go back and play with Merlin, okay?"

"Okay." Chewing on her fingernail, she turns and disappears back down the hallway.

"Keep your hand under there, the burning will stop soon." I go in search of a first aid kit, which after five minutes of searching, I find at the bottom of my bathroom cabinet. I return to the kitchen to find her sat at the island.

"How is it?" I ask.

"Better, but it still hurts."

I take a seat next to her, taking her hand in mine and placing it palm up. There's a thick stripe across her hand where she gripped the handle that burned her, the skin red and angry. I blow gently on her palm to soothe the burn and I glance up to find her watching me, a faint blush staining her cheeks as my breath fans over her hand.

I begin rubbing petroleum jelly onto her skin, trying to be as gentle as I can around the tender area.

"How are you so good at this? Are you a doctor in some alternate universe?"

I chuckle. "No, but when you've been in enough fights like I have, you learn early on how to take care of injuries. Scrapes, burns... *cuts*... It's all second nature now."

"I get the feeling the other guy comes off looking worse than you do."

"Of course they do," I say with a shrug.

She laughs softly before we fall silent as I tend to her hand and she watches me with fascination.

Her mouth opens to speak, and I can already guess what she's about to say before a single word slips past her lips.

"Are we just gonna ignore the elephant in the room?" she asks. "I mean, that's why you escaped at the crack ass of dawn this morning, isn't it? To avoid me?"

I will never get over how Reese goes in straight for the kill, none of this beating around the bush bullshit, she just says it how it is.

"It shouldn't have happened."

"But it did. And I think we both wanted it to, I know I did. It was only a matter of time, anyway."

"A matter of time?"

"Before this tension between us got too much. I know you feel it, the same as I do, and at some point, that cord will snap."

"We can't let it," I say. Last night was a wake up call to whatever this is. That kiss has proven how much I need to fight this pull I have towards because it's more powerful than I first thought. That cord is holding on by a single tiny thread and just one more touch of her lips will be the end of me, I'm sure of it.

"Why is it so wrong to think we could be good together?"

I pause for a moment, taking the time to wrap her hand in a clean bandage. "I don't do relationships."

"Neither do I. I've been hurt too many times, gotten my hopes up way too often and I'm done, with all of it."

I secure the bandage at her wrist and clear my throat, forcing my eyes to remain on her hand. "All done."

I move to get off my seat, but her hand tightens around mine, holding me in place. "Rafe?"

I pull my hand out from under hers. "I'm sorry. I just can't."

18

Rafe

I wake up once again on the couch with the walking toilet brush lying across my chest, purring away as it nuzzles it's head into my neck, and tossing it out the window is becoming a more and more appealing idea.

That's not to say I'd ever actually go through with it, 'cause I wouldn't. I'm not a monster, but I'm still not it's biggest fan.

"Go on, get off me." I nudge Merlin off my chest and with a loud disgruntled meow, he jumps onto the floor and disappears under the couch.

I groan as I move to sit up. This fucking couch is wrecking my back. Every night my sleep becomes more uncomfortable and no matter what position I try to settle in, within half an hour I'm fidgety and restless. Pain shoots up my spine and I do my best to stretch out the ache and ease the crick in my neck, but it's no good. I'm going to be a cripple before I'm thirty.

Reese strolls into the room, spotting me on the couch as she heads towards to kitchen.

She gives me a small smile. "Morning."

I jump from the couch and follow her into the kitchen where she busies herself making coffee. "How's your hand?"

"It's fine. Want some?" She takes out a second mug.

"Yeah, thanks. Listen, are we... are we good?"

She looks up to meet my eye. "Why wouldn't we be?"

I scrub a hand over my stubbled jaw. "I don't know I— just wondered after yesterday..."

"We're fine, okay?" Her clipped tone makes me think otherwise, but I know Reese, the more you push, the harder she pushes back so I drop the subject for now.

I know exactly what she was suggesting last night as I bandaged her hand and I don't know how I feel about it. It's one thing fucking strangers you never have to see again, but living with them, seeing them everyday is another. It's too intimate, too personal, and whether you want feelings involved or not, there always will be, especially when the person in question you consider a friend.

I'm not going to lie and say I'm not attracted to her, because I am. I'm crazy attracted to her, more than I have been to any other woman and that alone scares me. There's things about me I don't want her to know, things that would change everything and alter the way she sees me if she ever knew. Things I don't particularly like about myself and if I gave into my attraction for her, there would be no hiding it.

And I can't allow that.

Reese pours our coffees and slides mine towards me along the counter. She doesn't take a single breath as she downs hers in one. "I've got an errand to run in town this morning, will you be okay? Ivy's still fast asleep."

"Yeah, we'll be fine. Where you off to?"

"Just got some stuff to do, that's all. I won't be long. I'll pick up some groceries for dinner tonight on my way back." Her vague answer has me wondering if she's hiding something, but we're already treading on eggshells after the kiss, I better not push anymore.

"Okay. Drive safe."

Without another word, she's out the door like she couldn't get away from me fast enough.

∞∞∞

Two and a half hours later, I'm sat on Ivy's bedroom floor, cross-legged while she kneels in front of me. The tip of her tongue peaking out the corner of her mouth in concentration while she does God knows what to my face.

A sea of different makeup items litter the floor around us.

After breakfast, I suggested watching a movie, to which she declined. I then offered to do what Reese suggested by playing dolls, which again she said no to. I was going to leave it at that, but then she suggested she do my makeup and as much as the thought filled me with dread, it opened a door to get close to my daughter, and I wasn't going to pass up an opportunity like that.

"You're gonna look so pretty!" she exclaims.

"And *very* pink, I'm assuming."

She giggles as she dips her makeup brush into one of the palettes beside. "Eyes closed please."

I do as she instructs and slam my eyes closed. I feel her dusting the brush over my left eyelid, and we sit like this for a couple of minutes while she switches to my right.

"You can open them now," she tells me. She fiddles around with something else and switches to a bigger, fluffier brush. "Now for the blusher!"

"You're not gonna go making me look like a clown now are you?"

Her cheeks turn a shade of pink. "No! You're gonna be Princess Rafe!"

Can't say I've ever been called they before.

"Ives, can I ask you something?"

"Uh-huh." She nods, dragging the brush against my face.

"Do you like living here? With me?"

She shrugs. "I guess. Your house is lots nicer than Sally and Toby's. They were real nice and all, but their house smelled like smelly feet."

I chuckle. "Well, that's not good, is it?"

She drops the brush and pulls out a bright pink lipstick.

Oh, Jesus...

"I never knew I had a daddy," she says, twisting the lipstick up and pressing it to my lips.

"Everybody has a daddy."

Her eyes widen as they shift to mine. "Even *you*?"

"Yeah. Even me. That would make him your granddaddy. He was a *really* great dad."

"Where is he? Can I meet him?"

I swallow thickly. "No, sweetie. You see, he's... he's in heaven now."

She frowns. "Like my mommy?"

"Yeah. Like your mommy."

"How comes you never saw me, like when I was a baby?" she asks.

I reach forward to swipe her hair from her face. "I didn't know you existed, Ives. If I had... Not a single person could have torn me away from you."

"But you have me now, though. And you're not gonna leave me to go where mommy is, right?"

I dart my eyes to the ceiling as I force back a wave of tears that burn my eyes. I give myself a moment before returning my gaze to Ivy, her big blue eyes full of innocence and curiosity. I open my arms, ushering her closer and to my surprise, she accepts.

She crawls into my lap, winding her arms around my neck, her head resting over my heart.

This is the first time I've properly held her and it feels so fucking good.

I press a kiss to the top of her head. "No. I'm not going anywhere, sweetheart. I promise. If you ever need anything, or if you're ever sad or in trouble, I'll always be here to take care of you. Okay? If you ever want to talk about your mommy, don't ever be afraid to. Just remember that I love you, sweetheart, I love you so much." *More than life itself.*

She snuggles closer. "Loves you too, Daddy."

My heart thuds in my chest. She loves me. I can't even put into words the magnitude of what I'm feeling right now, how my heart just expanded so much I'm sure it'll burst.

That's the first time she's called me that. I wondered if she ever would and I never could have imagined how it would feel like to hear that word leave her lips.

It feels like I'm fucking flying. It's like every high imaginable rolled into one, every drug injected directly into my heart.

I hold her for I don't know how long because I can't seem to bring myself to stop.

I always thought it so unimaginable how much a person could love their child, but now I know. It's all-consuming, unconditional, fulfilling and it has me feeling all kinds of things I've never experienced.

Daddy...

The best goddamn sound in the world.

The front door slams closed. "Hello? Where is everyone?" Reese calls.

"In here!" I reply.

My back is facing the door and as I hear her footsteps growing closer, I suck in a breath.

I still haven't been able to shake this feeling I felt when I kissed her the other night, and whenever I look at her, that kiss is at the forefront of my mind.

"Reesie!" Ivy twists from my grasp and skips to greet her.

"What's going on in here?" she asks.

"I'm making Daddy look like a princess," Ivy says.

Reese moves further into the room, her eyes falling on me as she breaks into a laugh. "Oh, my God!"

"Isn't he pretty?" Ivy asks, her eyes flicking between Reese and her handiwork on my face. I dread to think what I look like.

Her eyes are a little puffy which makes me think she's been crying. Where did she go off to this morning? What's made her so upset?

"He sure does, honey." Reese tries to keep a straight face, but I can see the twitch of her mouth from where I'm sat.

"I have an idea," I start, "why don't we make Reese a princess too?"

Ivy tuts. "She's already a princess, silly. She's the most beautiful princess ever!"

"Yeah, she is." I don't miss how Reese takes in a breath as I say the words, my eyes lingering on hers.

Is she so surprised that I'd call her beautiful?

"Have you guys uh… have you eaten yet?" she asks, changing the subject, a tinge of pink staining her cheeks.

"Not yet," I answer.

"Want me to make you a sandwich?"

"Yes!" Ivy exclaims. "I'm starvin' marvin'!"

Reese laughs. "Well, we can't have that, can we?" Her eyes drift over me once more before she leaves the room.

"I'm gonna go help Reese, okay? How about you tidy all this away for now, then we can do Reese's makeup later?"

Her eyes light up. "Can we?"

"We can do anything you want, Ives." I drop a kiss to her forehead before heading through the house to find Reese.

She's digging through the fridge when I reach the kitchen, pulling out a million different things and placing them on the counter.

"I see you two are finally bonding," she says.

"If by bonding you mean letting a five year-old make me look like a clown, then yeah, we're best buds now."

"And she started calling you Daddy," she points out.

"Yeah it's uh… It feels good." Like we're finally headed in the right direction.

Her eyes find my face and her shoulders shake with laughter. "You look absolutely ridiculous."

"I'm glad I amuse you." I pull off the lid of the peanut butter, digging out a lump on my finger and flicking it in her direction.

It spatters all over her face and she stares at me in shock with her mouth gaping open. "I can't believe you just did that."

A deep laugh rumbles through me. "Now who looks ridiculous?" I reach for another lump.

Her eyes go wide. "Rafe, don't you dare!"

She begins backing away from me, and I advance towards her with my peanut butter covered finger high in the air, and she grips the kitchen island tightly. I take a quick step to the right and she jerks, ready to run.

"Rafe…" she warns, an apprehensive smile creeping up onto her face. "Don't."

My smile widens. "You're going down, Miss Reynolds."

Without warning, I break into a run and Reese squeals as I chase her around the island, her infectious cackle echoing through the apartment as we run rings around the kitchen.

She's fast, but I'm faster and within a minute my arms wrap around her waist from behind as I pull her into me. As she squirms against me, I can feel my dick growing harder and I spin her around, backing her against the counter.

Her laughter slowly dies off as her eyes hold mine, waiting for my next move.

With a clean finger, I swipe at the peanut butter from her face and bring it to my mouth, sucking it off my finger. Her mouth parts as her eyes track the movements as I repeat it until there's not a trace of it left on her beautiful face.

Her eyes dart to the finger which is still covered in the peanut butter I was using to chase her, and without thinking, I smear it over her neck, leaving a trail from the space below her earlobe all the way to where her breasts dip below the neckline of her top.

She's breathing harder now as she watches me, her grip on my arm tightening as her pupils dilate.

She's as turned on as I am.

I lean in, swiping along the trail of butter with a single long drawn-out drag of my tongue, starting at her heaving chest.

She gasps when my tongue reaches the sensitive spot on her neck, goose bumps erupting over her skin as she shudders under my touch.

She feels so good in my arms, and as my lips linger on her skin, and her sweet scent fills my nose, a million dirty thoughts cross my mind. A million different ways I could have her, taste her, *fuck* her, make her scream my name and I'd love every single second.

Reese tips her head back, giving me better access and I know she wants me to go further, I want that too. But I step back, releasing her from my hold, putting some distance between us.

I shouldn't be doing this.

I went too far.

Her eyes meet mine. "W—What's wrong?"

I clear my throat. "I'm what's wrong. I got carried away. I'm sorry." Without another word, I turn on my heel and walk away, and every step is agony.

19

Reese

My sleep is restless tonight.

I'm constantly tossing and turning, unable to find a comfortable spot in which to fall asleep and I can feel the frustration building inside me with every incessant tick of the clock on the table.

After our little interaction in the kitchen earlier this afternoon, the one in which Rafe *literally* licked peanut butter off of me, leaving me a confused, panting and thoroughly turned on mess, Rafe barricaded himself in his office and I never saw him again.

I know he enjoyed it the same as I did, I felt how much he enjoyed it prodding against my belly.

We were *so* close. So close to that cord between us snapping and he stopped. *Again.*

I don't know why he keeps holding back, blowing hot and cold at the flick of a switch. I don't know what has him running in the opposite direction whenever we get closer, and whatever this war is that's raging within him, tearing him up inside, I want to save him from it.

I just don't know how to make him see that we could be good for each other.

I glance over at the clock on the bedside table. Two in the morning and I'm wide awake. I reach for my phone and scroll through TikTok for a while, diving headfirst down a rabbit hole about a girl who was locked in a basement by her twisted father who abused her for years on end only to become the mother of his children.

Gross. I shudder.

I carry on scrolling and before I know it, I can feel the tug of sleep finally pulling at my eyelids. Just as I'm about to drift off, the sound of the bedroom door opening has me sitting up straighter.

I blink through the dark to where a male figure stands at the foot of the bed, his frame silhouetted from the light filtering in through the blinds. "Rafe?"

"Can't sleep either?" he asks, rounding the bed to perch on the edge. Through the thin strip of soft moonlight filtering in through the window, I can make out that he's shirtless, wearing only a pair light grey sweatpants. He's ripped, with a hard wall of muscle a Greek god would be proud of.

"Not really, no. What's up?"

"Me." He leans forward, resting his elbows on his knees. "I've been an idiot haven't I?"

"Depends on what you're referring to."

"Us." He turns his head towards me, his eyes meeting mine through the dimly lit room, but even in the dark I can see the sparkle in his ocean blue irises. "I've been a fool to think I could fight this, but I've been fighting a losing battle from the very start."

Does he mean what I think he means? "Okay..."

He turns fully to me. "I want you, Reese."

Hearing his admission out loud has my heart beating out of my chest.

"I want to take you into that shower and fuck you against the tiles. I want your thighs squeezing my head like a vice as I lick that beautiful pussy of yours. I want you straddling my hips while you ride me like a bull, and I especially want to fuck you into this mattress, with your hands bound, completely open for me. I want you every way possible."

My pussy pulses between my legs as his words paint vivid images in my head.

I want it all.

Everything he can give me. Even if it's for a short while.

Before he can say another word, I grab the back of his neck and slam my mouth onto his, crawling out from under the covers and onto his lap. One of his hands dives into my hair while the other cups my ass, squeezing as he holds me to him, his tongue slipping into my mouth to tangle with mine as the kiss deepens.

Using his hand on my ass, he rocks me against him, his erection pressing against my core, and with every move of my hips against the hardness in his pants, pleasure zaps through me.

I pull back, breaking the kiss only to tug my shirt over my head before diving back in. His mouth trails along my jaw and down my neck before easing back to admire my tits on full display.

Goose bumps break out across my skin under his intense

gaze, my nipples hardening into sharp peaks when he reaches down and grazes the pad of his thumbs over them.

"You're so fucking gorgeous," he pants before gripping my hips and tossing me onto my back on the mattress with a soft bounce.

He hovers above me, dipping down to capture my lips once more, then kisses a trail down my body beginning with each breast, slowly working his way down so he's kneeling my feet that dangle off the edge of the bed.

His eyes meet mine as he reaches for my panties. "You were made to tease me, weren't you, Reese? I bet you didn't notice that every time you made a midnight trip to the kitchen for a drink that I was watching, did you?"

What? He saw me?

He grins, peeling my panties down my legs and bringing the fabric up to his nose and taking a deep inhale. "Naughty girl, walking around my apartment in just a thin vest and a tiny scrap of fabric covering this pussy."

"What are you gonna do about it?" I challenge with a smirk, deciding to play along in this little game of his.

I'm so turned on right now, and the way his eyes drink me in has me needing to squeeze my thighs together to ease the ache that's building there, but Rafe's hands stop me. He spreads my legs wide, keeping me exposed to him completely.

"Every time I watched you, all I could think about was doing this." With his hands pinning my knees to the bed, he sinks his face between my legs.

I cry out, unable to stop the sound from escaping my lips as he devours me, licking through my folds like he can't get enough.

My fingers dive into his hair as I writhe and squirm, the

pleasure that shoots through my body is unlike anything I've ever felt. I feel it *everywhere* and one thing is absolutely certain…

This man sure knows how to eat pussy.

"Rafe…" I moan, my fingers tightening in his hair as his tongue flicks and licks my swollen clit, circling the tight bundle of nerves with the tip of his tongue before sucking it between his lips, working me up into a frenzy.

"You taste like heaven." His words are muffled as he dives back in, plunging two fingers into my soaked channel, fucking me with them as he curls them against the spot that has me on the verge of release in an instant.

A few more swipes of his tongue and my orgasm is right there. I bite down onto the back of my hand to muffle the sound as I teeter on the edge and just as I'm about to tip over, Rafe pulls back, his mouth and chin shimmering with my arousal.

I go to protest but I'm flipped over onto my stomach and dragged onto all fours. His palm connects with my ass cheek and I yelp just as his lips meet my skin, soothing the sting. I feel him move from behind me, digging through the bedside draw before the distinct sound of a condom wrapper has my pussy contracting in anticipation.

I feel the mattress dip, as he climbs behind me and then he's there, the thick blunt head of his cock lining up with my entrance.

He teases me, pushing in no more than an inch and pulling back out only to do it over and over again. "I can't promise to be gentle, Reese. You good with that?"

I don't care how he does it, I just need to feel him inside me, anyway he wants me. "Yes. Fuck me."

Without having to be told twice, he grips my hips and surges forward, filling me to the hilt in one deep thrust and a cry catches in my throat.

I'm so full, I feel like I'm being stretched from the inside out. There's a twinge of pain as I adjust to his size, but it soon fades.

"Hang on tight, baby." Rafe pulls out and drives back in harder this time.

I fist the bed sheets in my hands as he fucks me hard and fast, one hand gripping my shoulder to hold me in place while the other grips my hip, his fingernails biting into the soft flesh.

"Oh... God... *Rafe...*" He literally fucks the words from my mouth, and I don't think I could string together a complete sentence if I tried, the pleasure radiating through my body is the only thing I can think, *feel.*

Every nerve ending hums with rapture, every part of my body alive as he uses me shamelessly, rutting into me hard enough there's no doubt I'll still feel him there tomorrow.

"So fucking good," he groans, cupping my chin and bringing me up so my back is pressed against his chest with his cock still buried deep inside me.

He tilts my neck up and slams his mouth down on mine, his tongue plunging past my lips in a deep, determined kiss while he continues to work in and out of my pussy.

"So good," he mumbles against my lips, his breath hot as it mixes with mine.

The crude sounds of our skin slapping together bounces off the wall, it's dirty and it only serves to turn me on more.

He presses me down so my chest is flush to the mattress leaving my ass high in the air as he eases out slowly, then surges back inside, hitting from a different angle that sends him even deeper inside me. *Impossibly* deep.

I cry out, the sound muffled against the mattress as he fucks me slow and deep this time, the steady rhythm as he grazes that spot inside that drives me closer to my release.

I need to come.

Rafe reaches around to play with my clit, the sensation of his cock inside me together with the slow circles he draws over the swollen bud has me coming within seconds.

My pussy clenches around him as my climax rockets through me, wave after wave crashing over me while fireworks dance behind my eyelids. It seems to go on forever and it's not long before Rafe thickens inside me.

"Fuck, I'm gonna come," Rafe says, his hands gripping me tighter as his climax hits him. He lets out a deep groan as he comes, spilling inside the condom as his thrusts turn slow and shallow.

I collapse onto the bed, my muscles lax and my body spent. Rafe follows me down, his forehead coming to rest between my shoulder blades as he pants for breath.

"Why the fuck did I fight that for so long?" he asks.

I laugh. "Uhh… Because you're an idiot?"

He gives me a sharp slap on the ass and I laugh harder.

He pulls out of me and disappears into the en-suite bathroom as I roll onto my back, climbing under the covers. He returns a moment later with his sweatpants back in place, then slides into bed beside me.

He rolls onto his side facing me. "I can't promise you anything, Reese. I told you before, I don't do relationships."

"I'm not asking for you to promise me anything. Only this."

"You're sure?"

"Yes."

"Okay. I don't want to hurt you, which is why I'm setting some ground rules so we both know where we stand. If we do this, there can be no strings between us, no commitments and no feelings."

I hate the way my heart sinks. "Okay…"

"In public we act normal," he continues, "like friends, as we have been doing for weeks. But here, in the apartment, in this bedroom, you're *mine*."

"So we're basically Justin Timberlake and Mila Kunis?"

His blank expression tells me he has no idea what I'm talking about.

"*Friends with Benefits*," I elaborate. "It's a movie about two friends who give up on dating assholes and decide to just fuck each other instead."

One corner of his mouth curves into a smile. "I suppose we are. Is that enough for you?"

Is it?

I know this will probably turn out to be yet another mistake to add to my ever-growing list, but what if it doesn't? I know not to get my hopes up, because he's as good as said I can't have him in *that* way, a relationship with him is off the table, but with how good it felt to have him inside me and how much I want to feel it again, I don't think I could say no even if I wanted to. And if this is all he can give me, then I'll be damn sure I'm going to take it. I just have to find a way to separate sex with this feeling I can already feel brewing deep inside me somewhere. This feeling that will no doubt result in me getting heartbroken if left unchecked.

I force it down.

I shuffle across the bed and plant a delicate kiss to his lips. "Yes."

What's the worst that can happen?

20

He stayed.

That's my first thought as I take in his sleeping form beside me, his arm thrown over his face, shielding his eyes as he lies on his back. He stayed beside me, he didn't leave. Not that he could go very far considering it's his apartment, but to see him beside me warms my heart.

My eyes slide over him, his hair is dishevelled, pointing in all directions. The light dusting of stubble on his jaw has me wondering what it would feel like grazing on the insides of my thighs. The sheet exposes the top half of his body, his abs looking like he was carved out of stone like one of those statues from Ancient Greece.

He's a literal work of art.

My eyes catch on the clear tenting of the sheet where his morning wood strains against the sweatpants he's wearing. I asked him last night if he'd be more comfortable with them off, but he insisted he preferred to keep them on.

He doesn't like sleeping naked... *Noted.*

"Like what you see?" he mumbles sleepily and my eyes shoot up to his. He watches me with a knowing smirk out the corner of his eye.

"Just admiring the view."

His grin widens. "It's great, huh?"

I shrug. "Mmm, I've seen better."

"Oh really?" He rolls over until he's hovering above me, his knees bracketing my thighs and my wrists pinned either side of my head. "You're a bad girl, Reese."

"What're you gonna do about it?" I challenge.

He shifts up onto his knees, pulling down the sheet that covers me, exposing my breasts.

"I'm going to tease you like you've been teasing me since I had you move in here."

"Yeah, that decision will probably come back to bite you in the ass," I laugh.

He dips down and I wait for his lips to land on mine, but they don't. Instead, they close around my left nipple as he sucks in into his mouth and I gasp.

His tongue flicks over the hardened tip and pleasure zaps through my body straight between my legs while he kneads the other, rolling the nipple between his fingers.

"Touch me," I moan.

While he switches to my right nipple and with his arm braced on the pillow above my head to hold him up, his other hand begins a slow decent down my body. His fingertips dance across my skin, over my belly and down between my legs.

His fingers glide through my folds with expert ease, grazing my clit and my toes curl as he works two thick fingers inside me, pumping them in and out of my tight channel that's already dripping for him. I don't think I've ever gotten so wet for a guy so easily and quickly as I do him. All this man has to do is look at me and I'm on the verge of an orgasm.

I need to touch him.

I work my hand into the waistband of his sweats and wrap around his hard length. He's long and thick in my hand as I work him from root to tip, eliciting a deep moan from him.

"Fuck, Reese. Don't stop," he pants before switching to the opposite breast, licking and sucking my hardened nipple while his fingers continue their sweet torture on my pussy.

My pussy clenches, knowing I'm bringing him as much pleasure as he's giving me. I squeeze the base of his cock, making him hiss before I stroke him harder and faster.

The sensations pulsing through me have me climbing to the edge so quickly, every nerve ending in my body is alive and it's a feeling I could get used to.

"I'm so close, Rafe."

"Me too." He kisses a trail up my chest, burying his face in the crook of my neck, his fingers still pumping inside me while he thrusts into my hand.

"I want you to come with me. *On* me," I say.

"Fuck… *Fuck*. Come, now," he commands.

I let go.

My toes curl and my body locks up as my orgasm hits at the same time his does. His cum splashes on my belly, a deep groan rumbling up his throat, as he spills onto me while my body trembles beneath him.

He pulls out his fingers from my pussy and takes them into his mouth, his eyes never leaving mine as he sucks them clean.

He sits back on his heels above me, readjusting his sweatpants as he looks down at the mess he made on my body.

He smirks. "I'm a sick bastard for liking the sight of my cum on you."

"Then I'm a sick bastard for *liking* your cum on me," I reply. I'm not lying, it does something to me, it turns me on. It's primal and dirty, like he's marking me as his, but deep down I know that will never be true.

He takes a finger and swipes it through the mess on my belly before bringing it to my lips. "Suck." His eyes darken as I close my mouth around his finger. "Good girl," he praises.

His words have my pussy clenching, the salty taste of him hitting my tongue as I suck it clean.

"The things I have planned for us, Reese. The things I'm going to do to you... They will ruin you for any other man besides me. This whole arrangement will most definitely come back to bite me in the ass, but I'm gonna enjoy it while it lasts, and I'm gonna make damn sure you enjoy it too." He leans down and pecks a kiss to my lips before shifting off the bed.

The thought of this ending before it's even gotten started has my stomach sinking. I'm not stupid enough to believe it will last forever, because he said so himself that he can't promise me that, but there's always that spark of hope that this could come to mean more to him than just sex.

"I'm gonna go take a shower," I say, sliding off the bed, heading to the bathroom.

His eyes scan my naked body with an unreadable expression.

"What?" I ask.

His eyes meet mine. "Nothing. I uh... I should probably wake up sleeping beauty," he says before disappearing out the door.

The sound of laughter fills the space as I move towards the kitchen. I find Ivy sat at the kitchen island, giggling away as Rafe attempts to make breakfast.

"What did we say about letting you loose in the kitchen by yourself?" I ask.

"I can't possibly burn down the kitchen making toast," he replies, tossing a glance over his shoulder.

"Rafe, no offense, but you could burn water."

"You can't burn water!" Ivy objects with a frown.

"Your Daddy can."

"I'm a magician, Ives." Rafe wink, making her giggle harder.

My hands reach out for him of their own volition, gliding over his midriff as I slide in beside him. "Let me help."

He opens his mouth to speak, but he's cut off when his phone rings in his pocket.

"It's Ivy's social worker for her weekly check-in. I won't be a sec." His hand brushes over my back softly as he leaves the kitchen to answer it.

"Are you Daddy's girlfriend?" Ivy asks curiously, bringing a beaker of orange juice to her lips.

The hope in her eyes makes my heart squeeze. "No, sweetie. I'm not. We're just really good friends, that's all."

"But if you were, that would make you my new mommy, right?"

I round the island and perch on the seat beside her. "I suppose it would, yes. But you know that no one will ever replace your mommy, right?"

"I know, and I miss her lots. I sometimes dream about her. But if I was gonna have a new one, I want it to be you."

Her words have a lump lodging in my throat and tears springing into my eyes.

"Come here." I open my arms and she climbs onto my lap. I press a kiss to her head as I squeeze her tight.

"Love you, Reesie."

Reesie...

Only one other person has ever called me that and she's the one remaining family member I have left. My grandmother. Hearing her use that nickname has my heart soaring.

"I love you too, Ivy." I'm falling in love with her as if she were my own.

Rafe returns to the kitchen a few minutes later, his eyes flicking between us with a look I can't read. I wonder if he overheard what Ivy said?

"Everything okay?" I ask.

He clears his throat. "Amanda's coming over from Austin for a meeting in few weeks to check in."

"Mandy's coming? Yay! I like her," Ivy says excitedly.

"Hey, why don't you go get dressed and Daddy and I will make breakfast?" I suggest.

"Okay!" She jumps off my lap and skips down the hall to her room.

"Ivy starts school soon, right?" I ask.

"A week on Monday."

"We should probably go shopping for some new clothes and supplies for her."

"Good idea," he agrees. "Now, there's something that's been bugging me..."

"Like what?"

"Like how I'm going to punish you for that little dig about me burning water."

He raises an eyebrow and I can't hold back my smile.

"Do your worst, Hudson," I challenge.

He eats up the space between us, trapping me between the counter and his solid body. "Oh, I guarantee you, I will, and you'll be screaming my name before it's over."

21

Rafe

I hate shopping.

I fucking hate it. Traipsing from store to store mindlessly for hours on end is *not* my idea of fun when I could be doing something much better with my time. I can't actually remember the last time I physically walked into a store for something other than alcohol. But today, much to my surprise, I don't mind it, dare I say I'm actually enjoying myself? Reese and I have brought Ivy to the mall, it's her first day at her new school tomorrow so we're shopping for supplies; clothes, shoes, stationary, anything she wants or needs.

I trail behind them most of the time, hanging back while they gush over pretty dresses and sparkly shoes and butterfly hair clips... Girly shit that I will never understand. I suppose that's why Ivy's taken to Reese so well since she came to live with us, she shares things with her, has things in common that she and I will never have.

I hate this feeling inside, the fact that a pang of jealousy stabs me in the gut when Ivy takes Reese's hand, how she clings to her, gravitates to her instead of me. I know that day we shared when she painted my face in makeup was a huge step forward in our relationship, I just can't help but still feel a degree of distance between us.

I hate it.

Why am I jealous? I should be glad that Reese makes my daughter happy, but I want to be that person too. I want to be the one to make her smile and make her laugh. I want to be the one she needs. If anything, I'm jealous of how easy Reese makes it all look, and how easily Reese has slotted into our lives.

Like she belongs here with us.

I didn't miss their little chat when I took that call from Amanda last week. I heard everything. How Ivy loves Reese, and if she were to ever have a new mommy, she'd want it to be her.

Is what Reese and I are doing the right thing? Am I putting my daughter at risk by giving into my attraction for Reese?

The longer she's around, the more attached my daughter will become to her and the harder her heartbreak will be when Reese eventually leaves when our arrangement is over. I hate to admit it, but the thought of this being over and Reese returning home makes me feel sick to my stomach. I think I'm becoming as attached to Reese Reynolds as my daughter is, and that thought alone terrifies me.

I follow a few steps behind them through the mall and as they veer into what's about the seventh clothing store today, I spot a face through the crowd that catches my eye, a face looking directly at me. He sticks out like a sore thumb among the throng of families and groups of friends that fill the space. I can't seem to place his face, never having seen him before in my life, but there is no doubt that he knows me.

When he notices me staring, he turns and heads in the opposite direction, disappearing like a ghost in the crowd as if he were never even there. If I was alone, I'd follow him, but I'm not about to abandon Reese and Ivy when they could be in danger. After all the shit that went down with my brother and his wife last year, I'm not taking any chances.

I pull out my phone and dial my brother's number. He answers on the third ring.

"What's up, brother?"

"I'm at the mall with Reese and Ivy. It could be nothing, but I'm sure a guy was watching us."

"A guy? Who?"

"No clue, never seem him before but he definitely knew me."

"He still there?"

"No, he clocked me watching him and he left. Like I said, could be nothing."

"But it could be something. Keep an eye out. Anything out of the ordinary and you get yourself and your girls the hell out of there. You hear me?"

My heart expands at the words *'your girls'*. "Of course."

Hanging up, I scour my surroundings for any sign of him still lurking, but he's gone. *For now.* He could come back, and I need to be ready if that happens.

I just need to figure out who he is and what he wants with my family.

∞∞∞

21

Hours after we arrive back home, I still can't get that guy out of my head.

What does he want? Who is he?

It's something to do with Bryce Tanner, it has to be. It's too much of a coincidence, but it's been months since all that shit went down, and there's not been a single trace of any retribution or fall-out since it happened.

Tanner made it his mission to get his hands on Della, and after repeated attempts, he finally succeeded by kidnapping her, leaving one of our guys dead.

Do I regret killing him? No. I'd do it a thousand times over to ensure my family is safe, but what if I've put them in danger worse than before?

Back then, I only had my siblings, Della and my father to think about. I didn't know I had a daughter then, and the thought of putting her in danger terrifies me.

"*Hello?* Earth to Rafe."

My eyes flick up to where Reese is sat on the sofa beside me, watching some girly show on Netflix. "Sorry, what?"

"I asked if you were okay. You've been really quiet since we got back from the mall."

I can't tell her about the man watching us, it could turn out to be nothing and I don't want to worry her unnecessarily.

"Oh, yeah. Fine. Just work stuff has got me distracted, is all," I lie through a forced smile.

She shoots me a coy smile, flicking off the TV and shifting across the sofa to straddle my lap. "Anything I can do to take your mind off of it?"

My hands squeeze her hips, tugging her closer so her pussy grazes my dick and I groan. "I have a few ideas, but none of them are appropriate for a Sunday afternoon on the couch with a five year-old just down the hall."

"Maybe, but I'm sure there's something we can do..." She leans down to kiss my neck while her hands wander over my chest.

Jesus, she feels good.

My hands cup her ass, rocking her back and forth over my cock that's hard as a steel rod in my jeans.

"What're you doing?" a little voice asks.

Reese yelps and she's up and off my lap in a flash, straightening her clothes as her eyes land on my daughter.

Ivy wears a confused frown as she stands at the entrance to the living room, her eyes darting between the two of us.

"We, uh... We're just... Playing a game! It's a really *really* fun game," Reese stutters, her cheeks flaming red as she looks to me for support.

"A game? Can I play?" Ivy asks excitedly.

I hide my laugh behind my hand, enjoying watching Reese try to squirm out of this situation a little too much.

"It's a grown up game, sweetie. How about we play hide and seek instead?"

"Sure!"

Reese's face is one of mortification as she begins counting, covering her eyes. "I'll seek first. One. Two. Three..."

"You'll never find me!" Ivy tears down the hall.

Reese keeps counting. She looks over at me. "I guess you were right about the couch."

I break into a laugh, as does she, that beautiful sound of her laughter ringing in my ears and it dawns on me...

I need this woman, I need Reese Reynolds more than I thought I'd ever need anyone in my life, and I'm gonna keep her in it for as long as I can.

22

Reese

"What if no one wants to be my friend?" Ivy asks from the backseat as Rafe drives us to her new school.

I spin around in my seat. "How could anybody *not* want to be your friend? Any kid at that school would be lucky to have a friend like you, sweetie."

"But I won't know anybody."

"That's the most exciting part! You get to meet lots of new people, experience new things. You're gonna have the best day ever!"

She fiddles with her fingers in her lap as she chews on her bottom lip. It's not surprising she's nervous, I'm nervous for her, but the first day is always the scariest.

"We're here," Rafe announces, pulling up to the curb beside the school gates before switching off the engine.

We help Ivy out of her car seat and strap her new pink backpack onto her back. It's almost half the size of her tiny body, and I'm surprised she doesn't tip over completely with all the stuff we bought from the mall, not to mention the huge lunch I made for her this morning. The amount of food I packed for her is overkill, but I hate the thought of her going hungry like I did most days.

She looks over at the yard where a swarm of children chase and laugh, running rings around the other parents who chatter between themselves.

Ivy cranes her neck to look up at us and her chin wobbles. "I'm scared."

"Hey," Rafe crouches down in front of her, straightening her coat. "The first day is always the worst. I know it's scary, but once you're in there, and you've made lots of new friends, you'll see that all this worrying was for nothing."

"You sure, Daddy?" My heart expands at hearing her call him that. Not just for her, but for Rafe too. I know it means everything to him to have her trust him, *love* him.

"I'm positive, and you know what, at three-thirty, Reese and I will be right back here waiting for you."

She chews on her lip. "Okay."

Rafe opens his arms and Ivy steps into him, wrapping her arms around his neck. "Go knock 'em dead, Ives."

He releases her and she turns to me. I drop down and press a kiss to her cheek. "Have *so* much fun today, sweetheart. I want to hear all about it later, okay?"

"Okay." She smiles before turning on her heel and disappearing into a group of other kids.

My heart pulls watching her walk away, she looks so tiny. I feel like a proud mother waving off her child and a cry lodges in my throat. According to my grandmother, one of the few times my mom actually gave a crap and did something even remotely motherly, was my first day of kindergarten. Apparently she cried when I entered the school yard, standing by myself against the wall while every other kid laughed and played with their friends. She cried all the way home with the image of me alone at the forefront of her mind.

A part of me thinks the story is complete bullshit, because not once did I ever see my mom cry for any other reason other than when she was in one of her drunken hazes.

But the tears that spring into my eyes as the school bell rings and Ivy disappears inside the building are real, and it takes me a moment for my brain to kick back into reality.

She's not my daughter, and she never will be.

But I can love her like one, right?

Just as she reaches the gate entrance, she turns to look back over her shoulder. When she spots us, her face lights up. "Love you, Reesie! Love you, Daddy!" she calls, blowing a kiss before she enters the school gates onto the yard.

I see Rafe suck in a breath and I take a step closer, placing my hand in his, giving it a squeeze. He squeezes back.

Standing here, I could almost imagine a life like this, a ridiculously happy and domesticated one with Rafe and Ivy. Whether it's real or not, I like how we fit, but I know it's not. It can't be.

I'm gonna enjoy living in this little fantasy, this little family bubble we've created until it's over. It's gonna hurt like hell, but it'll have been worth it the heartbreak.

"Can you drop me off in town on your way back, I've got an errand to run?" I ask on the drive back to his apartment.

"What's with all these errands?" he quizzes, sneaking a curious look over at me before turning his attention back on the road. "You got another fuck buddy I don't know about?"

"It's nothing, just have some things to take care of, that's all."

"If it's nothing, then tell me. Is everything okay? Should I be worried?"

"Yes to the former, no to the latter and in the nicest way possible, it's none of your business."

"Okay. *Ouch*."

I glance over to him to see a frown marring his brow as he concentrates on driving.

I'm not trying to be rude, but him knowing things about my personal life makes this whole *friends who fuck* arrangement too complicated, too personal, the one thing that has no place in this arrangement between us.

I reel off the address and he gives me a look like he's trying to work out what I could possibly be doing there.

Ten minutes later, we pull up outside *Cedar Tree* and I jump out. "Thanks for the ride. I'll see you at home?"

Home... Fuck, I'm already sinking too deep.

I shut the door and head towards the building, expecting to hear his ridiculously noisy car drive away but it doesn't, instead the engine goes quiet and the sound of a door opening and shutting has me halting.

"What're you doing?" I ask as he jogs towards me.

"There's only three reasons I can think of to explain you visiting a retirement home. One: You work here, or volunteer at the least, but for a few hours a week, I don't think it's that. Two: You're visiting someone, someone you love who for some unknown reason you don't want me to know about. Or three: You're a dirty girl who's got herself a geriatric sugar daddy, or *granddaddy*, if we're being technical."

I fight back a smile that wants to come through. "Would

you be jealous if I said yes?"

"Of a geriatric sugar daddy? Hell no." He steps into me, leaning in with his lips level at my ear. "Because either way, I can do so much better than that. Just please tell me it's not option three."

I roll my eyes as I turn and continue towards the building, knowing there's only one way this can go. "I guess you better come in and find out then."

He follows me inside, and I spot Gloria immediately, sat behind the desk in the reception area, typing on the computer.

She smiles when she sees me. "Reese!"

"Hey, Gloria, how is she today?"

"So so." Her eyes catch on Rafe who hovers over my shoulder. "And who do we have here?"

"Rafe Hudson." He holds out his hand to shake hers. "I'm a… a *friend*."

"A pleasure," she replies before turning to me. "You can head on up, hon."

Rafe follows me up the two flights of stairs before I come to a stop outside her room and turn to him. "You know how I said my grandmother was the only family who gave a shit about me?"

He nods.

I turn the handle and step inside, finding my grandma sat on her usual chair staring vacantly out the window.

"Nanna?" I ask, coming into view. Her face is thinner than the last time I saw her, her skin has lost some of the little colour it had. She smiles when she sees me and my heart warms, though it's short-lived.

"Abigail! Oh, what a wonderful surprise." She struggles out of her chair and shuffles towards me, pulling me in for a hug.

"My darling daughter come to visit her old mother."

She's mistaken me for a stranger, an intruder a few times, someone she doesn't recognise, but not once has she ever mistaken me for my good-for-nothing mother who's never once visited. I hate the fact that I'm the spit of her, that we share the same auburn hair and green eyes. I hate that she's my mom and I'd rather Nanna believe I was a stranger than Abigail fucking Reynolds.

I smile as wide as I can and play along, fighting off the torrent of tears that threatens to flow. Telling her I'm not who she thinks will only upset her and confuse her even more, and I can't do that.

"How are you, *Mom*?" Just that one word is like a punch to the gut.

"Better for seeing you, Abby." Her eyes find Rafe who stands stock still like he's made out of wood against the door. "Which boyfriend is this one?"

"This is Rafe."

"It's lovely to meet you, Ma'am," Rafe says, perching on the edge of her bed.

"Call me Mavis. So nice to be young and in love... How did you meet?"

I stiffen at the word *love*, but Rafe doesn't seem to mind. He rattles off a story about how we met at his brother's wedding, the only part of the story that is even remotely close to the truth. The rest is closer to a fairy tale, a story you'd find in a romance novel, but my grandma hangs off of every word.

"I'm thirsty," Nanna says.

"Here, let me get it for you." Rafe reaches for the glass of orange juice beside the bed and hands it to her, and she accepts it with shaky hands.

"I'm sorry, I didn't catch your name," my grandmother says with a kind smile.

"It's Rafe," he reminds her.

"Are you Abby's friend?"

He smiles softly. "Uh... Yes, I am."

"Abby, you should really b—bring, uh..." I can see her searching her mind, her brows knitting together in thought as she stumbles over her words. "Bring R—Renee around sometime. I'd love to see her. Such a sweet girl."

Tears swim in my eyes but I fight desperately to keep it together. She doesn't even remember my name. "It's Reese," I correct.

She frowns. "Is it?"

I can see the confusion in her eyes as she looks at me. No, not *at* me, but *through* me as her gaze turns vacant the way it does these days. Her body awake but her brain on standby.

My fingernails dig into the palms of my hands so hard I'm sure I'll draw blood as I will myself not to cry. "I uh... I have to go now. I'll come back soon." My chin wobbles as I speak, and after placing a kiss to her cheek, I tell her I love her, not that she'll hear me, and dart out of her room as fast as I can, a sob crawling up my throat.

I collapse to my knees at the end of the corridor and double over, clutching my stomach as hot tears leak from my eyes.

I hate this.

Every visit is worse than the one before and hurts more than the last. I can't stop the tears. I'm crying so much I'm hysterical, it's like I'm having a panic attack or something. I can't seem to catch my breath.

"Reese? *Reese!*" Rafe's voice is panicked as he hurries over to me, his footsteps echoing down the narrow corridor before dropping to his knees beside me. "Are you alright?"

I shake my head, clutching at my chest. "I… can't breathe."

"Hey, look at me." He takes my face in his hands and forces me to face him. "Breathe with me. Deep breath in," he says, inhaling deep and I do my best to copy him. "Good girl. Now, breathe out slowly…" I do. "Now in…"

We do this three times until my breathing steadies out and I collapse against him, seeking the comfort of his arms, my tears staining his shirt.

"She has dementia." I sniff. "I had her admitted here when it got too dangerous for her living at home, that's why I have Merlin. She could barely take care of herself most of the time." I wipe my eyes on the back of my hand. "Every time I come here, my heart breaks a little more and I… I don't know how much more I can take. Most of the time, it's fine, but then there's times when she doesn't even recognise me at all."

He holds me tighter and I lean into his body, his warmth seeping through our clothes and deep into my skin.

"This is what you meant isn't it? That night at the bar months ago when we… You said that losing the ones you love isn't just about losing them, it's about losing a part of yourself too."

"You remember that?" I pull back, finding his eyes through my blurry vision.

He nods. "Why didn't you want me to know about her?"

"Because it makes whatever this thing is or isn't between us too personal, which is what we're trying to avoid, right? No strings. No feelings."

"Doesn't mean I don't care. We're friends, right? If you can even call us that. Not to mention my daughter loves you, and you her, I'd call that pretty fucking personal." He has a point.

"You wanna know why I got kicked out of my apartment?" I start. "Because some of the money I should have been using to pay the rent went towards keeping my grandma in this place. Years ago, I sold her house and ever since, the money from the sale has been paying for her to stay here, but it was never going to last forever and I… I couldn't stand the thought of moving her from here. She's comfortable and cared for. Moving her somewhere cheaper would've only confused her more. I'd have gone homeless before I let that happen."

"I'm so sorry, Ree. To be going through all of this on your own, at such a young age is… Do you have any idea how amazing you are?"

"Amazing? You have mascara stains on your shirt and I probably look a complete mess. I'm sorry for crying on you."

"There's nothing to apologise for. Nothing at all." He sweeps a strand of hair from my face, staring down at me in awe like he's seeing the sunrise for the first time or like he just found the holy grail, and it's the most dangerous look of all. It's a look that has me feeling things I shouldn't be feeling, and yet I don't stop myself when I lean up and my lips meet his.

His hand cups the back of my head as he deepens the kiss and unlike the other times we've kissed, this is slower, softer, *deeper*.

His tongue slips past my lips, licking into my mouth as mine meets his, the groan that leaves him sending a bolt of pleasure between my legs.

"We should stop," Rafe says against my lips, easing back.

"Why?"

"Because it's highly inappropriate to be sporting an erection in an old people's home."

I choke out a laugh. "I think I can help with that."

He grins. "Oh yeah?"

I nod. "Take me home."

∞∞∞

Three-thirty on the dot, Ivy comes hurtling through the school gates and down the sidewalk towards where Rafe and I are standing.

"Daddy! Reesie!" she calls, just as she crashes head-on into Rafe who's waiting on his knees with open arms, ready to gather her up.

"Hey, sweetheart." He rises to his feet with Ivy's tiny body wrapped around him. "How was your first day?"

"It was so cool! I got a new friend called Rachel, and she has a cat just like we do! There's Katie who has the same backpack *and* pencil case as me. I can't wait to go back tomorrow!"

"See, didn't I tell you you'd love it?" I ask, pressing a kiss to her cheek.

"I can't wait to go to sleep tonight, 'cause then I can be back here!"

"We better get you home then." Rafe carries her to the car and buckles her in before we begin the journey home.

It's not long after we've eaten dinner that Ivy falls asleep in front of the TV with her head resting on Rafe's lap and her legs draped over mine.

My eyes meet Rafe's as Ivy snores softly in our laps, and it's a look of complete contentment and peace. It might not seem significant, but sitting just like this means everything.

He reaches for my hand and squeezes, and my heart warms under his touch. He leans in and places a gentle kiss to my forehead as I rest my head on his shoulder.

22

I don't know how long we stay like this, but I can feel myself already getting used to it.

It's beginning to feel like home.

23

Rafe

"You're looking uncharacteristically cheery lately. Care to share?" Gage eyes me curiously as I stride into his office at *De La Rosa*. Alec is sat in one of the chairs opposite as I take the one beside him.

It's true, I haven't had anything to smile about of late, but I guess regular mind-blowing sex with a woman who sets my body on fire whenever I'm close to her will do that to a guy.

We've been like a couple of sex-starved teenagers, fucking like rabbits unable to keep our hands to ourselves, so much so, we're both running on three hours of sleep per night and sporting a million different bruises, marks and aches that leave nothing to the imagination.

"No reason," I lie. "So what's the emergency? Your text this morning sounded important."

I woke up to a message lighting up my phone telling me to get to the club as soon as I could. I left Reese fast asleep with a note on my pillow telling her I'd get Ivy to school myself and that I'd be back soon.

"We had a break-in last night," Gage replies.

"The fuck? Do we know who it was?"

Gage spins his laptop around and hits play. I lean forward in my chair as I watch a hooded figure on the CCTV footage searching around the offices, all of them, including mine.

"As far as we know, nothing was taken," Alec offers.

"But he could have planted something," I say.

"I got Derek to do a sweep this morning, he didn't find any bugs or hidden cameras," Gage says.

"So he was looking for something." *But what?* My eyes fall back to the footage on screen as his face is lit up by the light coming in from the street. "Wait, go back."

Gage rewinds a few seconds until I say stop, freezing the frame that allows me to see a portion of his face, one that looks familiar. "That's the guy who was at the mall."

"You're sure?"

"Yeah, I'm positive." I can spot an ugly bastard when I see one.

Gage huffs. "Shit, so this isn't random. He's watching you, breaking into this place... He's targeting us."

"It has to be about Bryce, it's too much of a coincidence not to be."

Gage makes a face, the kind of face I only ever see him make when he's unsure of something, or *hiding* something.

"What?" I ask.

"I uh... I probably should have said something sooner..." He pulls out his phone and taps a few times before turning it to face Alec and I. It's a text message sent months ago. On the day our dad died.

Unknown number: I know what you did to Bryce. You and your family will pay for what you've done.

"Why the fuck did you keep this to yourself?" I ask, rising from my seat, the chair legs scraping across the floor.

"I didn't want to make something out of what could turn out to be nothing."

"A threatening text message stating that some fucker knows I killed Bryce might be *nothing*? Are you fucking kidding me?" I rage.

"I know I fucked up, Rafe. Okay? But I'm telling you now because it might be connected. The main thing is that we find out who it is."

"What's his fucking game?" Alec asks.

"No idea, but we should be vigilant. Watch over the girls, be on the look out for anything remotely suspicious. I'm not taking any chances. Alec, I don't know what the fuck is going on between you and my sister, but I know you'll do anything to protect her. Rafe, watch over Reese and Ivy, don't let them out of your sight, not even for a second."

I'd sooner die than put either of them in danger. "No more secrets, brother. We've had this conversation a thousand times, do you want a reminder?"

His face pales. He doesn't need a reminder, he knows exactly that the fuck I'm talking about. My dad was dying of cancer, but suffered a stroke a few months before he died which showed the cancer had spread through his body, shortening his life expectancy substantially. He kept that knowledge from me and my sister to protect us, he said. It was my dad's wish, he said. Regardless, it doesn't make his betrayal any easier.

"No more secrets," he agrees, regret filling his eyes.

I give him and Alec a curt nod goodbye before stalking out

of the office.

Fuck, I could really use a drink right now, but I promised Reese I wouldn't, so instead I climb into my car and peel off onto the road.

As much as I'd love to indulge in a couple of double vodkas, I've got something waiting for me at home that will be just as much fun to indulge in.

∞∞∞

The shower is running when I get back. I slip off my jacket and toss it onto the chair before slipping into the bathroom.

Reese hums along to a tune in her head while she lathers shampoo in her hair, her rich, copper waves cascading down to the middle of her back.

Through the glass of the shower that's partially steamed up, I can make out the outline of her body, the curve of her hips that have my fingers itching and my hardened dick leaking to touch her. Her full tits have my mouth watering for a taste.

Her eyes find mine as she washes out the shampoo from her hair.

"You look good enough to eat," I comment.

She smiles mischievously. "So come on in and have a taste." She runs her fingers down her body until they disappear between her legs.

I groan, my dick painfully hard in my pants as I watch her touch herself. She falls back against the tiles as her fingers work her clit, her eyes boring into mine like a dare. Daring me to come in and finish what she's started.

I hang onto my restraint for another minute before it snaps, the need to touch her too strong.

I stalk towards the shower and I tear open the glass door that separates us. I turn off the water and wrap an arm around her waist, hoisting her over my shoulder and carrying her out of the bathroom.

Her body is soaking wet and my shirt is saturated in seconds, but I don't care. I deposit her onto the bed with a bounce and crawl on top of her, slamming my mouth on hers.

She gasps against my lips, her tongue seeking mine as our kiss deepens. She reaches up to wind her fingers through my hair but I pin her wrists to the mattress either side of her head.

"What are you doing?" she asks.

"No point in taking a shower when I plan to dirty you up all over again. Do you trust me?" I ask, searching for any signs that what I have planned might not be what she wants.

"Always," she replies breathlessly.

I press one more kiss to her lips before climbing off her and crossing the room to my closet where I rummage for what I'm looking for.

I pull out three neckties before returning to the bed. I sit back on my heels, towering over her as she watches with an eager gaze.

I grip her knees and pull them up and they fall open with ease. I then take her left wrist and bring it down until it lies beside her left ankle and bind them together. I do the same on the other side and lean back to admire her.

She's spread wide open for me, her pink, bare pussy on full display for my eyes only, and I don't miss the slight tremble in her legs and the moisture pooling between them as she gazes up at me with a mix of excitement and nerves in her eyes.

"If you want me to stop at any point, you tell me, okay? I promise, I'll stop."

"Okay." She nods.

I lean over, settling myself between her spread thighs and seal my lips over hers before bracing myself above her to secure the tie over her eyes, stealing away her vision.

"Have you ever been blindfolded before?" I ask her.

She shakes her head. I can see how fast her heart is beating by the pulse point in her neck. It's going crazy and I lean down to lick it, and she gasps as my tongue glides over her skin.

Stepping off the bed, I tug off my shirt and unbuckle my belt, letting my pants and boxers fall to the floor, tossing a condom onto the mattress by her foot.

I stand totally naked as my hand wraps around my cock, giving it a long, hard tug before climbing back over her.

Her legs widen to allow me room.

"All five of our senses work in harmony with each other, sight being the most dominant." I swipe my thumb over her bottom lip, gently pushing inside and she instantly begins to suck on it. Christ, I wish it was my cock. "Take one of them away, and your other senses are heightened, more alert, more *sensitive*."

Her mouth releases my thumb with a pop as my fingers find the stiff peak of her left nipple and give it a pinch. Her body jerks as a gasp escapes her lips.

"Without your sight, you have no idea what I'm going to do to you next..." I trail my fingers down the valley of her breasts, around her belly button and down to her pussy, letting the tip of my finger graze over her clit. "Does that excite you, Reese?" She nods and I grin. "I thought so. Your pussy is leaking like a fountain, baby."

Without warning, I slap her pussy, and she cries out, tugging on the fabric that binds her wrists to her ankles. Her juices coat my hand and I can't help myself from licking it off, her sweet, tangy taste exploding on my tongue.

I slap her again, this time a scream catches in her throat. "I can't wait to eat this pussy. I want you screaming loud enough for all of Halston to hear. I want them all to know you're mine."

"*Please*," she begs, unable to keep still as she squirms on the bed.

I lean over her and take a nipple into my mouth, tugging it gently between my teeth before soothing the sting with my tongue. "I think I'm gonna play with you first."

I feast on her tits, switching between left and right until I have her panting and writhing beneath me. Her tits are wet and red when I finally pull back before kissing a line down her stomach. Just when she thinks her pussy is my next stop, I bypass it and begin kissing a slow, agonising trail from her ankle, moving from one to the other all the way up until I reach the tops of her thighs where I sink my teeth into the soft flesh there.

She trembles beneath me, desperate for release as my mouth hovers over her pussy that's weeping onto the bed sheets beneath her. I don't think I've ever seen a woman as wet as Reese is for me right now.

It's hot as hell.

"Rafe!" she cries, struggling against her ties.

"What do you want me to do?" I ask in a voice that's barely a whisper as my lips drift over her skin.

"Lick me."

"Where? Here?" I lick a line up her leg.

"You know where, Rafe. *Please*." I never thought I'd enjoy

hearing a woman beg, but *fuck me,* coming from Reese? Best goddamn sound in the world.

"Say the words, baby. I wanna hear them."

"My pussy! I want you to lick my pussy!"

Her words are like a direct line to my cock and it hardens even more, something I didn't think possible. "That's my good girl."

I sink my face between her legs and lick a trail from her cunt to her clit and her hips buck off the mattress as I feast on her like a king at a royal banquet, savouring every drop of her, devouring her like my favourite meal.

I play with her clit, sucking it between my lips before nipping at it gently, a trick that has her screaming.

Her hips move up to ride my face as my tongue dips inside to fuck her.

She tastes like heaven.

"Rafe, you're gonna make me come. I'm so close," she moans, her thigh squeezing my head as she nears her release.

"Come on my face, baby. I wanna feel you gush on my tongue."

Seconds later she explodes, crying out my name that bounces off the walls, her grip on my head tight enough it feels like my skull will crack, but it'd be worth it.

Her body jerks and squirms as she rides out her high. I lick her through the aftershocks of her climax as they spasm through her body every few seconds until her breathing begins to even out and her legs fall apart limply.

I pull my face away, my lips and chin covered in her arousal as I tear open the condom and roll it down my length. Once it's on, I cover her body with mine and claim her mouth, curling my hand around her throat, giving a gentle squeeze, but not enough to choke her. "Don't you taste incredible?"

She mumbles something against my mouth as I squeeze a little harder, wedging myself between her legs as my cock lines up with her entrance.

"I'm going to drive you as crazy as you make me, baby."

I'm not sure when or why I started calling her baby, but it feels natural. It feels right.

I inch in slowly, a groan rumbles through my throat as I watch where we're joined, her cunt slowly swallowing my cock until I'm buried as deep as I can go.

I pull out as slow as I drove in before sliding back so slowly it's taking all of me to hold back from taking her hard and fast how I want to, but I do it again and again, teasing her until she's begging me to go faster.

"Rafe, please!" An indescribable sound catches in her throat, it's halfway between a moan and a cry and all of my restraint snaps.

I drive into her hard, thrusting my hips with a rhythm that has her tits bouncing with every jerk of my hips and her pussy clenching around me in seconds.

The sounds of my body slapping against hers, and the moans of pleasure that leave Reese's lips have my balls tightening.

Sweat beads on my back and my brow as I pump in and out of her, my pubic bone grazing her swollen clit with every thrust.

"You take my cock so good, Reese," I praise. "So fucking good..."

I flatten myself over her, bracing myself on my elbows beside her head as I bury my face in her neck while I continue to thrust inside her.

"So good, baby," I mumble against her skin. "You like

this don't you? Spread wide open just for me, tied up and completely at my mercy. You're my dirty girl aren't you, Reese?"

She makes me feral. This primal instinct to own her, dominate her and hear her scream my name is a feeling I've never experienced before, it's never consumed me as much as it does in this moment. It's a feeling I never want to end.

She cries out and I sit up to untie her wrists and ankles before flipping her onto her belly, dragging up her hips then plunging back in, this new angle allowing me to hit deeper.

"Rafe, make me come!" she cries and I reach around to play with her clit, and within a minute, her pussy is squeezing my cock like a vice.

"Come for me, Reese. Come all over my cock," I tell her and she does.

She goes off like a bomb, unable to contain her screams as her orgasm takes a hold. She trembles as I ride her through her release, following her over the edge moments later as her orgasm triggers mine.

It seems to go on forever and I wish to God I wasn't wearing a condom. I want to come deep inside her, mark her body and make her mine.

She slumps down onto the mattress, her body going limp beneath me as I collapse on top of her.

We lie there panting for a minute as I dot lazy kisses over her back before I move off her and dispose of the condom in the bathroom.

When I return, she's sat up on the bed, pulling at the blindfold knotted at the back of her head.

I turn my back as I tug my sweatpants on, then join her on the bed, pulling her to my chest as I prop myself up against the headboard.

"Are you okay?" I ask, pulling the sheet to cover our bodies.

She cranes her neck to look up at me and smiles. "More than okay. That was… incredible."

I take her hands in mine, rubbing her wrists where a faint red mark bands around them. I hate the thought that I've hurt her. "I wasn't too rough with you? I got a little carried away."

She shakes her head. "I liked it."

"I liked it too." In fact, I fucking *loved* it.

"I um… I've never done that before, the whole being tied up and blindfolded thing but I've never come so hard in my life."

My chest swells as I shoot her a grin. "Stick with me, baby. I'll give you orgasms that'll rock your world so hard you'll never wanna leave me."

I know I've fucked up the second the words leave my mouth because her face falls as she darts her eyes away.

Why the fuck did I say that?

24

Reese

The next morning, the sun that beams through the curtains is what rouses me from a long, restful sleep.

It takes a moment for my brain to kick into gear, but then it all comes flooding back. Everything that happened between us yesterday comes to me in flashes, letting me relive every single beautiful moment all over again.

I roll over onto my side where Rafe lies beside me, a sight I'm quickly getting used to waking up to. After everything he did to me yesterday, we stayed in bed, the both of us dozing before he rolled us over onto our sides and nestled up behind me, fucking me slowly, lazily while he whispered words of encouragement into my ear that had me coming in minutes.

I ended up taking another shower, one I offered to share with him but he declined. Instead, he used the guest bathroom down the hall and then was out the front door to pick up Ivy from school.

I glance over at him. The bed sheet covers his lower half where the top of his sweatpants peaks out. He's hard, I can tell that much. The memory of his tongue gliding over the most intimate parts of me fills my mind, and all I can think about is that I want to do the same for him.

I shuffle up the bed, carefully peeling back the sheet and untying the string of his waistband, I gently ease his sweats down and his cock springs free.

I wrap my hand around him, squeezing the base before sliding my hand over his hard length. He groans lazily, half-asleep, and I'm just about to lean in when my eyes catch on something.

I pull down his sweats a little further to reveal a group of pink, raised scars, each one roughly two or three inches in size on the inside of both of his thighs.

It's almost as if he's…

"What are you doing?" The low grumble of his voice makes me jump, and my eyes lift to his.

His horrified expression tells me he knows I've seen them and the fact that I can't seem to form a single word makes the anguish on his face even worse.

"Reese?" he presses, his eyes boring into mine.

"I—I just… After yesterday, the way you went down on me… I wanted to do the same for you." My heart hammers in my chest as I fall over my words.

His jaw clenches. "Well, I didn't ask you to," he snaps, swinging his legs off the bed, pulling his sweatpants back up and heading for the door.

"Rafe, wait." I push off the bed and take his arm. "What are those scars?"

"It doesn't matter. Forget it." He shrugs off my grip.

"Of course it matters or you wouldn't be so defensive," I argue as he continues towards the bedroom door. "I just want to understand."

He stops, his hand resting on the handle, his shoulders sagging.

"Hey." I move behind him, reaching up to turn his face towards me, forcing his eyes to meet mine. "Talk to me, please. Whatever it is, you can trust me."

His eyes search mine and after a moment, he allows me to guide him back towards the bed. He perches on the edge and leans forward, his elbows on his knees with his head in his hands.

I take a seat beside him and wait for him to speak.

"I never wanted you to see that part of me," he says.

"Those scars, did you…" I trail off.

He nods regretfully, rubbing the back of his neck. "It started when I was eleven. My mom had died and I… I didn't know how to handle it. I've never been great at expressing my feelings and it was the first time I'd ever experienced grief. My dad was inconsolable, Gage was too busy trying to hold us all together and Si was too young to fully understand what was happening. I bottled it all up. When someone asked if I was okay, I'd smile and nod and lie through my teeth."

He swallows hard. "One night it just all got too much, it literally felt like I was drowning, like I was locked inside a box that was gradually filling with water. I didn't know whether to scream or cry like a baby… I just let go. All the rage inside me came to a head and I tore shit out of that bathroom. Somehow I ended up cutting my hand on something sharp and the pain of it somehow eased the pain in my heart." He inhales deeply, clearly struggling with the feelings the memory of it all is dredging up.

"It gave me an idea, so I tried it using a razor blade, but on my legs instead. I figured I could cut myself there and no one would see the scars," he continues. "The only time that I felt peaceful was when I dug that razor blade into my skin, the relief that flooded me, it gave me a high that I can't even begin to describe. That feeling… it became addictive."

"Did you do it often? Cut yourself?" I ask.

"I tried to stop. Knew it was bad for me but I did it anyway. It was my way of coping. I couldn't allow myself to feel, I hated the feelings that built up inside me, and the only relief I got was sitting in my bathroom with a blade in my hand, all that pain inside me just bled out of me, *literally*. I thought I'd be okay, that I could keep my secret hidden, but I couldn't."

"What happened?"

"My first girlfriend, Anna, saw them. We were fooling around and she went down to give me head, I was so caught up in the moment I completely forgot about them."

I hate the wave of jealousy that rises up inside me at the mention of her. I have no reason to be. He's not mine.

"She took one look and ran a mile. She was horrified. That was when I decided to go about things differently. I loved sex, the high I got from the cut was nothing compared to an orgasm, so I stopped cutting myself, and filled that void with booze and sex. No relationships, no strings, no chance of anyone finding out. The only way I kept them hidden was to not allow anyone to see me, to only allow people to see the parts I *wanted* them to."

"That's why you never fully undress. Why the room is dark, or you use a blindfold." It's not a question, because I already know I'm right.

He's never allowed me to see him naked. I'm either facing away from him while he fucks me from behind, blindfolded, and he's always dressed again straight after we've had sex.

With a man like Rafe, it's hard to imagine he has body image issues and insecurities.

He nods. "That's not the only reason I use blindfolds, though. I enjoy the control, the pleasure I get from *giving* pleasure. I've always enjoyed seeing a woman come undone because of something I did. It's rare that I'm able to come if the girl I'm with isn't able to."

"I admire your nobility and I'd usually comment on how you could make even the most frigid of women cream their panties, but I don't want to go inflating that ego of yours anymore than it already is."

A smile crosses his face as a laugh rumbles through his chest.

"Have you... cut yourself recently?" I ask.

He shakes his head. "I never needed to, never wanted to until the night my dad died. When I got that voicemail from Della, I was in your bathroom. I saw your razor on the sink and I... I was so close, so fucking close."

"What stopped you?"

His eyes find mine for the first time since he began talking. "You."

"Me?"

He nods. "The knowledge of you on the other side of the door somehow stopped me from going through with it. All I've ever been is a let-down, and I didn't want to let you down, but I did it anyway the second I left you there. I'm so fucking sorry."

I take his chin and guide his eyes to mine. "No. You don't have to apologise. Not anymore. I get it. I'm the one who should be sorry..."

"I don't want your pity, Reese."

"It's not pity. It's that you went through all of this alone, that you felt the need to hide them at all. Those scars are nothing to be ashamed of."

"It's easy for you to say when you've never harmed yourself," he replies.

"Who says I haven't?"

A frown cuts through his brow as his eyes search mine.

"Self-harm comes in many different forms, Rafe, not just with a blade. Some people do it without even realising it," I begin. "Growing up, I wasn't the skinniest of girls, I had thighs the width of tree trunks and boobs and a belly that jiggled when I jumped up and down. I'd see catwalk models and reality stars on Instagram and in magazines with their toned stomachs, thigh gaps and perky tits and I'd look at myself in the mirror and wonder why I didn't look like that. I would take that metaphorical blade and pick out parts of myself that I hated. I'd compare myself to every girl I came across including my friends, even Della."

His hand comes up to my face, cupping my cheek. "But you're beautiful, Ree. You're fucking gorgeous."

"I didn't think so then. For years I tore myself apart, but then I decided I couldn't carry on hurting myself like that, so I decided to own my insecurities and instead of criticising myself every day, I'd pick out the parts that I liked, parts that made me *me.* What I'm trying to say is," I take his hands in mine and bring them to my lap. "Those scars... every single one represents a battle that you've fought and won. You survived, and you're still here."

"They're ugly."

"They don't define who you are. And with or without them, in my eyes… you're the most beautiful man I've ever met."

His eyes meet mine then. "You're pretty amazing, you know that?"

"I know." I give him a wink that makes him smile. "I'm sorry if I crossed the line by trying to suck you off while you were asleep."

He chokes out a laugh. "Yeah, I'm not gonna lie, it took me a little by surprise."

"I just *really* wanted to suck your dick."

"It would've been the best wake-up call a guy could have."

"Has anyone ever given you a blowjob?" I ask, and when he shakes his head, I sit there stunned, my jaw dropping open.

"I couldn't risk anyone seeing my scars," he replies, almost embarrassed by it.

"You're practically a virgin," I say, picking my jaw up off the floor.

He shoots me a look out the corner of his eye and smirks. "Baby, there's nothing virginal about me, haven't I proven that already?" His gaze darkens, though I don't miss the tiny mischievous glint in his eye. "Maybe I'm not trying hard enough."

"I think I need another demonstration. But first, I want you in my mouth." I slide to the floor and settle between his spread knees, tipping my head back to meet his eye.

"You don't have to."

"I want to, but only if *you* do."

"Are you kidding? I've thought of nothing else but the feel of your lips wrapped around my cock for weeks."

"Good." I grip his waistband and tug down his sweats and pull them off, leaving him naked, his hard cock standing to attention.

He sucks in a breath and I peer up where I'm met with a look of desire and excitement, but there's also a hint of vulnerability mixed in there.

I want to chase it away.

I run my hands up this thighs, spreading them a little wider as I reach for his cock, leaning in and taking him deep in my mouth before releasing him and taking him in my hand, stroking from root to tip, using my saliva as lube.

A deep groan erupts from his chest as he leans back, propping himself up with his hands spread out on the mattress behind him.

As I stroke him, I kiss a path up the insides of his thighs, not stopping when my lips brush over the raised skin on his scars. He tenses beneath me, but I continue dotting kissing over every single one and doing the same on the opposite thigh. I want to show him that they don't bother me, that they won't scare me off. That his scars make him no less than the beautiful man he is, both inside and out.

I then turn my attention to his hard length, licking a line along the thick vein that runs along the side of his shaft and running my tongue over the tip.

"*Fuck...*" he moans as I take him in my mouth, sucking on the swollen head before taking him deeper while my hand reaches down to cup his balls, massaging gently, earning me another moan.

My eyes flick up to his as I watch *him* watch *me*, his eyes fixed onto where his cock disappears into my mouth, like he's never seen anything so fascinating in his life.

"That's my girl... Suck me just like that..."

I moan around his length, his praise has my pussy clenching

as I let my tongue glide along the underside while I suck on him harder, working him in and out.

His chest heaves as he reaches for me, brushing his fingers across my cheek. "You look so fucking beautiful swallowing my cock, baby. I've never been so turned on in my life. *Fuck*."

His hand fists my hair as his hips thrust gently off the bed, sending him deeper into my mouth. I gag as he hits the back of my throat but the sounds that he's making are worth it.

I squeeze my thighs together to quell the ache that throbs there. I've never gotten so turned on by giving a blowjob before and I'm worried I'm going to leave a wet patch on the rug.

In the past, a blowjob has been more like a chore, a requirement expected of me that was as far from pleasurable as you could get, but with Rafe, I want this. I want to please him, I want to give him everything he's been missing out on.

I want to make him happy, so I suck him like my life depends on it, using everything at my disposal to give him the best head of his life.

"Jesus, I'm not gonna last much longer," Rafe says, his grip in my hair tightening as he climbs closer to his release.

I suck him harder, using my hands as an extension of my mouth, and a minute later, thick ropes of cum hit the back of my throat as a sound close to a growl rumbles through him, his body shuddering as he comes.

I don't look away for even a moment as I watch him come undone and it's the most erotic thing I've ever seen. The wave of ecstasy that crosses his face, his eyes fluttering closed as pleasure ripples through his body.

It's mesmerising.

I swallow him down and just as I'm about to pull back, he

lifts me up by my armpits to straddle his lap as he claims my mouth, his tongue seeking mine as his slips between my lips, not caring that I taste like him.

The kiss makes me heady, so much so it's hard to form a coherent thought, but it always does when it's with him.

I break the kiss, smiling down at him. "Thank you for trusting me, it means a lot."

"And thank *you* for listening."

My arms wrap around his neck. "Earlier you mentioned not having relationships, just casual one-night stands that didn't allow room for anyone to find out about your scars. Well, what about me?"

"You're different. You could never be just a one-night girl, Reese."

My heart hammers in my chest, those words filling me with so much hope, hope for something that can never be.

"Don't." I push off him, reaching for my bath robe that hangs on the back of the door.

"Don't what?" he asks from behind me.

"Don't say things like that unless you want me getting the wrong idea about us."

"And what idea's that?"

"You know what ideas, Rafe, and saying shit like that..." My eyes return to his over my shoulder as I twist the door handle. "I don't think I could take your kind of heartbreak."

25

Rafe

"You're it!" Ivy calls, tapping Reese on the leg then turning to run in the opposite direction.

It's a beautiful day out today, and Ivy begged us to take her to the park. I was supposed to go into work, but I figured it can wait. Spending quality time with my daughter is more important.

Reese catches up with me with ease, slapping me firmly on the ass. "You're it!"

She shoots me a wink while she takes off in the opposite direction to Ivy. I opt to go after Ivy.

She looks over her shoulder and giggles, pumping her arms faster. "You'll never get me, Daddy!"

I could. One of my strides matches three of hers and I could catch her in a second if I wanted to, but I'm okay with slowing myself down, letting her think she's winning.

Her laughter is a sound I want to hear for the rest of my life, it fills my heart with so much love and joy it's fit to burst.

I gain on her slowly and once she's within reach, I wrap my arms around her middle and lift her off the ground.

"Daddy!" she screams.

"Seems you're it again, little one." I press a kiss to her cheek and place her back on the ground, but before I can run, she taps my hand.

"Nope! You're it!" Ivy sprints away, and I spot Reese out of the corner of my eye, distracted by something on her phone and I start towards her.

"Run, Reesie! Don't let Daddy catch you!" Ivy calls to her and Reese's eyes lift to mine.

In a flash, Reese is running, but I advance on her quickly banding my arms around her and tugging us to the ground. She lands on top of me and rolls over to face me.

I brush her hair away from my face and take her cheek in my hand.

"Got you," I murmur, leaning in to dust my lips over hers.

She gives me a small smile that barely lasts a second. "Seems you did." Her voice is soft and shrouded in sadness as her eyes drop from mine and I know she's still thinking about earlier.

We haven't spoken about our conversation from this morning, and even though we don't bring it up, it's still there. It's the elephant in the room, the bad odour that lingers between us whenever we find ourselves on close proximity, the thing we avoid.

You're different. You could never be just a one-night girl, Reese...

This is why I never open up or allow people too close, because things get complicated and awkward and I almost always end up saying or doing the wrong thing. But what I said to her was the realest thing I think I've ever said to someone.

Sure, it might not have been something Mr. Darcy would be proud of, but it was my way of telling her that she's important, that she's not expendable, that she *means* something to me.

For the first time in forever, I actually felt good about myself today, a feeling that I don't experience often. She showed me that I don't need to hide my scars and that I don't need to be ashamed of them. They're a part of me and I should own them.

She did that.

"What I said earlier, I— *Oof*!" I'm cut off when a five year-old body lands square on top of us, knocking the wind from my lungs.

"Can we get ice cream? *Please Daddy!*"

Reese and I exchange a look. I can never say no to her. "Sure we can, come on."

We get back up to our feet and cross the wide expanse of the park towards a row of stores on the opposite side of the road.

It's busy in here, and spotting one of the few remaining tables, Reese heads to the table by the window while Ivy and I remain in the queue.

"How many flavours of ice cream are there?" Ivy asks curiously, peering up at me.

"I expect there's hundreds. You can make ice cream out of anything you want."

"Even rhubarb?"

"Even rhubarb."

She scrunches up her nose. "*Ew*. I hate rhubarb."

We're next in the queue and we step forward to the counter.

"What can I get you?" the blonde girl behind the counter asks with a smile. My eyes drop to her name tag, Emma.

"Hey, I'll take one chocolate chip and one raspberry ripple and whatever this one is having." I incline my head to Ivy, whose face is pressed against the glass counter where dozens of flavoured ice-creams in every colour sit on display. "What flavour would you like, Ives?"

"All the flavours! I want that one and that one and that one..." she points out each one by one.

Emma laughs, peering down at my daughter, then back at me. "She's cute."

"She's being unrealistic. She can mix the flavours right?"

"Uh-huh. Each extra scoop is a dollar-fifty," Emma, replies.

"You can choose three flavours, Ives. Pick wisely."

"Um... Strawberry, chocolate and rocky road please!"

"Coming right up." Emma sets to work, making Ivy's ice cream who watches with wide eyes as she piles on scoop after scoop before handing Ivy hers and passing mine and Reese's.

I pay for our ice creams and head over to the table by the window where Reese is sat.

"Reesie! Look at my ice cream!"

"Wow! That's huge," she says as Ivy tucks into her ice cream. I hand Reese her raspberry ice cream as I sink into the seat opposite her.

"You know the girl behind the counter was totally checking you out, right," she says before taking along lick of her ice cream, the image conjuring memories that have no business being in a place like this surrounded by children.

"No, she wasn't," I laugh off.

Her eyebrow lifts. "Oh come on, don't tell me you don't see it. Every woman's ovaries exploded the second you walked through the door. Single dads are hot."

"And your ovaries? How are they doing?"

"Perfectly fine, thanks, they're immune to your charm."

"Is that so? I'm gonna have to work on that."

She laughs before delving back into her ice cream while her eyes drift out the window.

"Have you ever been here before?" I ask her.

"No, my mom only took me to a grand total of three places when I was a kid; School, if she wasn't hungover from the night before. The supermarket to buy food and booze, though the food to booze ratio was always favourable towards the latter. And to my grandmother's house, usually to guilt-trip her into lending her some money she'd never be able to pay back to buy yet *more* booze."

"Jesus..." My heart aches for that little girl who was subjected to a childhood with a mother like that. I hate her mom for doing that to her, I'm just glad I'll never get to meet her because I won't be held responsible for my actions if I did.

"Did *you* ever come here?" she asks.

"Yeah, all the time."

"With your mom or your dad?"

"Mom. She uh..."

"What?" she presses.

"Here's me with wonderful memories of my mom and you have none. It seems insensitive to talk about it."

Reese covers my hand with hers. "Rafe, I wouldn't be asking if I didn't wanna know. Tell me about her. What was she like?"

I clear my throat. "She'd bring us here on the weekends. My dad was usually working, and when my mom wasn't volunteering or gardening, she'd always make time for the three of us. She was the best mom anyone could wish for. She'd put everyone before herself and she never complained, not once. No wonder my dad adored her, I don't think I'd ever seen anyone so in love with each other as my parents."

"Della said they met through her dad, Randall. She was with him first?"

I bristle at the mention of that bastard's name. "Yeah. He was awful to her and she confided in my dad, he and Randall were friends at the time and they fell in love straight away. She brought out the best in him."

"She sounds amazing. Rafe, I know you have a tendency to bury your feelings and choose not to open up, but you should see your face while you talk about her."

It does feel pretty good to talk about her, and where I thought talking about her and my dad out loud would hurt, it felt good to relive those memories, ones I've forced back since I was a kid.

"Oops." My eyes drift to Ivy whose mouth and hands are covered in a thick sticky layer of ice cream.

"Let's go get you cleaned up." Reese rises from her chair and leads Ivy to the restrooms in the back.

While they're gone, I let my eyes wander out the window where I spot a blacked-out SUV sat on the curb on the opposite side of the road. It's innocent enough, but something about it has my interest piqued, only I don't know why. It sticks out like a sore thumb, parked between a faded Toyota Corolla and a Station Wagon. Maybe I'm just being over cautious, but with everything that's been happening lately, I'm not taking any chances.

Once Reese has gotten Ivy cleaned up and we've finished off the last of our ice creams, we step out onto the sidewalk, heading back towards the car parked a few blocks away.

I scan the area for the SUV, but it's gone, it's no longer parked up across the street and I feel myself relax.

Ivy walks between us, hand in hand with Reese and I, our arms swinging as she chatters about something to do with a couple of the girls at school.

Reese goes to speak but a screech of tyres and screams from behind us cuts her off.

I spin around to see the same SUV from earlier ploughing towards us at high speed. It mounts the curb. Children and their parents jump out of the way, the car narrowly missing them by inches.

Everything happens so fast, it's like something out of a movie. Adrenaline floods my veins as I see the scene play out in front of me.

Ivy is in my arms faster than I can blink, tucked against my chest as my other arm wraps around Reese's waist, hauling them both into the open door of a cafe. It's a matter of seconds before the SUV blazes past the building. Customers dart away from the window, the piercing sound of metal screeching as the side of the vehicle scrapes against the bricks splits the air. The wide bank of windows shatters into a million tiny pieces of glass as the SUV speeds away.

The sound of its engine fades into the distance, the voices and the cries of the people that surround us is muted because all I can hear is white noise. It's deafening as it rings in my ears, my heart pumping so hard it could break my ribs, and it's only then that I realise I'm on my knees with my girls clutched tightly to my chest.

"...y'all okay? Are y'all alright?" A guy's voice growing louder as the ringing in my ears slowly fades into nothing.

The reality of what's just happened hits me like a brick to the face and a panic sets in.

"Reese? Ivy? Hey! Are you okay?" My voice comes out

shaky.

Reese eases back, her face pale as she peers up at me, her eyes wide with terror. "What the hell just happened?"

"I don't know." I turn my attention to Ivy. "Sweetheart? Are you alright?"

"Ivy?" Reese asks.

I brush her hair away from her face before checking her over for any sign of injury.

"Was that car trying to hurt us?" she asks with a frown, her eyes peeking up at me filled with tears.

"No, of course not." My eyes meet Reese's and by the expression on her face, she's caught me out on my lie.

The whole thing is too much of a coincidence for us to *not* to have been the target. It's scary as it is for them coming after me, but my daughter too? The thought of losing her terrifies me.

"Daddy's my hero." Ivy's arms go around my neck, and I gather Reese up to join our embrace. My hold on them both tightens as I breathe out a heavy sigh of relief.

We're okay, we're safe...

For now. But for how long?

26

Reese

Rafe doesn't speak a word as we drive to his brother's house, he just stares dead ahead while he white-knuckles the steering wheel. With every minute that ticks by, I feel the anxiety inside me rising as the questions and confusion of what happened swirl around my mind.

I'm still not fully sure of what *did* happen, it's all a total blur. It doesn't seem real. One minute Ivy was chewing my ear off about her and friends and what they got up to at school the week before, and the next thing I know, I'm on the floor of some random cafe in Rafe's arms as a huge-ass black truck steams past, smashing the windows. It almost feels like a scene I've watched play-out on a movie theatre, only deep down I know it wasn't pretend.

It was *real*.

We almost got mowed down by a rogue car. We almost *died*.

The thought sinks to the pit of my stomach that rolls with

nausea. My heart still hammers in my chest as my mind whirls. The only thing that grounds me is that we're alive, and that the little girl who's sound asleep in the backseat behind me is safe.

Before we left the cafe, Rafe called his brother, telling him to meet us at the house, and it was then I realised we weren't just in the wrong place at the wrong time, that car was coming for us.

We were its target.

After the third or fourth question I put to Rafe fell on deaf ears, I decided to keep quiet.

I'm guessing he's still in shock like I am. His jaw clenches and unclenches every few seconds anxiously.

We pull up outside his childhood home, which is more like a mansion than a house. I've been here a few times to visit Della, but it never fails to amaze me how huge it is.

Gage is in the living room when the three of us arrive, pacing restlessly by the window, talking in a hushed voice to Alec who wears a worried look.

When we enter the room they stalk towards us shoulder to shoulder.

Rafe touches my arm gently. "Ree, can you take Ivy through to the kitchen?"

"So you can all talk about what just happened like I wasn't there myself? Hell no. Some prick tried to kill us. I'm staying." I fold my arms over my chest defiantly. One of them will have to carry me out before I move a single muscle.

"I'll take her," Viola, their housekeeper offers as she hovers by the door.

"Thanks, Vi." Rafe crouches in front of his daughter. "Hey, you go with Viola and if you ask her nicely, she'll make you a milkshake."

"Chocolate?" Ivy's eyes light up.

Rafe chuckles. "Yeah, chocolate." He drops a kiss to her forehead before Viola leads her out of the room.

"So?" Gage asks, his eyes hard as they search his brother's face.

"A car tried to mow the three of us down," Rafe replies.

Gage's eyes widen. "What?"

"It mounted the curb and missed us by seconds. We were in that ice cream shop Mom used to take us to when we were kids. I saw this SUV sat across the street, but by the time we left, it'd gone. Next thing I know, it's ploughing towards us on the sidewalk."

"You get a license plate?" Gage asks.

"Funnily enough, no. I was too busy trying to haul us out of the way of a car trying to run us over."

"You think this, the text message and the break-in are all connected?" Alec asks.

"I bet my life on it," Gage says.

"There's no way this is all a coincidence," Rafe says.

"And the guy at the mall," Alec adds.

My eyes bounce between the three of them as my mind whirls. They go back and forth so fast, I'm getting whiplash. What the hell are they talking about? What text? What guy? What makes it worse is that they talk as though I'm not here and it pisses me off.

"Wait, *wait*... Slow down. What are you talking about?" I ask. My eyes fall on Rafe and I can tell he doesn't want to tell me, but I shoot him a look that tells him I'm not going to give in. "Well?"

Rafe blows out a breath. "There was a guy at the mall that

day we took Ivy shopping. He was watching us, and when he saw me looking, he disappeared."

What?! Why wouldn't he tell me something like that?

"Just over a week ago there was a break-in at the club, a guy searching through the offices. We got CCTV footage and it turns out it was the same guy as the mall."

"And the text message?"

Rafe's eyes lift to his brother over my shoulder and I spin to face him. "I got a text a few months back telling me that me and my family would pay for what we did to Bryce."

"Bryce? The guy who attacked Della? The one Rafe shot?" I ask.

He nods. "It was the night Dad died, my head was all over the place. I didn't think anything of it."

"You didn't think anything of it?" I scoff. "A text threatening your family and you just what? Swept it under the rug, decided to wait around for something to happen that would prove it was real? Are you kidding me?"

Gage's face hardens. "No offense, Reese, but this really doesn't concern you."

"You weren't the one who was almost ran over, asshole. Last time I checked, that was me, your brother and your niece, so yes, it *does* concern me. Question is, am I the only one who didn't know about all of this, or are Della and Sierra in the dark, too?" I get my answer when both Gage and Rafe remain silent. "Where are they anyway?"

"They're upstairs. Della's resting and Sierra is in her room," Gage answers.

I turn to Rafe. "When were you going to tell me? Were you *ever*?"

"Ree—" he starts, but I cut him off.

"You know what? Save it. I thought we understood each other, but it seems secrets are one thing this family specialise in the best and I can't deal with it right now. I am going to go check on *your* daughter and make sure she's alright." I storm out of the room in search of Ivy.

I find her sat on one of the stools at the large kitchen island in the centre of the room, swinging her legs happily while she watches Viola make her a milkshake.

I brush my hand over her hair and press a kiss to the top of her head. "You okay, baby?"

She yawns. "I'm sleepy."

"It's been a long day."

"You can take her to Rafe's old room if you'd like, let her take a nap in there?" Viola offers. "It's upstairs, turn right down the corridor and it's the third door on the left."

"Thank you. If we're gone for the rest of the afternoon, send out a search party, chances are I've gotten lost in this place."

Viola chuckles. "Will do."

I manage to find the bedroom easier than I expected and just like the rest of the house, it's obnoxiously big, bigger than the entirety of my apartment.

I tuck Ivy into the huge bed, bringing the covers up to her chin before climbing in beside her. I bring her little body closer to mine and press a kiss to the back of her head.

"Reesie?" she asks.

"Yeah, baby?" I brush her hair from her face.

"Did that car try to hurt us?" she asks.

Yes. "No, sweetie," I lie. "I think he just lost control, is all."

"Maybe he saw a cat in the road and turned the car to stop from hitting it."

I smile, loving how her little mind works. "Yeah, maybe that was it."

Within seconds, her breathing evens out and her body rises and falls with a soft, steady rhythm that soothes me, and I allow my mind to wander, thanking God that we managed to make it out today alive.

It's strange to think that an hour ago, it could have been a totally different story, I might not even be sitting here. We'd be a breaking story on the local news channel, the poor victims of a hit and run, a rogue, out of control car on an otherwise quiet Saturday afternoon. It's a weird feeling knowing that I could be dead right now, that it could have been my number that was up, my time. It's a thought that messes with my mind, but a brush with death will do that to you, I guess. I can't help but think that if I had died today, what would I have to show for my life? What would I be remembered for? Who would remember me? Certainly not my mom, and apparently not even my Nanna who can't even remember who I am while I'm alive, though that's not her fault.

I'm not going to lie and say that it doesn't hurt that he lied to me. I just wished he'd been honest with me, because when has hiding the truth ever worked out for the better?

I don't even realise that I've fallen asleep until I'm roused awake when the mattress dips behind me. I blink against the sunlight pouring in through the window to find Rafe peering down at me. "Dinner's almost ready."

"Okay." I turn to Ivy who's still nestles up tightly against me and nudge her gently awake. "Sweetie? You hungry?"

"Uh-huh." She nods, rubbing her eyes lazily.

The three of us head down for dinner with the rest of his family where we spend the majority of the time while we eat in an awkward silence. Gage sits at the head of the table with

Della sat to his left and Sierra to his right. I sit beside Della and directly across from me is Ivy with Rafe next to her. It's clear that Della and Si have now been brought up to speed because the tension between all of us in palpable. Della tries to keep the mood light, making small talk and idle conversation in an attempt to get us all through this shamble of a meal. The food itself is wonderful, a special family recipe according to Viola who avoids the dining room like the plague, a wise move if you ask me.

Ivy gasps excitedly, the sound cutting through the thick atmosphere and has all of us looking in her direction. "Has Daddy told you how he saved me and Reesie from a car? He pulled us out of the way. He was *sooo* fast, just like a superhero!"

My eyes meet Rafe's across the table and his jaw tightens.

"That's great, sweetheart," Della replies with a forced smile.

"Daddy's my hero," Ivy gushes, beaming up at him like he's her whole world.

Rafe gives a her a tight-lipped smile in response before his face crumples with remorse as he picks at the food on his plate.

The end of dinner can't come quick enough and once I'm done eating, I excuse myself from the table. I head out into the back garden to watch the sun set on a day that began so well and held so much promise and yet ended in disaster, a day I'm hoping to forget.

As with everything here, it's a huge expanse of open space lined with trees. The sky turns a rich shade of reds and oranges as the sun begins it's descent on the horizon. The cool air is crisp and clean as it fills my lungs.

The back door opens and closes behind me and I don't have

to turn around to guess who it is. Not a moment later, Rafe takes a seat beside me.

I don't have to say a word for him to know I'm pissed, the uncomfortable atmosphere between us is enough, but although I'm angry with him, even a little disappointed, I won't be able to stay mad at him for long, I know that much.

I don't think I ever could.

"I'm not going to apologise, because I'm not sorry I didn't tell you. But I am sorry that I *hurt* you. I did it to save yo—"

"Don't give me the whole *'I wanted to protect you'* crap, because we both know that's bullshit," I say, cutting him off.

"But it's true. I didn't tell you because I wanted to keep you out of it, away from this shit as much as I could."

"But I'm *in* it. I get why you thought it was a good idea, but after today, I'm in this as deep as you, your brother, Della..."

"It's all my fault. All of this wouldn't be happening if it wasn't for me," he says, bowing his head.

"How it your fault?"

"I set all this shit in motion the second I shot Bryce. I'm the target, and whoever this prick is that's doing all this, he wants to hurt me by hurting my family too. I put all of you in danger and I'm so sorry."

Anguish radiates out of every pore, the torment evident on his face as he shoulders all of this guilt he doesn't need to suffer on his own. How can he possibly think any of what happened today is his fault? He wasn't driving the car. He didn't make the driver do what he did.

I sigh. "You couldn't have known what was going to happen, Rafe."

"I'm still the cause of it." He scrubs his hands over his face and blows out a heavy breath. "I'm a bad person."

"Why would you say that?"

"Because I keep doing the wrong thing. I let the people I care about down and always find a way to disappoint them. I saw the look on your face when you found out I lied about that guy in the mall, the text, the break-in… You were disappointed in me, it's the look I'm used to seeing."

"You're not a bad guy, Rafe," I say.

His jaw clenches. "I've killed people."

"You did it to save your brother and Della, if you hadn't, they probably wouldn't be here right now."

"But I still took a life. I did it so easily, without so much as a second thought and that's what scares me," he admits.

"I'm not saying taking a life is a good thing, because it's not. But you know, good people can make bad choices with the best intentions, it doesn't make you a bad person. What you did, you did it out of love, to protect them and that is what matters. Would a bad guy take in a daughter that he never even knew existed, a choice that changed his life completely? Would a bad guy have opened up his home to a woman who was about to become homeless? Would a bad guy carry all of this guilt? Guilt he doesn't have to shoulder all on his own? You're a *good* person, Rafe, and a *really* great guy. Why else would I still be here?"

His eyes flit between mine as he reaches for my hand, covering it with both of his. "I almost lost you today. I almost lost my *daughter* today and I… I can't stomach the thought of anything happening to you, to *either* of you. You're too important—" His voice cracks and he swivels his face away from me.

Is he crying? It's almost as if he's embarrassed to express what he's feeling.

I take his chin and guide his eyes back to me, noticing them glossy, his blue irises sparkling in the setting sun. "You're important to me too."

Without warning, he leans in and his lips connect with mine. The kiss is sweet and tender. *Loving*. My arms reach up to wrap around his neck as his lips glide over mine, his tongue licking gently over the seam of my mouth as he deepens the kiss.

"I can't lose you," he murmurs against my lips.

My heart flutters in my chest as I stifle a cry, forcing back the tears that threaten to fall.

"You won't. I'm here for as long as you need me." I shuffle closer to him, looping my arm through his and resting my head on his shoulder as we watch the sun set on the horizon.

His hand comes to rest on my knee, squeezing gently. "I'm afraid I might always need you," he mumbles.

I'm not sure if he intended for me to hear his confession or not. Maybe it was a mental thought that slipped through accidentally, but either way, hearing his words make my heart swell.

"Can I show you something?" he asks, and I pull back to meet his eye.

I smile. "Sure."

He stands and holds out his hand for me as he leads me across the garden, his hand warm and tight around mine.

I always knew this man would be a danger to my existence, his touch and his tender words are the lit match that sets my soul on fire.

And if I'm being truthful, I'm afraid I'll always need him, too.

27

"I should've brought my hiking boots," I joke as Rafe leads me by the hand across the garden that seems to have no end.

He laughs, his eyes finding mine over his shoulder. "It's not much further."

The sun has now set as night slowly closes in, and the further we get away from the lights of the house, the darker it becomes. It's another few minutes before I notice a huge oak tree in the far corner of the two acre garden. It's tall and wide. It's thick trunk splits into three, the branches darting in every direction.

And there right in the middle, sits a tree house on a square platform of eight metres or so. The house is build entirely out of wood, with small panelled windows and shutters, a slanted roof, and a swing that hangs from one of the thicker branches to the left.

It's stunning.

"The tree has been here longer than our house. They say it's been here for over two-hundred years. It's strength was the reason my dad chose this one to build me a tree house on," Rafe explains.

My eyes widen. "Your dad built this? It's incredible."

"You wanna take a look?" he asks and I nod.

A series of wooden blocks mismatched in shape and size are secured to the tree's trunk like steps leading up to the tree house, with a thick rope to hold onto for support.

Rafe follows me up, keeping a protective hand on my lower back as I take my time with each step.

When we finally reach the tree house, he lets us inside, heading to a small wooden cabinet against the wall and pulling out a box of matches. A few seconds later, we're bathed in a soft orange glow from a half a dozen candles, placed in various spots of the tiny house.

It's roughly the size of my small living room in my old apartment, maybe a little smaller, but enough room for a few children to sit and play comfortably and not feel claustrophobic.

Some of the branches stretch across the house, poking out of the roof that has been built around it.

Off to the left is a tiny bookshelf and beside it a chest which I can only imagine is filled with toys from his childhood, and there are three beanbag chairs against the opposite wall.

It's cozy, full of memories from a time gone by.

Rafe pulls out two of the beanbag chairs and offers one to me and I take a seat beside him, sinking into the chair that feels like I'm sitting on clouds.

"My dad built this for me not long after my mom died. I spent a lot of time barricaded in my room, I didn't want to talk to or see anyone and my dad worried. I think this place was for him as much as it was for me. It allowed him to focus on something other than his grief, and gave me a place I could come to when I needed an escape."

"It's beautiful, Rafe."

He runs his fingers through his hair. "I've never allowed anybody else up here, not even Gage or Sierra have been in here, well, not that I know of."

"Seriously? Why?" I ask.

"This place is mine. My haven. My safe space. My siblings knew my boundaries and that this place was one of them. I guess I just wanted something for myself and not have to share it with anyone else."

"But I'm here," I say.

"Because I *want* you here. The only person I want to share this with, is you."

My heart skips a beat. "I'm glad you did. Thank you."

He can never know what it means that he brought me here, that he cares and trusts me enough to want to share a place so close to his heart with me.

"So what did you get up to in here?" I quiz.

"Mostly reading, despite what my sister is lead to believe. I'd draw, think… Sometimes I'd bring a portable DVD player and watch movies all day long."

"A *portable* DVD player?" I scoff. "You old fossil. I'm guessing you were too old for Netflix, right?" I joke and he shoves my shoulder playfully.

"I'll punish you for that."

"Do you promise?" I reply coyly, the smirk on my lips telling him that I'll love every minute, thought my smile soon fades. "Did you… Did you ever *hurt* yourself here?"

His eyes hold mine for a moment before he shakes his head. "No, like I said, this was my safe space."

I nod slowly. I'm glad. I'm glad he had a place he could escape to, a place that made him happy. I hate to think of him as a boy so consumed with sadness and grief that the only place he could go to was the sharp edge of a blade to find an escape.

"Will you promise me something?" I ask him.

"I don't make promises I can't keep, Reese."

"You can keep this one, I know it." I reach for his hand, holding it between both of mine. "If you ever feel like that again, that you need a release, that things get so bad you consider cutting yourself or drowning in a bottle of booze… Drown in *me*, get lost in *me*." My eyes sting with tears as I force back the urge to cry. "I'll always be here to help you through it. No matter what we are to each other, whether this thing between us leads somewhere or nowhere, whether we remain as friends, become more or nothing at all, promise me that you'll find me. Don't ever feel like you have nowhere to turn, or that harming yourself is the only option because it's not. Get lost in *me*."

He looks at me stunned, taken aback by my words as his eyes flick between mine. Without warning, he grips the back of my neck and slams his lips down on mine in a harsh, desperate kiss.

He slides to his knees in front of where I'm sitting and moves between mine, his fingers tangling in my hair as his other arm comes around my waist, pulling me closer.

My fingers dive into his hair as I slide to the ground to straddle his lap. His hands knead my ass, grinding me down on his hardening cock and within seconds, I'm growing wet and needy for him, the ache between my legs begging to be quelled.

"Rafe, fuck me," I mumble against his lips, my words coming out in deep huffs of air as I gasp for breath. "I want you to fuck me."

His eyes flare as he dives back in, his tongue slipping into my mouth to taste me, and *I* him. He reaches down for the hem of my shirt and tugs it over my head, and I do the same with his. We fumble with each others' clothes like a pair of impatient, horny teenagers desperate for each other and once we're naked, he lays me down on the plush rug that covers the majority of the floor.

He trails his fingers down my body and through the slick folds of my pussy before sinking a finger inside me. Tingles of pleasure zip up my spine as he strokes against my g-spot.

I grow wetter with every smooth motion of his finger. I need him.

I reach the waistband of his underwear, tugging gently. "Take these off."

There's a hint of hesitation in his eyes as he looks down at me and I give him a reassuring smile. After a moment, he pushes down his underwear, exposing the raised pink scars on the insides of his thighs.

His body stiffens, but when I press a kiss to my fingertips and place them over his scars, something softens inside him.

He hovers above me, holding himself up on his forearms either side of my head while he settles himself between my legs. He kisses a path from my lips to my cheek before burying his face in my neck where he sucks on the sensitive skin there just below my ear, earning him a moan.

He reaches between us, running the tip of his cock through

my wet folds before pushing inside me. It doesn't take long to adjust to him, and I gasp when he fills me completely, sliding out and pushing back in more forcefully this time.

A deep groan rumbles up his throat, the vibrations radiating through my skin as he bites my neck gently, finding a steady rhythm as he moves inside me. With every slow, drawn-out thrust of his hips, his pelvic bone grazes my clit, sending sharp bolts of pleasure through my body.

His movements begin slow, savouring my body like he'll never feel me again. It's deep, intimate, *sensual,* but he soon picks up speed, his thrusts coming harder and deeper, sending me spiralling towards my release.

My ankles lock at his back, my hands clinging to his neck as I hang on for dear life while he fucks me into the rug. My tits bounce with every snap of his hips and my pussy clenches around his cock as he whispers dirty words of encouragement in my ear.

"You take my cock so good, Reese... So fucking good..."

He rises up onto his knees, pulling me up with him to straddle his lap while he remains buried inside me.

"Ride me, baby," he groans.

And I do.

I ride him hard and I ride him fast, bouncing up and down on his cock like it's a sport, circling my hips to hit that spot that will have me hurtling towards the finish line.

I can't get enough of him. He's like a drug and his kiss, his touch is the high I get from him.

He grips my hair and tugs it so my head drops back, my neck aches at the angle, but the pain is soothed when his mouth connect with my throat.

My thighs burn with exertion as I lift up and drop back

down over and over while his hands wander over every inch of me.

"Fuck, I'm gonna come," he groans. "I want you to come with me, Ree. Come with me, baby."

His words tip me over the edge and before I know it, my orgasm consumes me and a cry slips free from my lips as wave after wave crashes over me.

Not a second later, Rafe thickens inside me and a deep guttural groan rumbles up his throat as he comes deep inside me.

My mouth finds his as I ride us through our release, my pussy contracting around him, wringing out every last drop of what he has to give me. My movements over him are slow and lazy as my muscles turn lax and I drop my head to his shoulder, my chest heaving.

He lifts me off him and lowers me back down onto the rug and rolls onto his side, wrapping me up in his arms. He presses a delicate kiss to my forehead and I melt into him.

"This place is like something out of a fairy tale. It's magical," I say, letting my eyes roam around the tiny tree house.

"All those fairy tale books of Ivy's have gotten to you, huh?"

"Just a little."

"Is that what you dreamed about when you were her age? Prince Charming swooping in to save you?"

I chuckle. "Are you referring to yourself after your heroics earlier?"

"Nah. I think I'm closer to the Beast in this story than Prince Charming." I hear the hidden meaning behind his words, even if he doesn't say them out loud.

"No, that would imply you're ugly, and you could never be ugly and you're definitely not a beast. I don't want Prince

Charming, he's handsome and all, but he's boring. He's too perfect. I want you with all your rough edges, your jagged scars and your broken heart. I want every tiny perfectly imperfect piece of you so that I can put you back together, if you'll let me." My confession has my heart hammering in my chest.

"Hmm... Some fairy tale," he says quietly.

A twisted fairy tale, but I wouldn't have it any other way.

We lie in each others' arms for a little while longer before heading back towards the house. We walk hand in hand across the garden and my heart has never felt so full. The fact that he showed me the tree house, a place that is clearly personal to him means everything.

He leads me through the back door into the kitchen and I turn to him.

"I'm gonna grab something to drink, I'll be up in a minute," I tell him.

"Okay, don't be long." He pulls me in for a kiss, walking me backwards until I'm sandwiched between him and the counter.

When he pulls back, I come away breathless and he gives me a wink before he disappears out of the room.

I head to the fridge, pulling out a jug of orange juice and pouring myself a glass.

"You're good for him." I jump at the sound of Viola's voice as she moves towards me. It's dark in here, and I didn't see or hear her come in. "I didn't mean to startle you."

"Him?"

"Rafe," she clarifies. "Forgive me for interfering but he needs someone like you. I've never met a man more deserving of love than Rafe, he just doesn't know it. I've known him since he was a baby, and I've never met a boy more emotionally guarded. He chooses to be alone because that's what he thinks he deserves. He suffers in silence, never giving away too much because he thinks showing his feelings will make him weak, but anybody with eyes can see he's crying out for someone to love him. His heart is guarded by a thick wall of brick, but I have a feeling you're the one to break it down. The change in him since you've been in his life... He's happier than I've ever seen him."

Her words have a boulder-sized rock lodged in my throat.

"You're in love with him, aren't you?"

My chin trembles as I nod, blinking back my tears. "He's going to break my heart. He won't mean to, but he will."

"Why do you say that?" she asks.

"Because he'll never love me back. This thing between us was only ever supposed to be fun. I knew it would never be limited to that, not for me, but I agreed to it because I thought it was the only way I could have him like that. He'll break my heart and it won't even be his fault, it'll be mine."

I knew what I signed up for, so I'm not surprised I feel like this, but there's always that shred of hope in my heart that he'll surprise me. That he'll love me back.

Viola pats my hand. "That boy rarely knows what's good for him, even if it's staring him in the face. He might just need a little push in the right direction. Just don't give up on him, not yet." And with that, she heads back out of the kitchen.

When I reach Rafe's old bedroom, I find him lying beside Ivy who's nestled up to him in the centre of the mattress. I kick off my shoes and climb in beside them so Ivy is positioned in the middle.

His eyes are closed so I assume he's asleep, but when he reaches across to take my hand, I glance up and find his eyes fixed on me. We watch each other through the darkened room, neither one of us speaking as Ivy's soft breaths are the only sound we hear.

It's moments like that that have me envisioning a life that can never happen. A picture of the three of us as a family; happy, content.

But how can it? This whole thing between us was based on the agreement that feelings wouldn't be involved, that we'd keep things from becoming complicated but that's exactly what it's become. I love Ivy as if she were my own, and Rafe's sweet words earlier had my mind spiralling and my heart soaring. Rafe has the power to make me fall in love with him, but he also holds the power to shatter my heart with the slightest touch—something I swore I'd never let happen again. But the longer this goes on, it's getting harder and harder to conceal the truth of what I'm feeling, because when it finally comes out, my heart will be broken beyond repair.

I just don't know how long I can keep pretending that I feel nothing when I feel everything.

28

Rafe

The next morning, I roll out of bed as gently as I can and sneak around the room, trying my best to not make a sound that will wake Reese and Ivy. After the events of yesterday, they need it.

I come to stand over Reese, resisting the temptation to reach out and dust my fingers across her beautiful face. Her fiery red hair are like flames against the crisp white pillow beneath her head. The colour should be warning enough that this woman is dangerous, I've always known it, I just underestimated the hold she had over me.

I'm not sure where exactly this whole *'friends who fuck'* thing started to feel different, because the things I feel for Reese are like nothing I've ever felt before. My feeling are definitely not limited to friendship *or* desire. It's more. I feel every fucking emotion going and it's screwing with my head, blurring the lines I put in place to stop this exact thing from happening.

No strings. No commitments. All those rules, all those lines I laid down that I swore I'd never cross, and all it took was a woman with copper hair, a sharp tongue and an addictive smile to have me breaking every single one of them.

Last night we spoke of fairy tales and I likened myself to the Beast, which undoubtedly makes her the beauty in the story. But forget Beauty and the Beast, Prince Charming and all that crap. She's Goldilocks, only with flaming red hair, and rather than inviting herself into the three bears' house, she's broken into the fortress that is my heart and made it her home.

She's invaded my every thought, both awake and unconscious, she's embedded herself so deep inside me that I don't know where I end and she begins. She's changing me in ways I never thought possible, and I don't know how much longer I can let this carry on.

She's already seen so much of me, uncovered all of my secrets and the darkness that resides within. She knows me better than anyone which makes her dangerous. This arrangement between us was never meant to get this far, I should have stopped it long before now, but we've been spiralling out of control for so long now, we're in *way* too deep as it is and I don't know if I could let her go of her I tried.

Letting them sleep, I head downstairs and into the kitchen where Sierra sits at the kitchen island with a plate full of toast in front of her.

I slip my hand around from behind her and swipe a piece of toast from her plate.

She slaps my hand. "Hey asshat, get your own."

I laugh, dropping into the seat opposite her. "Good morning to you, too," I say around a mouthful of toast.

"Not as good a morning as you, clearly," she comments.

"And what's that supposed to mean, little Hudson?"

She smirks. "You and Reese."

My heart thuds. "What about us?"

"You know what. You think we're stupid, but we all know something's going on. I know you two snuck off to go fuck in your tree house last night."

"Nothing's going on," I lie. "You don't know anything."

"I'm not judging or condemning whatever is *not* happening between you, just don't hurt her. She never does anything by half and that includes love. She loves with everything she has and gets hurt twice as badly when things go wrong."

"It's just a bit of fun, nothing more." It *is* more, I'm just not gonna tell my sister that.

Sierra rises from her stool. "Keep telling yourself that, but we both know it's not true, not to you and definitely not for Reese. She's one of my best friends, and if you hurt her, I'll have no problem helping her castrate you. I should have yours and Gage's balls regardless for lying to us about that text and all the other shit."

"We didn't lie, we just didn't tell you, there's a difference," I say.

She crosses her arms. "We're a part of this family too, we deserve to know the truth especially if we're all in danger. I'm tired of being the last one to know about everything in this family. Got anymore secrets you wanna unload, brother? I'm all fucking ears."

"It's too fucking early for this, Sierra," I grumble.

"Fuck you." She snatches a piece of toast and turns for the door.

"Si, wait," I call after her, rising from my stool.

She stops and spins on her heel with a sigh. Her eyes are

glassy as she nibbles the inside of her lip, a clear sign she's trying everything not to cry.

"Come here." I open my arms and pull her in for a hug and she gasps.

I *never* hug. I never show affection and do all that mushy shit so this is as new to me as it is her. I can't remember the last time I ever willingly hugged my little sister, but it feels pretty good.

"Who are you and what have you done with my brother?" she asks.

I chuckle, pressing my lips to the top of her head. "I'm still here, I guess my aversion to public displays of affection isn't as strong as it used to be." I'm not lying, the prospect of a hug or a kiss a few months ago would turn my stomach and fill me with dread.

"Being in love will do that to you I suppose," she replies, pulling back to look me in the eye.

I frown. "I don't know what you mean."

She smiles softly. "I think you do. Don't worry, I won't tell." She reaches up to kiss my cheek before disappearing out of the kitchen.

Maybe I'm not as good at hiding my feelings as I thought.

∞∞∞

The second we step inside my apartment, the cat runs to us, meowing and whining like it hasn't seen us in a week when it hasn't even been twenty-four hours.

Reese drops to her knees and gathers Merlin into her arms and it rubs itself against her face. "I'm sorry, baby. Let's go get you fed."

She carries him into the kitchen and sets about making his food while I set up movie on the TV for Ivy, something about a dog that's a superhero.

"Daddy, can I have a sleepover with Auntie Sierra sometime? She said that she will braid my hair and that we can watch movies *all* night long!"

"She did, did she? I guess that would be alright," I reply to which she rejoices with a punch of her little fist into the air.

The sound of glass smashing from the kitchen has my head snapping up.

"Crap!" Reese shouts from the kitchen and I rush in to find her on her knees, picking up the broken pieces from the floor.

"Are you alright?" I ask, crouching down to help her.

"I will be when the fucker who tried to kill us is dead." There's a slight tremble in her hand and I cover it with my own.

"Whoever it is will be dealt with, I promise you."

"But they're getting closer to us. It's not just a text message or break-in, they tried to run us over, Rafe."

"I'm not gonna let anything happen to you or our daughter." The word *'our'* is out before I can stop it and Reese's wide eyes reflect my own.

Shit. Why the fuck did I say that?

"I, uh...um..." My mind's a total blank as I stumble over my words like a fool.

She rises to her feet and drops the glass into the trash, clearly flustered by my mistake and leans back against the counter with a heavy sigh.

"So what happens now?" she asks, changing the subject. "Do we wait around for the next time they try to hurt us? Spend the foreseeable future looking over our shoulders for another car trying to run us down?"

I stand, moving towards her. "No. Gage, Alec and I are gonna try to figure out who this guy is so we can get some answers. Alec knows a guy in the FBI from his Army days who might be able to help, and we've got Derek. It's not gonna be easy, but we'll get him. For now, I don't want you going anywhere unless you're with me or one of the men from the house. I need to know you're safe."

"And what about you? *I* need to know *you're* safe. I… I can't lose you."

I step closer, taking her face in my hands. "You won't. I'm not going anywhere." I rest my forehead against hers. "I'm sorry I dragged you into all this."

"You didn't drag me into anything, I knew what I signed up for."

"You didn't sign up to have a target painted on your back because of me. When I find this guy, I'm gonna kill him and he won't be able to touch us ever again, I swear."

I press a kiss to her forehead, letting them linger there for a moment, praying to God we find this guy before he finds us.

29

Rafe

"Did we manage to get anything on this prick?" I ask, leaning forward as I sit on the sofa in Gage's office. Alec stands against the wall off to the side while Gage sits behind his desk with Derek opposite, tapping away on his laptop.

Sleep has evaded me these past few nights. No matter how much I will my mind to quieten down, I just can't seem to switch off, the knowledge that there is a threat to my family that seems to grow closer with every passing day has me on edge. The slightest noise throughout the night has me on high alert, enough that I have my gun loaded and ready to go, stuffed under my pillow in case I need it.

I've never been one to worry, but lately it's all I seem to do. I've never had anything to lose before, but the near catastrophic events from the other day shocked me awake and made me realise what's right in front of me. Now I have a daughter to think about and a woman who's more important to me than I first thought.

Two people I'm terrified of losing.

Two people I can't seem to live without.

We need to find this prick. *Fast.*

The shit with the car was way too fucking close for my liking, we barely got out of it alive and we were lucky, any closer and it could be a totally different story.

Derek clears his throat. "I ran a check on the vehicle our guy was driving, and as suspected it wasn't his. It was reported stolen a couple of hours before the incident. I did however manage to pick up his face on one of the CCTV cameras as he fled the scene, it's not a clear image, but I think you'll recognise him." Derek spins the laptop around on his lap to face us.

"The guy from the break in, and the one I saw watching us at the mall."

Derek nods. "The very same. Got a name for you too, I got a couple actually, but one being Stephen Thomas."

My heart lurches. *What the fuck?* "Wait, Stephen Thomas as in Yvonne's abusive ex?" Gage and I exchange a look.

"Who's Yvonne?" Alec asks.

"Ivy's birth mom," I answer. "We think he used to abuse her. Think he had something to do with her death too."

Gage rounds his desk and comes to stand over me, cursing under his breath when he sees the face staring back at us on the screen. "That's definitely him. Who is he? Did we get any background info on him?"

"Turns out his real name is Warren Vickers," Derek continues. "Thirty years old. Ex-Army, got dishonourably discharged six years ago for interrogating a prisoner using unethical methods of torture. He was also found to have sexually assaulted a number of women while they were detained."

"Fuck..." My hands form fists as rage floods my veins.

He abuses women... He's a dead man walking.

This man was around my daughter. He could have done anything to her. He could have done anything to her mother, or maybe he did...

"So he has form, but why would he want to kill Yvonne?" Gage asks.

I stand up and pace the room. "Does there have to be a motive? For all we know he could be some sick sadistic prick who enjoys hurting women. Maybe it was a sex game gone wrong and he covered it up to look like she fell? Maybe they were fighting and he pushed her? Maybe Yvonne found out what a sick bastard he was and killed her to keep her quiet. He could have been abusing her for months... Fuck knows if he laid a hand on Ivy, she has nightmares about him, she could be too fucking scared to speak out."

"But what does he want? Why would he go to such lengths as try to run you down in broad daylight surrounded by dozens of witnesses?" Alec asks.

"To fuck with us? Who knows. But we need to find this prick. I hate how close he got the other day and I won't allow Reese or my daughter to be in any more danger than they already are. I..." My voice falters as I sink back down onto the sofa, scrubbing a hand over my stubbled face. "I can't lose them."

This fear building inside me has my throat closing up with the thought.

A hand squeezes my shoulder and I glance up to meet Gage's eyes. "We'll find this son of a bitch, brother. I swear. *Your* girls are going to be fine." I don't miss his emphasis of the word *your* girls.

My girls.

Alec steps forward. "So this guy, he's the one who's been behind all of this. Was he behind the text message too?"

"We don't know, but nothing suggests that they're related. If he wanted to get to Rafe, why was the message sent to me? Right now, they're two separate things, but we need to find him and figure this shit out," Gage replies.

"Where is he now? Does he have any family, any connections at all?"

Derek shakes his head. "I haven't found anything that would suggest it, no links to anybody else, not yet at least. I tracked him down one of the side streets on the outskirts of town but I lost sight of him, the CCTV there is near non-existent. He's laying low, but I'll keep looking. I'll find him."

"I just don't get why he'd break into the club? For what reason?" I ask.

"To find a loophole, any weaknesses or ways in to allow him to gain access to you and Ivy," Gage suggests.

"And the fact he was so blatant in the mall. He didn't even try to hide, it was like he wanted me to see him watching us. Like him being there was a warning."

None of this makes sense.

My phone buzzes in my pocket and I reach in to see Reese's name lighting up my screen.

"Hey."

"You need to come home, *now*."

Her words have my blood running cold. "Why, what's wrong? Are you okay?"

Three sets of eyes find me as my voice comes out panicked as I clutch the phone tighter.

"Yeah, I'm fine, it's nothing bad. The social worker's here, Amanda... *something*, I can't remember."

"Sampson," I offer, sighing with relief.

"Yeah, that's it."

Shit. I forgot that was today. With everything going on it completely slipped my mind. "I'll be home in ten."

"Oh, and she's under the impression I'm your girlfriend, God knows why." *Oops, my bad.*

"Tell her I'm caught up in traffic or something and that I'll be there as soon as I can." I hang up and rise from the sofa. "I gotta go, Ivy's social worker showed up from Austin. I forgot the meeting was today."

"No worries, you go to your daughter," my brother says.

"Let me know when you find this bastard, *I* wanna be the one to pull the trigger."

Gage smiles. "You'll be first in line."

∞∞∞

Reese and Amanda are sat in the living room when I arrive home, with Ivy sat cross-legged on the floor in front of them playing with her dolls while Merlin nuzzles himself against her leg.

Ivy's eyes snap up when she sees me, a wide smile breaking out on her face. She jumps to her feet and races towards me. "Daddy!"

Before she can crash head-on into me, I bend to lift her into my arms while her arms and legs go around me. I press a kiss to her cheek. "Hey, sweetheart."

"I'm so happy you're back, I missed you."

My heart swells. "I missed you too, Ives."

"Mandy's here! See? I told her all about how you saved Reesie and me from that car and that you're my hero!"

Shit. I had hoped Amanda wouldn't hear about that.

Amanda rises from the couch. "It's good to see you again, Mr. Hudson, or should I say Superdad?" she says with a laugh, extending her hand to me.

"You too, I apologise for being late, I'm sure I don't have to tell you about city traffic."

"You definitely don't."

I take a seat beside Reese, placing Ivy on my lap while I pull Reese against me and press a kiss to her lips. "Hey, baby."

She smiles up at me. "Hey yourself."

Out of the corner of my eye, I can see Amanda watching the exchange between us. When she called to arrange the meeting, I happened to mention that Reese was my girlfriend. Don't ask me why I said it, I guess it sounded better than fuck buddy, but maybe it's not such a bad thing. Maybe it gives her the impression that we have a more solid foundation on which to raise Ivy, as a family.

"Ivy, why don't you go and play in your room, while I talk to your daddy?" Amanda suggests.

"Okay." Ivy slides off my knee and reaches for the cat before disappearing down the hallway.

Amanda closes her folder on her lap and leans forward. "Before you arrived, I spoke with Ivy, and I must say, she is a completely different girl to the one I left you with. I never expected such a profound change in her in just a couple of months. She seems to have settled in very well. It's lovely to see her so at ease and happy here with her family where she belongs."

"It took her a while to open up, but I think Reese helped

with a lot of that, and I suppose I should also show the cat credit where it's due." Merlin has quickly become Ivy's best friend, so much so, that the fur ball even sleeps in her room, curled up beside her on her bed. And as much as I hate to admit it, Reese was right, he *is* good for her, and seeing the two of them together makes me hate the cat a little less.

Reese chuckles beside me. "I told you he'd grow on you."

"And how are you, Rafe?" Amanda asks. "I remember how bewildered you were that day walking into my office with your brother."

I settle back into the sofa, my arm slung around Reese's shoulders. "When you first called me, telling me I had a daughter, I was dealing with some stuff. I'd recently lost my father to cancer and I was close to spiralling into depression or alcoholism, whichever came first, I guess. But as cliché as it's going to sound, Ivy's changed my life. She saved me. I never in a million years would have imagined my life turning out like this, but now I can't imagine it any other way. She gave me purpose, something to fight for. I've got my girls and that's all I need."

Reese softens beside me.

"And you Reese? How are you with everything?" Amanda asks.

"I love her like she was my own daughter. My own childhood was far from a happy one, and I don't want that for Ivy. She's an incredible girl and she deserves the world."

"She certainly does. I'd just like to ask about your relationship, if I may?"

"It's a relatively new development. Reese is a close friend of my family and we've known each other for some time. Ivy struggled the first couple of weeks and I asked Reese for help.

From there, we found we had a connection and I honestly don't know where I'd be without her. She's an incredible woman and I'm lucky to have her."

I glance down at Reese whose eyes are swimming with tears. I'm not sure whether she's crying because she thinks I'm saying all of this for Amanda's benefit, but I mean every single one of them.

That night at Sierra's party when I told Alec I had no more room left in my heart to care, I'm not sure that was true, because I'm positive that since the night I spent with Reese all those months ago, there was space in there somewhere reserved for the girl with emerald eyes peering up at me now, I just hadn't realised it yet.

Half an hour later, and after saying goodbye to Ivy, Reese and I walk Amanda to the front door.

"It was wonderful to meet you, Reese. I'm confident that Ivy is going to thrive here with you both," Amanda starts, "I'll check in with you in a few weeks, but should you need any support in the meantime, just give me a call."

"Thank you," Reese says.

"You have a beautiful family here," Amanda comments with a warm smile.

I bring Reese into me, tucking her into my side. "Thank you."

Reese stiffens beside me, and once Amanda has gone, Reese swivels out of my hold.

"You okay?" I ask.

She forces a smile. "Yeah. I'm gonna go take a shower."

I watch as she disappears down the corridor, the bathroom door opening and closing a minute later.

I consider leaving her to it, but I hate that something is

bothering her, and dread sinks in my stomach at the thought that it might be me.

I head into the bedroom and strip off my clothes, finding Reese under the hot spray of the shower with her back to me, the view in front of me has my cock hard in an instant.

Stepping into the shower, she tenses when she feels me behind her, but relaxes when my arms wind around her middle.

"You sure you're okay?" I ask, smoothing her hair away from her face and resting my chin on her shoulder.

"Fine," she says quietly.

"Then why don't I believe you?"

"It's nothing. Just..." She spins to face me. "Just make me feel good."

My mouth is on hers the second the words leave her mouth, backing her up against the cold tiles behind her while my mouth slides over hers.

I reach down and lift her, guiding her legs around my waist, rocking my hips so that my cock rubs against her pussy, gliding through her slick folds.

"You drive me fucking crazy, baby," I say against her lips while her fingers tangle in my wet hair. "Need to fuck you so bad."

"So fuck me. I want it hard. Fuck me like you hate me."

"But I don't hate you." *I could never hate her.*

"Maybe it would be easier if you did."

I have no idea what that means, but I'm too turned on to think on it. "You want it hard?"

She nods.

I release her, spinning her to face the tiles and push down on her back so it bows, her tits pressed up tightly against the tiles, her beautiful ass sticking out, ready for me.

I unhook the shower head from the bracket on the wall and bring it down and aiming it directly on her clit and a strangled moan escapes her lips.

"Give me that pussy, baby." I grip her hip with my free hand and tug her back so she arches even more. I kick her feet apart and sink my cock inside her tight heat with ease.

I don't give her time to adjust before I take her roughly, pounding into her from behind with wild abandon.

My grip tightens on her hip as I thrust harder, *deeper*, a moan escaping her with every single one.

I'll never get enough of this woman. She's like every wet dream and every fantasy I've ever had rolled into one.

"Oh my god, Rafe." Her fingernails bite into the grouting between the tiles as I bring the head of the shower closer to her pussy, making sure the angle hits her clit just right that I'll have her screaming for me.

"You gonna come for me, Reese? You gonna come on this cock like a good little whore? That's what you are aren't you? My dirty little whore?"

My dirty words tip her over the edge and she squeezes my cock, her body shuddering as her orgasm wracks through her.

I ride her through her release, keeping my pace steady as I chase after my own.

"Where do you want me to come, baby?"

"In my mouth."

I pull out of her and push her down to her knees in front of me. She wastes no time in guiding me into her mouth, sucking off her juices that coat my dick as she takes me to the back of her throat.

Putting the shower head back onto the hook above us, the

hot spray rains down on us as she licks my cock like her favourite lollipop before sucking me back down into her throat.

The palm of my hand slaps against the tiles as my stomach clenches with the need to release, while my other hand fists her hair.

She moans around my cock as I begin thrusting into her mouth, and I look down to see her eyes on me as my length disappears between her lips.

It's the hottest fucking thing I've ever seen.

My balls tighten, and I don't have enough time to warn her I'm about to come before my orgasm takes hold. I come down her throat with a roar and she takes me so well, her eyes fixed onto my face as my cum spurts into her mouth, dripping out of the corners of her lips.

When I finally start to come down, I pull out and she releases me with a pop, swallowing everything I had to give her down with ease.

I lift her from her knees and smash my lips to hers, pulling her body closer as my cock begins to soften between us.

I rest my forehead against hers.

This woman has me feeling like I'm in heaven when I should *definitely* be in hell, repenting for all the things I've done, but that would mean being without her, and I'm certainly not ready for that.

When we step out of the shower, she keeps her back to me as she reaches for a towel to dry herself off.

"I'm gonna go order us some food. Is pizza okay with you?" I ask.

She shrugs. "I'm not really hungry."

"Hey, are you sure you're alright? You've been really quiet

since Amanda left."

"I'm fine. I have a headache, is all. I'm gonna go lie down for a while." Her feeble attempt at a smile doesn't have me convinced, and as she disappears into the bedroom, I decide to give her the benefit of the doubt, but in my gut, I'm certain something is wrong.

30

Reese

I should've seen this coming, or maybe I did and chose to look the opposite way. No, it was my own selfishness that lead me here, my desire for a man I could never truly call my own clouded my better judgement.

I thought I could do it. I thought I could keep my feelings in check, but it was always going to be impossible.

What did I expect was going to happen when I entered into a strictly no-strings relationship with a guy I already had feelings for? There was only ever going to be one outcome—me ending up with a broken heart. And as history has proven, I have a habit of making the wrong decisions, and none of them I've learned from, *clearly*.

Maybe I'm a coward, or maybe it's my self-preservation instinct that has me throwing handfuls of clothes into a suitcase that lies open on the bed—jumping ship before I get hurt even more. The longer I drag this out, the worse it's going to be, so it's best I rip the Band-Aid off now before I get any deeper.

I stuff my suitcase full, not particularly caring what I'm packing, just throwing in random things because I can't see for the tears blurring my vision.

The funny thing is, none of this is Rafe's fault. For the first time in my life a man wasn't the one breaking my heart. No, that was all *me*. He's the innocent party in all of this, as is Ivy.

Shit… Ivy.

My heart clenches when her face flashes before my eyes. What do I tell her? How do I explain that I'm leaving in a way that won't hurt her? Who the hell am I kidding, whichever way I try and explain, she's going to be crushed.

What kind of sick person earns the trust of a broken little girl with abandonment issues, only to break her heart all over again by leaving? *Me*. That's who.

"Ree? What's going on?" My stomach sinks at the sound of Rafe's voice behind me.

I square my shoulders as I turn to face him and the frown he's wearing deepens when he sees the tears pooling in my eyes. "I can't do this anymore, Rafe."

"Do what?"

"*This*, you and me. Whatever this is or isn't between us."

His eyes a mix of fear and confusion as they search my own. "I don't understand."

I shift my eyes to the ceiling, willing myself to stay strong and not break down in tears before returning my gaze to him. "I lied to you when I said I was okay with our relationship being purely physical, that there'd be no feelings involved because I already had feelings for you before we even started."

He blinks at me wordlessly, and there's a long pause before

he speaks. "We agreed it was just sex."

"I know, which is why I lied. I figured if it was the only way I could have you, then I'd force my feelings aside and do my best to ignore them, but I couldn't." I was lying to myself for thinking I could do it.

He swallows hard, processing my words. "I..."

"You don't have to say anything, Rafe. I brought all of this on myself, I know that. I shouldn't have let it go on for so long." I zip up my suitcase and drag it to stand on the floor beside me, making a move for the door.

He steps sideways, blocking my path. "Hold up a sec. What brought all this on? What's changed? We were fine."

"Everything's changed, Rafe. Everything changed between us the second I agreed to this, but the longer I spend here with you, the deeper I get and the harder it hurts knowing I can never have you like that," I say, my stomach twisting as I force myself to meet his eyes.

"It was earlier wasn't it? The whole pretending to be my girlfriend thing with Amanda? I'm sorry I told her that you were, I just figured it would be easier to lie than explain the truth."

"But that's just it. I didn't have to pretend. I wanted it to be real and for an hour or two, it was, but I deserve more than to be the stand-in girlfriend whenever it suits you."

"You know it's not like that. You mean more to me than that," he protests.

I cock my head. "Do I?"

"Y-Yes," he stammers.

"Do you love me?" I blurt out.

He hesitates. His mouth opens and then immediately closes, like something in his brain is telling him not to speak.

"Rafe, do you *love* me?" I repeat.

The longer the silence hangs between us, my eyes holding his, I can feel my heart splintering into pieces in my chest. He doesn't need to speak, his silence is answer enough.

I step closer to him so there's a matter of inches separating us. "Look me in the eye and tell me that you feel nothing for me. That everything that's happened these past couple of months meant nothing to you."

I search his eyes. "You can't say it can you? Well, I'll tell you what you mean to me, shall I? You're everything I've always wanted, Rafe. Being here with you, helping raise your daughter, being part of a family is everything I've dreamed of." My fingernails digging into my palms to keep the tears that sting my eyes at bay. "I never expected to fall as hard and fast as I have for you, but that's why I have to leave. It's killing me inside. I'll come back for the rest of my stuff another time." I grab my suitcase and shove past him out of the bedroom, dragging it behind me as I head towards the front door.

"Reese, please don't go," he calls after me and I stop, my heart pounding in my chest as I fight off a wave of tears.

I turn back to face him. "Give me one reason why I should stay."

"The job." I'd almost forgotten that he's been paying me ever since I moved in. Jesus, that makes this whole thing sound so cheap.

"Then I guess this is my official resignation."

"Reesie?" I glance behind Rafe where Ivy stands, her teddy bear clutched to her chest as she looks between me and the suitcase. "Where are you going?"

Dropping to a crouch, I open my arms for her and she's hesitant as she nears me. I pull her into me and she rests her head against my chest. "I have to go away for a while, sweetie."

She peeks up at me, her eyes glistening with tears. "But why? Don't you love me anymore?"

My heart squeezes. "Of course, I love you, Ivy. I'll always love you, don't for one second think that I don't."

Her chin wobbles as a single tear trickles down her face. "You're not going where my mommy is, are you?"

A cry escapes my lips as I press a kiss to the top of her head while a tear drips down my face. "No, no I'm not. I promise. I'll always be here if you need me. I just need to be by myself for a while."

She clings to me, her little arms banding around my neck. "But I don't want you to go," she cries, her tears wetting my shirt.

"I know, sweetie. I'm so so sorry."

How did I not see this coming? How did I think Ivy was going to react to watching me walk away from her? After everything she's been through, she more than anyone doesn't deserve any of this.

"Can you still visit me?" she asks with a sniff.

I hug her tighter. "Of course, I can. Try keeping me away from you. But can you do something for me while I'm gone? I need you to take really good care of Merlin for me for a while. Wherever I go, he might not be welcome there, but I know you'll look after him for me. Can you do that?"

She nods weakly. "I'll look after him real good."

"And you take care of your daddy for me, okay?" My eyes find his over Ivy's shoulder. "He needs all the love he doesn't think he deserves." My voice cracks and I'm almost certain there's moisture gathering in Rafe's eyes.

"Don't worry, Reesie. I'm gonna give Daddy *all* the hugs

and kisses," Ivy says.

"Good girl." I give her one last drawn-out hug before she disappears back down the hallway to her bedroom, giving me a small teary-eyed wave as she goes.

"You don't have to leave, Ree," Rafe says as I rise back to my feet.

"Yeah, I do. Seeing you every day, wanting something I can't have is too painful, so I'm taking myself out of the equation."

"I told you a long time ago that I'm not the hearts and flowers sort of guy." It's true, he did, but I fell for him anyway.

"And I told you I don't want Prince Charming, I don't need the fairy tale because what I want is right in front of me," I say. "You want to know what I think? I think you're scared. You're terrified to admit that you feel something for me because you somehow think you don't deserve it, that it makes you weak, but it doesn't. Love gives you strength you never knew you had. I know you feel the same about me as I do you, the only difference is, I have the courage to say it. What are you so scared of, Rafe? Why are you so afraid to admit you feel something for me? Why are you so scared to let me love you?"

He swallows hard, his gaze dropping from mine for a split-second. "Where will you go?"

"I don't know. Maybe a hotel, or crash at Della and Gage's place for the night until I figure something out."

"You can go back to your old apartment," he suggests.

"I got evicted, and I'm sure as hell not grovelling to that prick for my apartment back."

"You don't have to. It's yours. Had it renovated and refurbished. I actually bought the whole building for next to nothing after it turned out he'd been tax-dodging and intimidating his lodgers. Told him I'd report him if he didn't agree to my terms."

Oh my God. "But... Why?"

He shrugs. "I know how much you loved it there, despite its questionable neighbourhood and it being the size of a dog kennel. But it was yours. It was so that after the job with Ivy was over, you'd have somewhere to go."

I don't realise I'm crying until a tear drips onto my boob.

Is he doing this on purpose? Is he trying make it twice as hard to walk away from him?

Who knew this incredibly reserved man who keeps his cards tight to his chest, who shies away from his feeling could be so thoughtful in his own way?

"Let me give you a ride, or at least let me see you to your car."

I shake my head. "You don't have to worry about me. The way I'm feeling right now, no attacker would dare try it on with me."

One corner of his mouth twitches, but only sadness fills his eyes.

Taking in a deep breath, I close the gap between us and reach up onto my toes, pressing a chaste kiss to his mouth, letting it linger there a little longer than I should, savouring the feel of him one last time. When I pull back, his eyes are red and glassy as he peers down at me, though his eyes dart down to the floor briefly as if trying to hide it.

"Reese," he whispers.

"You're an amazing man, Rafe, *believe* it. For the first time in my life, you're the only man who has never broken my heart. This time I broke my own." I give him a tight-lipped smile before spinning on my heel and starting towards the door, but I stop and turn to look back over my shoulder.

"I love you, Rafe Hudson. I just wish you were brave enough to love me back." And with that, I grab my suitcase and pull open the front door, disappearing out into the corridor without looking back.

31

Reese

My eyes are raw and heavy as I make my way up my old apartment. My head thumps out a hard, steady rhythm while my heart feels like it's been clawed out by a werewolf, my chest now a gaping chasm to where my heart used to be.

I don't think I stopped crying once on the drive over here. It was as if someone turned on a faucet and left it running and no matter how hard I tried to stop, the tears kept on falling, every single one of them more painful than the one before.

As hard as it was walking away from Rafe, I know in whatever is left of my heart that it was the right thing to do, for all of us. Dragging it out any longer would have only prolonged the agony and hurt us all even worse.

Why is Rafe so afraid to confess his feelings? I know he feels something, I'm not imagining it. I *felt* it in the way he touched me, how he held me close while we drifted off to sleep in each other's arms. I felt it in his tender kisses and through his soft words, so why won't he admit it?

Is it out of fear? Pride? Whatever it is, it's holding him back, I just wish he'd be strong enough to confront it.

Once inside the apartment, I flick on the light and take a look around. It looks *nothing* like the apartment I left. Rafe wasn't kidding about the renovations. All new furniture fills the space, a grey leather sofa taking up the centre, a glass coffee table and flat screen TV secured to the wall opposite. Gone is the peeling wallpaper and the discoloured paint. Gone is the threadbare carpet my landlord refused to replace on a number of occasions. Now it's a full plush grey that feels like clouds beneath my feet. The old kitchen has been switched out with all new appliances, everything a gleaming white that's almost blinding.

I head for the bedroom to find that it too has been updated. A brand new double bed commands the centre of the room while the built in mirrored wardrobes makes the room look twice the size as it bounces the reflections back. And to top it off, it's been decorated in grey and purple, my favourite colour.

I sit down on the edge of the bed and feel a rush of emotion surge up inside of me like a tidal wave as the tears begin to fall again. He knew my favourite colour, and I don't remember ever telling him about it.

What's more, all of my belongings that I sent to storage are all here, in almost exactly the same place as they were originally.

Since the fridge is completely empty, I order a takeout and spend the rest of the night in front of the TV, watching some ridiculously apt movie about unrequited love and heartache that has me bawling with tears for the last thirty minutes.

I can almost hear Rafe's laughter beside me, how he'd find it hilarious that I become so invested in a movie that it has me crying like a baby at the slightest thing.

My heart jumps when my phone pings with an incoming message, my pulse spiking when I see Rafe's name on my screen.

Rafe: Checking in to make sure you made it home safe.

I don't know what I was expecting to find, maybe a confession that he'd made a mistake and that he loves me after all, but the fact he cares enough to see I got home safe eases a little of the ache in my chest.

I'm about to type out a reply when another message comes in.

Rafe: I never wanted you to get hurt.

Me: I'm home, thanks. And... Ditto.

I toss my phone on the couch next to me and let out a heavy sigh.

God, it's only been a few hours and I miss him already. It seems walking out was only the beginning. The withdrawals from not seeing him and Ivy every day are going to be much harder, I just need to find a way through this so that I make it out the other side.

∞∞∞

The next morning, for the first time in months, I wake up alone, and the empty side of the bed somehow feels colder than it should. It feels weird to be back in my old apartment, I feel like a stranger in a place that was my home for years. No matter how hard I try, I can't seem to drag myself out of bed, and it's only when I'm dozing back off to sleep that my phone vibrates with a call.

My heart sinks when Sierra's name lights up the screen rather than Rafe's.

"Get your lazy ass out of bed and get dressed," she orders. "Della and I are taking you for brunch. We're parked outside your apartment."

"How did you know I was here?" I ask groggily.

"Uh… Rafe might've mentioned it."

"I appreciate you're trying to cheer me up, but I'm really not in the mood."

"I don't care. You're coming, end of discussion. Now hustle! You have ten minutes until I'm coming up there." The line goes dead and I fall back against my pillow with a groan.

Swinging my legs out of bed, I take a quick shower and pull on a pair of jeans and a sweater. I don't even bother to style my hair or do my makeup, because if truth be told, I really don't care enough.

After climbing into the car that idles outside my building, to my relief Della and Si leave me alone as Alec drives us to wherever the girls decided, and the silence is a welcome reprieve.

"What do you want to eat?" Si asks, sliding a menu across the table to me as we sit in a cafe I've never been to before.

"I'm not really hungry."

"You have to eat something," she insists.

"No, I don't. I didn't even want to come here in the first place," I snap.

"We just wanted to help," Della says softly and guilt claws at me.

"Look, I'm sorry. I— This is why I didn't want to come. All I'll do is make you guys miserable so you should've just left me be."

"You could never make us miserable," Si says.

Della smiles. "Besides, you were there for me when Gage and I had problems, I just want to be there for you too."

"We both do," Si adds.

I give them a small smile. "Thanks. I'll survive. I've gone through more breakups than Taylor Swift, I should be an expert in this by now."

"But I'm sensing this is the hardest one." It's not a question, and Della knows it.

I nod. "I should've known it would turn out like this. More fool me, huh?"

"My brother's an idiot if he let you go."

"But that's just it, he isn't. What happened between us was never supposed to involve feelings, he kept his end of the bargain and I didn't. I brought it all on myself and in the process, I've hurt Ivy. It would be so much easier if I could hate Rafe, but I don't think I ever could." I blink back tears as I speak.

"Hey." Della's hand lands on mine, giving it a comforting squeeze. "It'll be okay."

My eyes fall to Alec who's sat on the table just behind us, his eyes scanning the room before training on the door. "Enough about me. What's happening with Kevin Costner over there?" I ask Sierra, nodding my head towards Alec.

"Huh?"

"Please tell me you've watched *The Bodyguard*."

Her blank expression gives me the answer I need.

"Okay, movie night needs to happen, we need to get some culture in this girl. How is it possible you've never seen it? It's a classic. Whitney Houston falls in love with the bodyguard assigned to protect her," I explain.

"That is not what's happening," she denies.

"Really? Because he watches you like a hawk and you literally have drool coming out of your mouth every time he's near you, so..."

"Yeah, it's... never gonna happen," she replies, a flash of disappointment in her eyes.

"Never say never. You two would make the hottest couple."

My phone buzzes in my pocket and I pull it out to see my grandmother's care home calling me.

"I have to take this," I say before excusing myself from the table.

"Hello?"

"Reese? It's Gloria. I thought I should let you know your grandmother had a fall earlier today."

My stomach lurches. "Is she okay?"

"She's a little shaken but she's alright. She doesn't appear to have broken anything and there's no sign of concussion, she's at the hospital just as a precaution. You're welcome to visit her if you'd like?"

"Of course. I'm on my way." I hang up and head back to Della and Sierra. "Hey, I'm so sorry, I have to go. My grandmother's had a fall."

Della gasps. "Oh my God, is she alright?"

"I think so. I'm gonna go see her now."

"Let us know how she is, okay? And if you need us, you know where we are."

"Thanks. Love you both."

Doesn't life just like to kick you in the tits when you're already down on the ground?

31

∞∞∞

"Hey, Nanna," I greet, standing in the doorway to her hospital room half an hour later.

She's tucked up in bed, staring vacantly off into nowhere like she does most of the time these days. The thin, pale skin of her left arm marred with dark angry bruises, but thankfully, there's no signs she hit her head when she fell.

"Nanna?" I repeat.

Her tired eyes meet mine and she gives me a weak smile. "Abby?"

My heart sinks. "No, Nanna. It's me, Reesie." I force a hopeful smile.

She tuts. "I know who it is! Come sit, Reesie girl."

An older man in a white coat enters the room and smile when he sees me. "Good afternoon, I'm Doctor Gaines, I'll be seeing to Mavis' care while she's here."

"I'm Reese, her granddaughter. Did she break anything with the fall?" I ask.

"We've X-Rayed your grandmother and as far as we can tell, she was lucky. However, we did notice a hairline fracture on her collarbone, most probably from the impact. I would like to keep her in overnight for observation just to be on the safe side."

"Thank you."

"If you need anything, one of the nurses will be along shortly," he says before leaving.

"Do you need me to bring you anything?" I ask.

She shakes her head, her eyes off elsewhere. "No."

"This room is isn't too bad. You've got your own bathroom and a huge TV... Maybe we should move in?" I joke.

I turn back to my grandmother who's entire expression has altered.

"Nanna?"

"I don't like it here, Reesie. Take me home with you?"

"Nanna, I—I can't. This is the best place for you, you know that. They can help you here."

The look in her wide eyes as they bore into me is one of panic, a wildness in her stare as it scares me.

"Nonsense. The best place for me is in *my* home. The people here are s-strangers." She grabs my hand in a suffocating grip, with a strength I never knew she had. "Don't leave me here, Reesie. Please. I don't like it here. I can't I— I do— I..."

I jump to my feet and wrap my arms around her, stroking her grey, thinning hair. "Nanna, calm down," I soothe. "It's okay. I'm here. It's alright..."

After a minute or two, her erratic breathing slowly returns to normal as I hold her, rocking her gently back and forth until she begins to calm down, repeating my words over and over until they start to take effect.

"Nanna? Are you alright?" I ask, pulling back only to find her staring off into space again, her eyes vacant, all of the pain and panic from a few moments ago has completely vanished.

A cry lodges itself in my throat.

Taking her calm state as an opportunity to leave without causing her further distress, I lean in and press a kiss to her wrinkled forehead, though she doesn't acknowledge me again. "I love you, Nanna. Never forget that."

32

Emptiness…

That's all I've felt since the moment she walked out my front door.

I somehow fooled myself into believing it would get easier, that missing her would hurt a little less the longer time went on, but *oh* how wrong I was. The past few days without her have been rough. Rougher than I ever imagined they could be. I can't believe how quickly I became accustomed to having her around in such a short amount of time. How her laughter bounced off every wall, how her joy and her light filled every inch of my apartment without her even trying. How good she made me feel.

The silence in my apartment is deafening, like all the sound and the laughter was sucked out like a vacuum the minute she left. She filled that silence, that empty space that isn't just in my apartment, but in my heart too.

She was right when she said that when you lose someone, you lose a part of yourself when they leave, because I haven't felt like myself since she walked out the door.

I miss her. The crippling ache in my chest is the only reminder that everything Reese and I had was real, that the last few months weren't all in my head. It's an ache I haven't felt since I lost my dad all those months ago.

Loss.

Guilt.

Heartbreak.

The loss of a love I had but was too stupid to realise at the time, and the guilt of hurting the woman who means so much to me, kills me. My heart breaks for her, and for me.

It's a feeling I hate.

It makes me feel sick to my stomach and I want it all to stop.

It's had me tossing and turning for the past couple of nights, unable to quieten my overactive mind and drift off to sleep. Tonight, the frustration and lack of sleep got too much, that's why I've been sat on my bathroom floor since three a.m. with a razor blade pinched between my fingers, hovering over the raised scars on my thighs I put there when I was a kid.

I need a release. I need a diversion, a distraction to the thoughts that plague my mind, thoughts I haven't had in so long.

Worthless…

A disappointment…

All you do is let the people around you down…

My hand trembles as I bring the blade closer to my skin, bracing myself for the initial sting as the metal slices my flesh, followed by the stab of pain that shoots through my body as it sinks deeper and the feeling of euphoria that follows, the rush of calm.

Of *peace.*

I crave that feeling right now.

Just as the tip of the razor touches my skin, the bathroom door to my right swings open a fraction, and Merlin strolls in heading straight towards me. He nuzzles his head into my arm, a deep purr rumbling through him before he jumps into my lap and makes himself comfortable there.

A few months ago, I'd have shoved him off me, but I can't get over the fact he picked *that* specific moment to come in.

I was as if he knew what I was going to do.

It was like a sign. From *her...*

If you ever feel like that again, that you need a release, that things get so bad you consider cutting yourself or drowning in a bottle of booze... Drown in me, get lost in me...

My heart sinks as her words echo in my mind. Without realising it, the blade clinks to the tiled floor beneath me, and I find myself holding onto this mass of fur I've come to love on my lap as a tear slides down my face.

All my life I've forced myself not to cry, determined to not let my emotions get the better of me, thinking it made me weak. But this time I don't hold them back. I let my tears fall. I cry for my dad, I cry for my daughter, for Reese, and I cry for *me*. Everything pours out of me as a sob wracks through me, all the while clutching onto the one connection I have left with Reese.

I made her a promise to find her when things got so bad I felt like hurting myself, and despite my track record for keeping them isn't great, I'm going to make sure I keep this one.

I won't let her down, not anymore.

∞∞∞

"We got him," Gage says through the phone, the next day, and my body goes still.

I know exactly what those words mean.

Warren Vickers *aka* Stephen Thomas.

I've been waiting for this phone call and here it is. My heart begins to hammer against my ribs as I grip the phone tighter.

"Where?"

"The old warehouse, you know the place. We're waiting for you." Gage hangs up and I'm on my feet, swiping my car keys from the table in the hallway and hurrying towards the front door.

"Daddy, where're you going?" A little voice asks. I whirl around to find Ivy stood against the wall behind me.

"I just have to go out for a while. I won't be long, if you need anything ask Reese okay?"

It isn't until I say her name out loud that reality hits me like a sack of bricks.

Reese...

"But Daddy, Reesie's gone," Ivy says, her eyebrows knitting together.

"Shit," I mutter, running a hand through my hair. "I'm sorry, sweetheart. I totally forgot." I move towards her and lift her into my arms.

"I want Reesie to come back," she says, her chin beginning to tremble.

I clutch her tighter, smoothing a hand over her raven hair. "Me too, sweetheart. Me too. Come on, I'll drop you off with Auntie Sierra for a while, okay?"

"But you'll come back for me, right?"

My heart squeezes. The fear of abandonment is evident in her voice and it kills me that fear is still there. I want to chase it away.

"Always. You're my whole world, sweetheart. Nothing will ever keep me away from you."

I kiss her forehead before heading for the door.

Once I've dropped Ivy off with my sister, I pull up outside the abandoned warehouse on the edge of town twenty minutes later, the memories from the last time I was here hitting me full force as I head inside.

I almost lost my brother and Della here last year.

I killed Bryce Tanner here. Shot him without a moment's hesitation. It was him or my brother, and I wasn't about to watch my brother die.

The warehouse is huge, sat neglected and abused by years of vandalism and bad weather. The windows have been smashed and the walls sprayed with graffiti. The smell of damp hangs in the air, and the odour of something decaying turns my stomach.

As I move further into the building, the sound of voices catch my attention, pointing me in the right direction, and not a minute later, I find who I'm looking for.

Thomas, or rather *Vickers,* whatever he chooses to call himself is tied to a chair. His back is to me, his hands bound together behind him with his ankles secured to the chair legs with zip ties.

Gage, Alec and a couple of other guys who work for my brother stand around him, each of their eyes lifting as I enter the space.

I move around the chair to face the man, and I'm surprised to find he's uglier up close, his lip is split in two places as dried blood begins to crust there. There's a cut to his eyebrow and sweat beads at his forehead and trickles down his neck.

"Warren Vickers, or should I call you Stephen Thomas?"

His eyes are cast down, refusing to meet mine as I speak.

"Whatever your name is makes no difference to me, but what I *do* care about is why you've been following me, why you tried to have me and my family killed."

Again, he says nothing in response and his silence only fuels my anger.

"I suggest you answer my brother," Gage says.

I draw up a chair and position it directly across from Vickers, and take a seat so that I'm sat just a few inches away.

"I heard about your time in the Army. Heard about your torture tactics. What were they? Waterboarding? Sleep deprivation? Beatings? Sexual assault? I hear you were very fond of the latter, particularly against helpless women."

His shoulders shake a fraction and I glance down to find a small smirk curling his mouth as he keeps his gaze trained to the ground.

"That what you did to Yvonne? Hmm? Why did you kill her?"

"Who says I did?" His voice is low and rough as sandpaper.

"*I* say. I find it very hard to believe she just tripped down the stairs. You terrified my daughter to the point of having nightmares, I'd say that's a big fucking red flag where you're concerned. So tell me, why did you hurt Yvonne? She didn't deserve what you did to her."

"The whore deserved everything she got," he spits. Our eye connect for the first time since I got here, with the same look of hatred and disdain I saw in the mall that day. "I'm only sorry I didn't get to her little bitch of a daughter, *boy* would I have had some fun wi—"

I don't realise I'm moving until my fist collides with the side of his face. Saliva and blood shower the both of us as his body slumps over, the chair balancing on two legs before tipping over. Still tied to the chair, Vickers lies on his side as I step over him.

"You piece of shit!" I hit him again and again, going at him like a raging bull as the bones in his cheek crunch beneath my fist. He lets out a deep groan as his eyes droop and his body goes limp.

A hand lands on my shoulder as I pull back my fist to strike the prick again. "Rafe, stop," Gage says. "He's goading you. He never touched Ivy, we know that. He's just trying to rile you up."

I nod, standing back, my breaths coming in heavy pants as I tower over Vickers.

I grip the collar of his shirt and pull him upright, the chair creaking beneath him. A string of blood hangs from his mouth down to the cold grey concrete beneath us. He spits onto the ground and returns his gaze to the floor.

I return to my seat, taking a deep breath to steady my rapid heartbeat. "Why try to run us down? Why the break-in at the club? Who do you work for?"

Silence.

"*Who* do you work for?" I repeat, but he continues to say nothing. I lean in closer to him. "I have ways of making you talk, Vickers."

He snorts a laugh as his eyes flick up to meet mine. "None that'll work, 'cause I'm not saying shit to you." His words are slurred by his swollen, bloodied lip. "So I guess you'll have to kill me, *Hudson*."

"We get his phone?" I ask my brother, not taking my eyes off the piece of shit in front of me.

"Yeah, it's a burner. There's nothing on there of use to us, the only numbers programmed into it no longer exist, no trace of who they were registered to."

"Shit," I mumble.

Vickers chuckles under his breath, his blatant smugness only adding to the anger that boils in my blood.

I rise from the chair and begin pacing the floor in front of him. I pull out my gun from my waistband and turn it over in my hand, checking the clip, and flipping off the safety.

Torturing him into talking isn't going to work on a guy like him. He's ex-Army. Don't they undergo some sort of training for a situation like this? Trained to not give away any information regardless of the methods used to extract the truth?

"What are you thinking?" Gage asks, stepping closer to my side.

I raise my gun, aiming the barrel directly between his eyes.

Can I kill him in cold blood? Am I that man?

"Just kill the prick, man. With him dead, your family's safe. *Ivy's* safe," Alec offers behind me.

He's right. With Vickers dead, he's no longer a threat to not only my family, but to other women who cross his path. He won't be able to hurt anyone else.

The world will be a safer place.

Vickers laughs, a low rumble that carries through his chest, his eyes lifting to mine once again. "You have no idea."

The shot rings out, piercing my eardrums, the sound bouncing off the walls until it fades into nothing and Vickers' body slumps back into the chair, a trickle of blood coming from the bullet hole in his skull as his lifeless eyes stare down at the floor.

My stomach churns as nausea creeps up my throat but I force it back.

It *was him or my family,* I remind myself. *He was a murderer, a woman abuser.*

I don't know what I expected. I guess I thought I'd feel relieved to see him dead, to know I'm the one who rid him from this world and to know my family was now safe.

But I don't.

I feel nothing, only that the last words that prick spoke left a bad taste in my mouth.

"Get rid of him," Gage instructs his men. "Leave no trace."

"Yes, Sir," they reply in unison.

Gage claps a hand on my back proudly. "It's over, brother. They're all safe."

"You okay?" Gage asks as we make it outside, the cool crisp air a welcome feeling against the film of sweat that clings to my skin.

"Fine," I lie.

"Della told me about you and Reese. I'm sorry, brother. What happened?"

When we make it to my car, I turn to face him. "Same thing as always. I fucked everything up like I usually do."

"Why? Because you love her but you're too scared to admit it?"

"It's more complicated than that," I protest.

"I don't think it is. Seems pretty fucking simple to me. Don't let your stubbornness and your pride get in the way of being happy, because I'm telling you now, it'll be the biggest fucking mistake of your life letting that girl go."

"I don't know how I can be what she wants, what she *needs*."

"And you won't do until you take that leap. But trust me, I've seen how she looks at you, you are everything she needs and more. Don't sell yourself short, bro. You're a good man who's got a lot of love to give a girl, you've just got to learn to let love in."

33

Reese

"I'm very sorry to have to tell you like this, Reese, but your grandmother passed away earlier this morning."

My heart stops. My entire body goes stock still.

I hear the words but my brain refuses to register their meaning, like when you look at something but you're not sure if you're seeing things or not, like your eyes are deceiving you somehow.

I repeat the words in my head, but they don't make sense. They don't sound real. I don't *want* them to be real.

They can't be, *can they?*

"Reese? Are you there?" Gloria asks on the other end of the phone.

"I… I— I don't understand. I only saw her a few days ago…" *How is this happening?*

She was discharged from hospital after spending the night under observation. The bruises were fading, the fracture to her shoulder would heal in no time with enough rest. The doctors told me she would be okay.

She was *fine. Wasn't she?*

"I know. It was sudden, but it seems she died peacefully in her sleep." Gloria's voice is soft and comforting, cushioning the blow that just ripped my world apart.

My stomach sinks.

This *is* real.

A cry catches in my throat as I picture my Nanna all alone at the end, lying in a bed that wasn't in her home probably wondering why I wasn't there with her.

Tears burn in my eyes. I swallow down the lump. "Can I um… Can I come and see her?"

"Yes. The funeral director will be here in an hour or so. I'm so sorry, Reese. I can't imagine what you're going through."

"Thank you for letting me know, Gloria. I'll be there as soon as I can." I hang up and stand frozen in the middle of my kitchen trying to process the last few minutes.

She's gone.

I knew her dementia diagnosis a few years ago was in essence, a death sentence for her, a slow but steady decline in both her mental and physical state as the disease ravaged her brain. I just always assumed she'd be around for a long time. I fooled myself into thinking she'd always be there, just as she had when I was growing up because it was all I'd known. I couldn't imagine a time when she was no longer there, my brain just couldn't comprehend it. She was the only constant in my life, the only person in my life that I could rely on, and now I'm more alone than ever.

I've never lost a loved one before, so dealing with death is all new to me. It's so strange to think that I'm never going to talk to her again, never going to hear her laugh or see her smile, but more importantly, I never got to say goodbye.

I *need* to see her.

I grab my keys and my jacket and haul ass out of my apartment, taking two steps at a time until I reach the ground floor. I burst through the front door and head in the direction of my car, but my steps falter when I glance up to see Rafe walking towards me across the grass at the front of my building.

Why is he here?

My heart slams against my ribs as I take him in, looking every bit the man I've fallen so hard for, only his cheeks and jaw are covered in stubble and it looks as though his hair hasn't seen a brush in days—but somehow it makes him hotter than ever.

All the emotion from the past few days gets the better of me and before I know it, I'm running to him, the need to be close to him too strong.

He frowns when he sees me coming at him, and a second later, I crash into him.

His arms go around me instantly, taking my weight as my legs give way beneath me. "Reese? Ree? Are you okay?"

I cling to him tighter as an uncontrollable sob rips free, the tears I've tried holding in free falling down my face. My whole body trembles as I cry, my breaths short and jagged as I struggle for air.

"Ree?"

I don't care why Rafe is here, I don't care about what's happened between us, all I know is that I need this. I need the security of his embrace to ground me when the world around me is crumbling.

I need *him*.

He pulls back enough to peer down at me. He moves my hair out of the way and cups my face, swiping the tears away with his thumb.

"What's going on, baby?" His eyes flit between mine, worry knitting his brow.

I sniff. "N—Nanna. My grandmother... She's *gone*." My voice cracks as a whimper slips through.

His face falls. "Shit, Ree. I'm so sorry."

He reels me back in, his hand cradling my head against his warm, solid chest while his lips find the top of my head.

Sobs wrack through my body, my tears staining the front of his shirt but he doesn't seem to mind, he just holds me.

I draw back. "I need to go see her."

I go to shrug out of Rafe's hold but he catches my arm. "Let me take you. You can't drive like this."

Normally I'd protest, but he's right. I'm hysterical and I'll more than likely get into an accident if I get behind the wheel in this state.

With a slight nod of my head, he leads me to his car and helps me slide into the passenger seat before rounding the hood and climbing in the driver's side.

I wipe my eyes with the back of my sleeve and stare out the windshield as huge spots of rain hit the glass.

The engine rumbles to life, but before we drive away, Rafe reaches across the centre console and takes my hand in his, giving it a comforting squeeze.

"It'll be alright. You're not gonna go through this alone. I'm here, for as long as you need me, okay?" He gives me a small but sure smile before peeling away from the curb and onto the road and somehow, I don't doubt him for a second.

33

When we arrive at *Cedar Tree,* Gloria is the first to greet us. She pulls me into a tight hug, and the tears I've managed to suppress on the drive over here slip free.

"I'm so sorry, honey." She rubs small circles over my back soothingly.

"I can't believe she's gone."

"I know, it was a shock to all of us. Do you think you're ready to see her?" she asks.

"As ready as I'll ever be, I suppose."

"I'm right here," Rafe whispers into my ear. His arm slips around my waist, holding me close as Gloria leads us up to my grandmother's room.

We come to a stop outside her door, but before I go inside, my hand hesitates on the handle.

I turn around. "I don't know if I can go in there."

"You don't have to do this, honey." Gloria says softly.

"Yeah, I do. I need to say goodbye. I need to see her one last time." My eyes find Rafe. "Will you stay with me?"

He nods. "I'm not going anywhere."

I give him a weak smile before I turn back to the door, and taking a deep breath, I open it. My eyes instantly move to the bed where my grandmother lies content and still.

I move closer and lower myself into the chair beside her bed. Her eyes are closed tight, her skin paler than usual, dull, almost grey in colour.

I feel Rafe move in close behind me, his hand coming to rest on my shoulder.

"It's like she's sleeping. She looks so peaceful like this." I reach out my hand to touch hers but jerk back when I find it stone cold. I knew it would be, but I hadn't prepared myself for just how cold it would be.

"I should have been here, holding her hand at the end." A tear trickles down my cheek.

"You couldn't have known it would happen, and she wouldn't blame you for not being here," Rafe tells me.

"It breaks my heart to think of her all alone—" My voice cracks.

Rafe tips my chin to look at him. "You're here now, that's more time than I ever got with my dad. I couldn't bring myself to be there, but you're *here,* that's what matters."

I know he's right, but it doesn't make it hurt any less.

I rise from the chair and step closer to the bed. I brush my fingers through the thin silvery white locks of my grandmother's hair.

"I love you, Nanna. You're the one person who never let me down, my one constant. I wouldn't be the person I am today without you, and I'm so grateful to have had you in my life. You'll always be with me." I lean down and press my lips to her cold forehead as a single tear drips onto her skin.

I take a step back, straight into the waiting arms of Rafe, who wraps me against his body like a blanket as I cry. He kisses my cheek gently and I can't help melting against his touch. It feels so good to be in his arms.

"Come on, I'll take you home," he says softly.

With one last look back at my grandmother over my shoulder, I let Rafe guide me out of the room, and after saying goodbye to Gloria, Rafe helps me into his car.

The next thing I know, Rafe is carrying me. I'm cradled in his arms with my head against his chest and my legs draped over his arm. I don't even remember falling asleep on the drive home.

I let my heavy eyes drift closed, lulled by the gentle sway as

Rafe walks.

"Hey, we're here," he says quietly, lowering me to my feet onto the hardwood flooring.

Wait... My apartment is carpeted.

My eyes fly open.

We're in Rafe's apartment and Merlin is curling himself around my ankles, meowing. *Why has he brought me here?*

My eyes shoot up to Rafe's and suddenly, I'm wide awake. "Why am I here? You said you were taking me home."

"You *are* home, Ree. This *is* your home, with Ivy and me. This is where you belong. The place hasn't been the same without you this past week."

"Rafe, nothing's changed. This still isn't going to work."

"Everything's changed. Everything changed the second you walked into my life, I was just too blind and too fucking stupid to see it. Being without you these past few days made me realise what a fool I've been."

"So, what are you saying?"

He takes a step closer, taking my face in his hand. "You were never just a friend to me, you're so much more than that. You're *everything*."

My breath hitches as I stare up into his ocean blue eyes, the same eyes I've been drowning in these past couple of months.

"What I'm trying to say is... is that I—" he cuts himself off, closing his eyes with a soft shake of his head, like he can't find the words.

"You what?" I press.

He takes my other cheek in his hand so he's cupping my face, his eyes burning into mine. "I love you, Reese Reynolds. I love you so fucking much that the thought of being without you terrifies me."

I stare up at him, searching for any hint that this isn't real, that the words I've dreamed of his saying to me *didn't* just leave his lips.

"I'm so lost in you that I don't know where I end and you begin," he continues. "You're a part of me, a part of my soul and I don't know what I am without you."

With his thumb, he swipes away a tear I didn't realise had fallen.

"I never should've let you walk out that door, I should have held you like this, told you how I felt but I was just..."

"Scared," I finish and he nods. My heart is thumping in my chest, my mind spinning a mile a minute. I can't believe this is happening.

I wrap my hands around both of his wrists, feeling his pulse pumping wildly beneath his skin. "I love you, too, Rafe. I've always loved you, even when I shouldn't have. This is all I want; a family, here, with you and Ivy. You're everything to me, too. I—"

I don't get to finish my sentence before Rafe claims my mouth, swallowing up my words as he lifts me off the ground, guiding my legs around his waist. He backs me against the wall, ravaging my mouth like he can't get enough, his tongue sliding into my mouth to tangle with mine.

My arms wrap around his neck, my fingers gliding through the thick silky locks of his hair.

"I need you so fucking bad right now," he rasps against my lips, his erection grazing my core.

"So get lost in me."

34

Rafe

I stare up at the ceiling, the scent of sex hangs in the air, the rhythmic tick of the clock on the beside table next to me slowly bringing my racing heart to a resting pace, the sheen of sweat gradually cooling on my skin. Fuck, I don't think I'll ever get tired of making love to my girl. She's addictive, she's the drug that gives me my high and without her, I think I'd die.

I never thought falling in love would be so easy, come so naturally that I didn't know it was happening to me. I somehow had this idea that it would slam into me like a kick to the gut and punch to the heart, and I guess it does for some. For me, it was like a gentle breeze on a sunny day, the grey clouds parting and there she was. Her warmth washing over me. My sunshine. Always there, but hidden from view. But now she's all I see. All I can think about and all I want for the rest of my life.

I'm in love with Reese Reynolds.

And surprisingly, I'm okay with that.

She makes it as easy as breathing and right now, all I breathe is her. She fills my lungs, my head, my heart. She consumes every cell in my body and all I see is her. The thought of my life without her is just… empty, and I can't imagine my world where she's not in it.

I'm lost in her.

The bathroom door opens and a naked Reese walks back into the room, her fiery hair a tangled mess from hours of sex, her beautiful curves silhouetted against the light filtering in from the bathroom.

"Fuck, I'll never get tired of this image," I say with a wide grin as I admire the way her full, perky tits bounce with every step, how her hips sway with seductive ease as she nears me.

She crawls onto the bed, settling herself on top of me with her knees either side of my waist. My hands naturally gravitate to her hips, tugging her closer to graze around my semi-hard dick.

She leans down and kisses me, her tongue seeking mine as she grinds down on me, the heat of her pussy seeping through the thin cotton bed sheet that separates us.

I groan into her mouth as my hand comes up to tangle in her hair, my fingers gripping the back of her neck to hold her to me.

She continues to grind on me and I pull back to look up at her. "Gonna have to give me a minute, baby, if you wanna go for round five."

She laughs softly. Her hair falls in loose waves down her back and around her shoulders, creating a curtain across her face. I tuck it behind her ears as her eyes hold mine, a shy smile tugging at her mouth. "I missed you this week."

"I missed you too, baby, more than I even expected. Ivy is going to lose her mind when she sees you after school."

She smiles. "I can't wait to see her, I'm just worried about getting her hopes up."

"What do you mean?"

"Well, what if this goes wrong? What if you change your mind about us?"

"Not possible." I shift up to sit, bringing my face closer to hers. "You're all I want. *This*. You, me and *our* daughter."

My emphasis on the words *our* doesn't go amiss because a small gasp passes her lips.

"It may not be by blood, but you and Ivy share a bond like a biological mother and daughter would, and I can't imagine a woman better suited to help raise her. She loves you so much and the progress she's made since she came here is all down to you, I don't think I can take any credit for that."

Her eyes fill with tears. "I love you both so much. I just wished I'd have gotten the chance to introduce Ivy to my grandmother."

"I know. I'd give anything for her to meet my dad, for him to have met her just once."

She nods slowly with an understanding both of us share. "Thank you for being there today. I don't think I could've done it alone," she says with a teary-eyed smile.

"You don't have to thank me, baby. We're in this together from now on, okay?"

She nods and I kiss her again.

"Can I ask you something?"

"Anything."

"Why did come to my apartment earlier?"

"I needed to see you," I say, swallowing hard. "You remember how you said that if I ever felt like cutting myself, to come and find you? No matter what we were to each other?"

Her eyes tear up as she nods.

"I wanted to. I hate to admit it, but I did. I never imagined being without you would be so hard, but being in that apartment… it being so quiet with you not there…" I tear my eyes from hers, shame seeping into my pores as I admit to her the one thing she was terrified of. I was a hair's width away from going through with it, but for the first time in my life, I kept my promise to her that I'd find her.

Her hand caresses my cheek as a tear slips down her own. "I love you," she says, leaning down to press her lips to mine.

I kiss her back, rolling us over onto her back, her legs falling open to allow me room between them.

"I love you too," I whisper against her lips. "You're everything to me, Reese, I'm just so sorry it took me so long to realise it."

I slide inside her with ease, fucking her slow and deep while my mouth eats up the moans that pass her lips. I make love to her, my feelings for her pouring out of me with every thrust, every lick of my tongue against hers, every squeeze of my fingers laced with hers.

∞∞∞

"Reesie!" Ivy's eyes light up when she spots her, and tossing her backpack onto the floor, she slams into Reese, who's on her knees, her waiting arms wide open to invite my daughter in.

Reese hugs her tight. "I missed you so much, sweetheart."

"Are you here to stay? Are you coming to live with Daddy and me again?" Her eyes are hopeful as she looks up at Reese.

"Yeah, I am. I'm never leaving you again, okay? You and your daddy mean the world to me, and I never want to be without you."

"Yay!" Ivy cheers. "I love you, Reesie!"

"I love you too, baby." Reese presses a kiss to her forehead. "So *so* much."

The sight of the two most important people in my life together warms my heart and I suddenly feel complete for the first time in my life. I've always felt an emptiness inside, like a tiny piece of me was missing. I tried to fill it with all the wrong things, but all it took was a little girl with my eyes and infectious smile, and a woman with copper hair and a heart of gold to steal my own.

My *family*.

"Oh! I drew you a picture while you were away! Lemme go grab it!" Ivy takes off in a run down the corridor towards her bedroom.

I close in on Reese, tugging her into my arms with my hands on her lower back. I press a kiss to her cheek. "Why don't we take her to the park later? Maybe grab a bite to eat?" I suggest.

"I'd like that." She smiles, but there's a flash of apprehension in her expression.

"What's wrong?"

"What about the guy who's been following us? Is it really safe to be going out?"

"He won't hurt us again."

"But how do you know?"

"Because he's gone. We managed to track him down and get a hold of him. He wouldn't talk but all you need to know is that he's been dealt with," I assure her.

"Dealt with, as in..."

I give a firm nod. "*Dealt* with."

She knows exactly what I mean, and to my relief she doesn't press any further. Sparing her the details is a blessing.

I can tell by her eyes she wants to know more, but she decides against it.

"I got it!" Ivy yells, waving a piece of paper in the air as she ploughs towards us. She skids to a stop and holds it out to face us. "Look! That's me, and Daddy and Reesie, and Merlin and there's my mommy up in the clouds." She points to each of us as she speak, and for a five year-old, it's a pretty decent drawing.

Each of us in the picture has one exaggerated feature that has it closer to a caricature than anything else. I have the biggest quiff that likens me to Elvis Presley and apparently, feet the size of a giant. Reese's hair is the colour of blood and her head a little too big for her body. Ivy, of course is coloured head to toe in different shades of pink, her hair jet black. Merlin's eyes are bright and vivid, his thick fur pointing in every direction. And then there's Yvonne, sat on top of a cloud with a halo hovering over her head, looking down on her daughter.

My heart squeezes.

"It's beautiful, sweetheart," Reese praises to which Ivy beams with pride.

"Daddy, Reesie's a part of our family, right?"

My arm tightens around Reese. "Yeah, she is."

"So... Does that mean she's your girlfriend now?" She purses her lips.

"It does." My heart swells.

Her face lights up as she jumps up and down on the spot excitedly. "Yay!"

"And I won't give you reason to regret it," I add, turning my attention to Reese who gazes up at me with teary eyes.

I press a kiss to her mouth before resting my forehead on hers.

"Everything is going to be alright now, I promise."

Epilogue

Reese

Two Months Later

"I still can't believe how gorgeous he is," I gush as the little bundle in my arms coos and squirms, his warm hazel eyes identical to those of his father.

"He's really something isn't he?" My best friend smiles from ear to ear as she leans over me, beaming down at her beautiful baby boy who's cocooned in my arms.

Della gave birth to her son a few weeks back, Theodore Joseph Hudson, the spit of his father, Gage, who looks down at his wife and son proudly from across the room. Theo Joseph, named after a fallen friend and bodyguard, and Gage's father, and I couldn't have picked a better suited name for him.

"He's gonna be one hell of a heart breaker when he's older," Rafe says, sitting tight up against me with a hand placed securely on my hip, his eyes soft and warm as he peers down at the baby, a smile curling his lips.

"Hmm, just like his Daddy." Della glances up at Gage, the look of love and adoration in her eyes reflected back in those of her husband.

"Won't be long for the both of you, huh?" Della comments, her gaze flicking between me and Rafe.

"We're *no way* near ready for that yet. You're forgetting who was by your side while you were in labour for thirteen hours. That shit was painful just watching let alone having a baby the size of a watermelon come out of my vagina," I reply.

She giggles. "It was worth it in the end, and let's be honest, the making was the fun part." She shoots Gage a cheeky wink.

"Don't worry, angel. It won't be the last time," he assures her, his gaze heated.

I'm not going to lie, I've always wanted to be a mother, grow a tiny baby inside me and bring them into the world, I just had no one to experience it with until I met Rafe. And not having anything of a mother figure in my life to go by, I'll make damn sure I do it right, be the mother that I never had growing up.

Since Della gave birth, my broodiness is undeniable. Whenever I'm near Theo, I gravitate towards him, he's like a magnet and I can't help but feel envious towards my best friend. Rafe and I have discussed the possibility of having a baby in the future, but we've decided not to rush into anything, much to Rafe's reluctance. I've recently discovered his eagerness to get me pregnant, an idea he relishes, but for the time being, our little family of three is enough for now.

Ivy has since began to call me her mom, and while it's heartwarming she considers me someone worthy of the honour, I never want her to forget the woman who gave birth to her, so I make a point to show her pictures of her mom whenever I can. We managed to get a hold of some of her and Yvonne's old belongings, and in them a box of photographs from when Ivy was a baby, something that Rafe holds dear seeing as how he never got to see her like that. He missed out on so many years of his daughter's life, something that still weighs heavily on him.

"Dad would've loved Theo," Rafe comments.

"It's a shame he'll never meet his grandparents, but his Uncle and his Aunties more than make up for that," Della says, smiling at Rafe and I sweetly.

"What about your dad?" I ask. "I know it's a sore subject but doesn't he have a right to know his grandson?"

"Randall March lost the right to be anything the day he decided to kill his wife and leave his daughter without a mother, not to mention being the cause of our own mother's death," Gage snaps, his expression turning hard.

"Damn straight." Rafe nods in agreement, his jaw clenching and I feel bad for bringing it up.

"W-What?"

All four of our heads dart in the direction of the door where Sierra looks on in horror, her eyes flicking between all of us. "What are you talking about?"

"Si—" Gage starts.

"No!" she barks with a warning glare. "Don't you dare lie to me. I want to know what you were all talking about. Please, carry on, pretend I'm not even here."

Theo grows restless in my arms with all the commotion around us, and after carefully passing him to Della, she hurries from the room.

"Well? Anyone going to say something?" Si's eyes pass between her brothers.

"We wanted to protect you. Telling you the truth would've

only hurt you," Gage says.

"What truth? Did Della's dad *really* kill our mom?"

After a long pregnant pause, Gage nods. "Yes."

A strangled sob leaves Sierra's lips, her eyes filling with tears. "H-How?"

"He was trying to kill Dad. He tampered with the car and he didn't know Mom was driving that night."

"But... Why? Why would he want him dead? I know our families never got along but, trying to *kill* him...?"

"Mom was with Randall first," Gage starts. "Their relationship got rocky and she sought the comfort of Dad, who was his best friend at the time and they fell in love. Randall didn't like it. He had it in his head Dad stole the legacy that should have been his as well as stealing his woman. He pushed Della's mom down the stairs when he found her trying to leave him with Della. I guess he thought that by getting rid of Dad too, they could live happily fucking ever after." I don't miss the bitterness in Gage's tone.

"Oh my God," she gasps, clutching the door frame like a lifeline. "How long have you all known?" Her voice is as shaky as her legs that threaten to buckle from under her.

Gage clears his throat. "Since Bryce kidnapped Della."

Her eyes widen. "That was a year ago!"

"We were going to tell you eventually, when the time was right," Rafe says.

She glares at him. "Save it. You've only come clean because you got caught out. You had no intention of telling me the truth. What else have you been hiding from me? *Huh?*"

"That's it, I swear," Rafe says.

"Forgive me if I don't believe a word that leaves your mouth. All the two of you do is lie and keep secrets and I'm tired of it." She lets out a frustrated huff before her eyes land on me. "Did you know?"

I nod regretfully.

"You're one of my best fucking friends!" The hurt of my betrayal contorts her features as a single tear leaves a trail down her cheek.

"It wasn't my secret to share, Si, I'm so sorry." I hated keeping it from her, in all honesty it's a truth *I* didn't even want to know, but it wasn't up to me to be the one to tell her.

"Gage, I—" Alec enters the room but stops when he takes in the scene before him.

"And you?" she asks Alec, spinning on her heel to face him. "Did you know Della's piece of shit father killed my mom?"

He squares his shoulders, the evidence of his own knowledge painted on his guilty face as he swallows thickly. "I did."

"Well, it's nice to know you all care so much about me." Sierra blinks back the tears pooling in her eyes. "You know what? Fuck this family and it's lies and it's secrets and fuck you all! I'm out of here!"

Alec takes a step towards her, reaching for her, but she puts a hand up to stop him. "Don't. Don't come anywhere near me."

Alec's face falters a fraction but he does his best to cover up the slip as Sierra storms out of the room. Her footsteps echo through the house before the sound of a door slamming cracks through the air.

"I'll go and talk to her." I move to get up, but Rafe's hand on mine stops me.

"Give her time to cool off, baby."

The knowledge of my friend hurting kills me, but Rafe's right, going after her now might stoke the fire that's already raging inside her, but I think it's going to take a long time for her to forgive her brothers.

∞∞∞

"Sierra's not in her room," I announce an hour later to the guys who are talking in the living room.

"What?" Alec asks, concern etched into his face.

"She's not anywhere. I've checked her room, the study, the garden... She's gone."

"Shit," Gage says. "Alec, check the security feed to the garage, see if she took one of the cars."

"On it." Alec disappears out of the room, moving so fast I'm not sure his feet even touched the ground.

Gage pulls out his phone, dialling a number and holds it up to his ear. "Fuck. Straight to voicemail."

"Where would she go?" I ask.

"No idea, but we need to find her, I don't like the thought of her out there on her own."

"But she's safe right? That Vickers guy is gone."

"We still have other enemies, and while I'm sure she is safe, I'm not taking any chances." Gage dials the number again, and judging by the string of curses that leave his mouth as he paces the floor, he's sent straight to voicemail again. "Damn it, Sierra, answer your goddamn phone," he grumbles. "I understand you're mad, but I want to know you're safe. Call me back now. *Please*."

Through his anger, I don't miss the tremble of his voice as he pleads the last word.

Just then, Alec returns to the living room, his footsteps loud and heavy as they eat up the floor in strong purposed strides.

"She took off in the Audi about an hour ago."

"Fuck," Gage mutters. "Okay, I can track her. All the cars in the garage are fitted with trackers." He flicks through his phone and a few moments later, his brows pull together. "It's parked down the street, what the hell is she doing?"

"I'll go get her," Alec says, hurrying back out of the room, the front door closing a second later.

"What's going on?" Della asks, pulling her cardigan around her body tighter.

"Where's Theo?" Gage asks.

"With Viola and Ivy, they're reading him a story."

"Sierra knows about what your dad did to their mom, she took off and Alec's gone to get her," I reply.

"Shit," she mutters.

At that moment, Gage's phone rings. "Alec… What do you mean she's not there?" His expression turns grave, his hand tightening around the phone as he listens to whatever Alec is telling him on the other end. "Get back here. Now." He hangs up and turns to us. "Alec found the car, she's gone. The passenger door was left wide open, the engine still running."

Della and I gasp in unison, Della's hand curling around mine in a death grip.

"I'll try her again." I pull my phone out and call her. After five long excruciating rings, she answers. "Sierra? Thank God. Are you okay? Where are you?" There's a muffled, crackling noise on the other end. "Si? You there?"

"Oh, she's here, but she can't come to the phone right now. She's… *indisposed*." The deep male voice on the other end shoots a chill up my spine, a voice that's vaguely familiar.

My heart thumps heavily in my chest, my eyes shooting up to Gage and Rafe who hang on with bated breath. "Who is this?"

Gage and Rafe take a step towards me, their expressions murderous.

"Are her brothers with you?" the man asks.

I swallow hard. "Yes."

"Put me on speaker, I think they'll want to hear this."

I pull the phone away from my ear, my hand shaky as I press the speaker button. "They can hear you."

"Gage, Rafe, it's been a long time coming."

"Who the fuck are you? Where's my sister?" Gage demands.

"She's fine, *for now,* and as for who I am, all in good time. You'll figure it out soon enough."

"What do you want? Whatever it is, it has nothing to do with Sierra," Rafe says.

"On the contrary. It has everything to do with her. I've been watching you for a while, working out your patterns, your weaknesses... Haven't you learned that love and family are the biggest weaknesses of all? They make you vulnerable. That's where we differ, I have none."

"Who *are* you?" I ask.

"Come now, Reese. I would've hoped our little dance was as memorable for you as it was for me."

Realisation dawns on me, why I recognise his voice. "Oh my God, you're the guy at Sierra's party."

"The prick who tried to drug her," Rafe adds through gritted teeth. "I should've killed you when I had the chance."

"Yes, you will come to regret that." He seems almost amused.

Rafe tenses beside me, just as Alec reappears in the doorway, his face a mix of anger and fear.

"I admit, you Reese were my original target. I decided to have a little fun with you and your boyfriend, make him think it was you and the kid I wanted. That way, the attention fell away from the sister."

"The car that tried to kill us, the guy watching us in the mall... You put Vickers up to it?" Rafe asks.

"It's not a coincidence that the man I hired to play with you just happened to be the kid's mom's boyfriend. Who do you think introduced them? It was so easy to find little Ivy; Enter your name on the internet and *voila*, there's her birth certificate with you named as the father. It's really a tragedy what happened to Yvonne... A trip down the stairs, how *utterly* unfortunate."

"You had him kill her?" Rafe's jaw clenches.

"The original plan was to have you gain custody of your daughter only to have her ripped from you so you knew what real pain felt like, but really? What fun could we have had with a five year-old? So I set my sights on beautiful Sierra Hudson instead."

"Who the *fuck* are you?" Alec asks.

"Like I said, all in good time. All you need to know is that she's mine now, for however long I decide she's useful. You'll get her back when I'm finished with her, can't promise she'll be in one piece, though."

"You're dead motherfucker. *Dead!*" Gage booms.

"You take my sibling. I take yours. And believe me when I say, we're going to have *so* much fun with her. You and your fucking family will pay for what you did to Bryce."

Oh my god...

Bryce had a brother?

Alec snatches the phone from my hand. "You piece of shit! I swear to God if you hurt her I—"

Alec is cut off when a piercing blood-curdling scream comes

through the phone. *Sierra's* scream. A scream of pure terror and excruciating pain that goes bone-deep. I can only imagine what they're doing to her for that sound to leave her lungs.

A sob rips through Della as she clings to me. My own tears leaking from my eyes at the sound of my best friend in pain.

The line goes dead, but the sound of her scream echoes through the room and rings in my ears, a sound that will stay with all of us long after the call was cut.

Alec is the first to move. He slaps my phone back in my hand and heads to the door.

"Where are you going?" Gage asks.

His jaw clenches as he tries to keep it together, but even as he tries to hide it, I know that Sierra being out there somewhere, in the hands of the enemy is killing him. "To find your sister. I don't care if it takes me a lifetime, I won't stop until she's safe."

The story concludes in Sierra's book, Catch My Fall.

Did you enjoy Rafe and Reese's story?
If you could spare a few minutes, I would be forever grateful if you could drop me a review, even if it's only a few words, your feedback is invaluable to little indie authors like me.
Thank You.

Want the latest news and updates about future releases? You can stalk me on Instagram, Facebook and Tiktok!

Author Notes and Acknowledgments

Book 9 is officially complete! This one was a tough one, and after several bouts of writers block, I finally managed to finish it, I hope I did their story justice. After writing *Drown In Me,* I was at a loss on how I wanted Rafe's story to go. It wasn't until one day I was at work and saw a young father sat on a bench with his little girl sat on his lap, that gave me the idea of introducing a daughter he knew nothing about. In *Drown In Me,* Rafe was very reserved with no real direction, so by giving him a daughter, I wanted him to have a purpose, something to strive for, to fight for.

I want to thank all of my fantastic readers who continue to read all of the crazy and wonderful things that come from my brain. I want to thank you for all of your continued support and especially all the help regarding the parental custody research, you guys were lifesavers. I know it may not be 100% accurate but there's always poetic licence isn't there?

I would also like to thank all of the bookstagrammers, bloggers, tiktokers who share my teasers and help spread the word of my books. Word of mouth and reviews mean so much to little indie authors like myself when our readership is small.

This whole journey has been unbelievable and I never imagined in a million years that I would ever get to this point on book 9, about to start book 10, let alone write one book!

Thank you all so much, I love you all.

Also by the Author

The Game - *Billionaire Romance*
The Promise - *Billionaire, Single Mother, Second Chance Romance*

Strip Me Down Series
Strip Me Down - *Student/Teacher Romance*
Fix Me Up - *Age Gap, Friends to Lovers Romance*
Promise Me Forever - *Second Chance Romance*
Guide Me Home - *Reverse Age Gap, Second Chance Romance*

Under The Mistletoe (A Christmas Novella) - *Small Town Romance*

Hudson Hearts Series
Drown In Me (Book 1) - Forced Marriage, Soulmates
Lost In You (Book 2)

Printed in Great Britain
by Amazon